Getting a Lawyer

... Borell's apartment. I figure ... t my
da ... said
he ... work-
ing ... head.

"G ... mily
an ... w be-
cau ... very
sel ... ll the
cra ... don't
kn ...

... said.
"S ... body
els ...

... nade
a c ... back
int ...

"You want some Grape-Nuts?"

Other Bantam Starfire books you will enjoy

NECESSARY PARTIES

BARBARA DANA

BANTAM BOOKS
NEW YORK • TORONTO • LONDON • SYDNEY • AUCKLAND

RL6, IL age 12 and up

*This edition contains the complete text
of the original hardcover edition.*
NOT ONE WORD HAS BEEN OMITTED.

NECESSARY PARTIES

*A Bantam Book / published by arrangement with
Harper & Row Publishers Inc.*

PRINTING HISTORY

*Harper & Row edition published October 1986
Bantam edition / November 1987
Bantam reissue / August 1991*
For permission to quote from The Rights of Young People.
*we gratefully acknowledge Martin Guggenheim and Alan Sussman.
American Civil Liberties Union, 1985.*

*The Starfire logo is a registered trademark of Bantam Books, Inc.
Registered in U.S. Patent and Trademark Office and elsewhere.*

ISBN 0-553-26984-4

Published simultaneously in the United States and Canada

*Bantam Books are published by Bantam Books, a division of Bantam
Doubleday Dell Publishing Group, Inc. Its trademark, consisting of the
words "Bantam Books" and the portrayal of a rooster, is Registered in U.S.
Patent and Trademark Office and in other countries. Marca Registrada.
Bantam Books, 666 Fifth Avenue, New York, New York 10103.*

PRINTED IN THE UNITED STATES OF AMERICA

RAD   0 9 8 7 6 5 4 3

To my beloved Guru Hari,
and
my beloved Paramguru,
Ralph Harris Houston

Introduction

It was not my idea to write this. That dubious honor must forcibly be bestowed upon the durable, sloping, and elephantlike shoulders of dear old Mr. Dunfee. Mr. Dunfee runs this divorce group thing at Wallace Beeley, my own and only high school, and it was assigned work for all of us poor divorce victims to keep a journal.

Maybe I should explain this divorce group business a little. They've had it here for a couple of years now, and Mr. Dunfee, this guidance counselor, runs it. He told us he discovered a couple of years ago that the majority of the kids in school had parents who were either divorced or about to be divorced, and thought it would be a good thing if the kids got together and discussed their feelings in regard to the situation, thereby getting things out in the open and also helping each other.

We meet twice a week for forty-five minutes, or three "mods" (tiny and minuscule sections of time into which our school days are broken down or up). Most of the kids end up talking, although not all of them. Nobody is forced. We do have to keep journals, however. We have to write something every day, at least a paragraph. It doesn't have to deal with divorce; however, since it's the biggest thing going on in our lives, a lot of us tend to write about it. These journals have to be turned in to Mr. Dunfee once a week. There's this sharing table, a Dunfee phrase if I ever heard one, on which you can put your journals on Friday. Then you can read each other's if you want to, but you don't have to. It's kind of interesting sometimes. The sessions run eight weeks and after that you can stay on if you want to, but you don't have to. There are always new kids coming in, which is a depressing comment on life's trends, if you want my opinion.

This book is based on my journal, not unlike the journals, of all the other poor, victimized, and guilt-ridden teenagers in the group. It was Amy's idea to get it published. Amy is a friend of mine in the group. She felt that the unusual, bizarre, and outlandish way in which I dealt with the whole thing might be of general interest. We'll see, but thank you, Amy. It's kind of a nice thing to have a published book at the age of fifteen, even if it's true and I didn't make any part of it up.

I tried to report this accurately, as a journalist might. I want to be a writer when I grow up so it was good practice. I also want to paint, which I do now, and possibly design special effects for motion pictures, maybe direct them, too, but that's in the future.

Anyway, all this happened, so I wrote it down and showed it to Mr. Dunfee, who wasn't too thrilled with my spelling. More importantly, I think, this book might be helpful to some kids who could be going through a divorce in their own families. I pointed this out to Mr. Dunfee just after he criticized my spelling and he had to agree. Anyway, here it is.

Christopher Mills

CHAPTER 1

We started out seemingly regular, the Mills family—my mother; my father; me, Chris (or Christopher for long); and my little sister, Jenny. She's six, an all-around wonderful person, very smart, very funny, and although she can get on my nerves, I love her a lot. It's a good thing, too, because I ended up having to take almost total care of her. But let me start at the beginning.

We live in Bedford, New York, which is in Westchester, a suburb of New York City, about one hour's commute. My father commutes to New York a few days a week and the other days he works out of his White Plains office. He's in land development. It's pretty lucrative even now with the whole economy falling apart. He's about forty and really good-looking. I hope I look like him when I grow up. I could do a lot worse, let me tell you. He's very athletic, tennis mostly and jogging (three miles before breakfast). We used to be really tight, until about four years ago. Then it started seeming like he never had any time for me, or that I was an intrusion of some kind, that I kept him from doing important things, like worrying about stuff I couldn't understand.

My mom is pretty. She's blond and looks about

thirty, I guess, although she's older. She's very smart. She has a master's degree from Smith in education and child development, although I'm not too sure how that figures in with me and Jenny. She doesn't work now, not a job in the literal sense of going to an office or anything, but she's very BUSY, more and more in the last few years. I feel in a sense that the mad dashing around has been largely an attempt to ignore the family falling apart at home. She writes articles, goes to the PTA, works for whale safety, organizes bringing groups of poor kids to Westchester for the summers, reads to kids at the library, plays tennis (paddle and regular), jogs, goes to exercise class, has her hair done, and does just generally everything. Except help make our family work at all. In her best moments, when she's in any way relaxed, she is very funny, a wonderful person to be with. We made a nice family.

Then there's my sister. As I mentioned, she's six and very smart—gifted, I guess you could say, although since this divorce thing came up she's been acting younger and younger. I've heard that kids do that sometimes.

Where is the beginning? As I said, for reasons too obscure for me to recognize, things had been disintegrating within our family for some time. My parents just gradually seemed never to want to be home. Month by month, week by week, they were a little more busy, a little more grouchy, a little more tired, a little less fun, and then the fighting began to build. Since I can remember, every now and then they'd fight, but it happened more and more until it seemed like that's all there was. It was like some freezing wind had come down from the Arctic, sweeping through and totally transforming them until they were all but unrecognizable from their previous selves.

I'm going to start with the day of the Beckners' doubles match. It was a Sunday in late November. The day started, as they were all starting around that time, with me making breakfast for Jenny. I had my tennis stuff on because the plan was for us all to go along to the Beckners', who have a tennis court and also a daughter named Trudy who's a friend of Jenny's. So we were all going to the Beckners', and Jenny would play with Trudy and I would sit around and wait for the doubles game to be over, at which time Dad and I would get to play some singles. As it turned out, that never materialized.

Anyway, there I was making Popeye eggs, which is a type of egg whereby you cut a hole in a piece of bread and then fry it with an egg in the center. I think some people call them One-eyed Sailors, the yolk being the single eye staring up at you. Whatever you call them, they're tricky to make because you want to cook the egg past the disgusting stage without burning the toast. I was working on this and Jenny was sitting at the kitchen table in her pajamas, drawing. She was holding Funny Bunny Richardson, who is her favorite stuffed animal. I'd noticed that since the fighting had gotten horrendous, she'd been carrying him everywhere. He's ancient and totally falling apart, but she doesn't care. Anyway, Funny Bunny Richardson (I don't remember how he got that name, she usually calls him Bunny) is this old but rather appealing rabbit who's been mended a million times, earlier by Mom and more recently by me (you get the trend). He has this startled look of alarm on his face, like he just heard a loud noise that might endanger his very soul life. You have to feel sorry for him.

Anyway, I was cooking and Jenny was drawing and holding Funny Bunny Richardson and my mom and dad were upstairs in their bedroom, screaming at each other. Their door was closed, but it was still inexplicably loud. Jenny and I were both pretty much used to the screaming by that point, but we didn't like it.

"What should I draw now?" asked Jenny.

My mother had just called my father a selfish bastard and he had just said she was a fine one to talk.

"I don't know," I said. "You want a Popeye egg?"

"Yes," said Jenny.

I jabbed a piece of bread with the rim of an overturned juice glass. It makes a hole of the correct size.

"But what should it be?" continued Jenny.

"Whatever you want."

"It's up to your decision."

"Why mine?"

"That's the way it is."

"I'm busy now. I can't think about it. Make whatever you want and show it to me later."

The screaming was getting louder.

"I don't understand you!" my father was shouting.

"Of course not," screamed my mother. "How the hell could you understand anybody? You're too damn selfish."

"How 'bout a turkey?" said Jenny. I knew she was hearing all the horrendous abuse being hurled around upstairs, but you couldn't tell.

"Fine," I said. I flipped the toast and just in time. One corner had started to burn.

The bedroom door slammed. I could hear my father's footsteps thundering down the stairs. Jenny bit her lip, the bottom one, on the side. She was digging her top teeth into it. Then the bedroom door opened.

"WHERE ARE YOU GOING?" shouted my mother.

My father didn't answer.

"WHERE ARE YOU GOING?"

The front door slammed.

"So many doors," said Jenny.

"I CAN'T STAND IT ANYMORE!" My mother was yelling and crying at the same time. Then she must have gone back into the bedroom, because that door slammed too.

I turned the heat off under the egg pan.

"What's wrong with Mommy?" asked Jenny. Her lower lip was starting to twitch.

"She's upset."

"But why?"

"She and Daddy are fighting. It makes her upset."

"Well, why are they fighting?"

"I don't know." I wanted to say something helpful, but I couldn't think of what. "Get the plates."

Jenny got up and went to the cupboard. She took Funny Bunny Richardson with her. "It's not good," she said. "Bunny doesn't like it."

CHAPTER 2

The tennis game was tense. I hadn't expected there to be one after all the screaming, but things were getting so strange around home at that point, I never knew what would happen next. It was unsettling. I figured what happened in this instance was that my folks were too embarrassed to cancel the game for fear of what the Beckners would think. My parents never used to be concerned about other people's opinions. I personally think it's a poor idea to do something, or not do something, because of what someone else will think. No matter what you do there's always going to be somebody, somewhere, thinking you're weird. It's a price you pay for living.

But, as I said, the tennis game was tense. I sat in my tennis things, ready to play, holding my racket and watching my parents and the Beckners play their doubles. My parents are good, although distracted on this particular day. They normally beat the Beckners. Mr. Beckner doesn't look like much of an athlete. He's on the overweight side, but he's a killer at the net. He plays with this oversized racket and is one of these vicious players who, you get the feeling, will kill you if you beat him. You also get the feeling he'll kill you if you play badly, or stupidly, because that adversely affects his game. I don't play with him if I can help it. Mrs. Beckner plays pretty well, but she's not real energetic and doesn't like to run, which bothers Mr. Beckner.

Anyway, they were playing, and there were all these undertones from Mr. Beckner about Mrs. Beckner's lack of get up and go, and worse undertones from my father about my mother's being in the wrong place at the wrong time, and from my mother about being criticized in front of the Beckners. When my mother's in a good mood she loves to tease people (in a nice way, never mean; we all kind of enjoy it) but she NEVER likes to be teased. Especially when she's in a bad mood. At those times you can't imagine she even has a sense of humor, which, as I mentioned earlier, she does.

Jenny was off to one side with Trudy, digging in the dirt and making unappetizing-looking dirt cakes. At one point they brought one over to me. Trudy held it out just under my nose.

"Eat it," she said.

"Maybe later."

"Eat it now."

"No thanks."

"You'd better eat it," said Jenny. I could tell she was serious.

"What is it, anyway?"

"It's a very certain dessert and you'd better eat it," said Jenny.

"No thanks," I said.

Trudy started to cry.

"Oh, come on, Trudy. It's dirt. You can't really expect me to eat it." Trudy kept on crying.

"Pretend," whispered Jenny.

I picked up the cake and pretended to chew contentedly, appreciating its goodness, which seemed to satisfy Trudy. I hate it when kids cry.

When the game was over we went inside for punch. No mention was made of my playing, which was fine with me because my dad is NO FUN when he's in a bad mood. I drank several glasses of punch while Mr. Beckner and my dad discussed business. Mrs. Beckner was showing my mother her hair and going into this whole big thing about it.

"Strand by strand," Mrs. Beckner was saying.

"My goodness," said my mother. She seemed distracted.

"He does Faye Dunaway," added Mrs. Beckner.

I remember wondering who he was and what he did to Faye Dunaway, but I didn't ask.

"You have to wait months for an appointment," continued Mrs. Beckner, "but"—she took a long sip of punch to prolong the suspense—"there's no root line."

"That makes all the difference," said my mother.

I wondered if she was putting Mrs. Beckner on. I certainly hope so. On the way home in the car Jenny and I were in the back as usual. We have this pretty roomy BMW sedan, which is a great car, my father's pride and joy, except for the oil leak. That's plagued him since we got the car a year and a half ago, that and a rattle in the back which only he can hear. When it comes to noises in his car he's like a dog who's driven crazy by high-pitched whistles only he can understand.

Jenny was next to me, completely covered in mud, totally unrecognizable as any previous person. She must have rolled in it, or mud wrestled with Trudy. From up front you could feel the waves of tension coming from my mom and dad. At first everybody was quiet. I was staring out the window, counting dogs, to keep my mind busy, I guess, to escape the horrendous and oppressive vibes. Pretty soon my mom started in about the tennis game and they were off. It was like me and Jenny were not even in the car, like we had ceased to exist.

"You have no right to belittle me in public," said my mother.

"Public?" said my dad. "That was two people, friends. And I wasn't belittling you. I was just trying to bring your attention to the fact that your mind was not on the game."

"Let's drop it."

"No. I'm curious. Where was your mind?"

"Guess."

"Don't be oblique."

"I don't want to talk about it."

"I have to go to the bathroom," said Jenny. Nobody paid any attention.

"Why do you leave holes?"

"I don't want to talk about it."

"I have to go to the bathroom."

"Jenny has to go to the bathroom," I said. I suspected she was lying, but I felt they should check it out, not just ignore her.

They kept on with the tennis business.

"I'm covering the net. I can't be looking back over my shoulder, wondering where you are. You have to counter."

"If you can't see me, how can you criticize my game?"

The whole discussion was so stupid that I wanted to grab my parents and shake them, to shout at them and say, "BE HAPPY! TENNIS IS JUST A GAME! IT'S NOT WORTH THIS! NOTHING IS!"

"I HATE TENNIS!" shouted my mother.

"Now you tell me! Five thousand dollars' worth of tennis lessons after the fact."

"I have to go to the bathroom," repeated Jenny, louder this time.

"Do you really?" I asked.

"You'll know when I explode."

When we got home, for some reason, Dad had trouble opening the front door. The lock was sticking, which Mom said was because Dad had agreed to sand the edge of the door three weeks ago and hadn't. Dad said Mom should have called Wally (the carpenter). It was her fault.

"Open up, Buster," said Jenny.

"Don't call your father Buster," said Mom.

"Well, whoever he is, he better hurry 'cause I'm gonna explode."

My father opened the door and Jenny rushed into the house.

"This person will self-destruct," she shouted, and ran into the downstairs bathroom.

Then my mother did a strange thing. She walked straight to the couch and lay down. She still had her tennis racket. It may not sound too strange if you don't know her, but it's not at all a thing she would do. She would always put her tennis racket away. She's very organized and also she's always busy, always moving, always doing something or other. My father set his tennis racket down on the coffee table and went over to the bar and poured himself a scotch. That's his usual. I just stood there. I didn't know what to do. I just sort of went numb, so I went into the den and turned on the TV. That's a problem of mine. When in doubt, turn on the TV. I have to get over that.

CHAPTER
3

When Jenny came out of the bathroom she joined me at the TV. I had gotten a bag of taco chips from the kitchen so we sat there eating chips, and I did a thing I often like to do when a show is poor, which is to shoot suction-cup darts at the image. It's fun to time it in this certain way so that you zap people right at some crucial point. "Heerrre's Johnny!"—Zap! Or "What can I do for these persistent tension headaches?"—Zap! Anyway, *The Flintstones* was on and I was getting pretty bored with them and also it was Sunday night and I hadn't even started my homework. I grabbed a fistful of taco chips and headed for the stairs.

"You should take a shower," I told Jenny. She was still covered with mud.

"*The Flintstones*," she said, which was supposed to mean that of course she couldn't take a shower at such a major point in time.

"I'd do it now if I were you."

"Well, you're not. There's only one me and I'm it."

"Mom won't let you eat like that."

"Mom's asleep."

"So what?"

"No mother, no dinner." She pulled hard on the seat of her jeans. "Indian underwear," she added.

"Right."

"You know what that means?"

I told her I did.

"They creep up on you."

"Right."

An arrogant and dense-looking man appeared on the TV screen, pointing into the camera and talking too loud. "You work tough, you play tough," he was saying. "You deserve tough underarm protection."

I regretted having set down my dart gun.

On my way through the living room I noticed that Mom was still lying on the couch. Dad was still in his tennis stuff, drinking his scotch and reading *The New York Times*. I was feeling pretty hungry in spite of the taco chips so I was curious about the dinner situation, but I didn't say anything.

I'll probably end up making Pepperidge Farm soup and grilled-cheese sandwiches for me and Jenny again, I thought as I made my weary way up the stairs to confront my homework. Corn chowder, or cream of mushroom?

I went into my room and shut the door. I was exhausted. Things were ganging up and now I had to analyze four amendments to the Constitution, finish my book report on *A Separate Peace* (as if I wasn't depressed enough), and copy a lab report on the inner blood flow of your common frog. My schoolbooks were piled high on my desk next to my fish tank, but I couldn't face them, so I sat down and stared at my fish. I've always wanted a pet of some kind, but I've had to be satisfied with fish (no offense) because Jenny seems to be allergic to animal fur. I love my fish. I find them fascinating, ancient harbingers of the deep.

Sometimes I can stare at them for minutes, or a half an hour maybe, contemplating what can possibly be locked in the inner recesses of their tiny fish brains. What do they think about? What do they know? I have seventeen fish.

I got the food out and fed them. Just then I began to hear my parents fighting downstairs.

Not again, I remember thinking.

I switched on my tape recorder, Beethoven's Ninth, a special favorite of mine. I hoped the music would drown out the noise from downstairs, but it didn't. I suddenly felt this kind of numbness of fear, like a terrible wave was overtaking me. At that precise point, I think I knew the terrible truth of what was about to happen. You know how they say when you die, just at that moment, your whole life passes in front of you? What happened next was like that. My family was dying and in that moment the whole goodness of what we once had passed in front of me, the whole thing of what was being lost. My parents were fighting and I heard that going on downstairs as a kind of background to the following: I'm staring at the fish. Fish. Fishing. My dad and me fishing on Monhegan Island, fishing together on the boat of this lobster fisherman, Manchester Crimp. He had three boats, three Crimp boats. Should have been Shrimp boats. Thoughts kept pouring into my mind. The whole thing flashed past, the classic, great family time.

It was four summers ago. We went on this vacation to Monhegan Island off Maine, part of Maine I guess, but not the mainland. We stopped at L.L. Bean's on the way, me and my dad's favorite, that and Eddie Bauer. We got matching sixty-forty jackets. Mom got one, too. Ours were green. Hers was rust. What did Jenny get? Something. I don't remember.

We had gone for family fun, but also, my parents love art and especially wanted to search out some paintings by a Russian painter named Nicholas Roerich. He's really great. I have a print of one of his paintings in my room. Mountains. He did an incredible Tibetan series. I'm studying him now in regard to my own work. My art teacher, Mr. Pucci, is letting me do an acrylic in Roerich's technique, using three colors and keeping it simple. I'm also exploring his use of perspective. He does a thing where you always seem to be viewing the scene from some obscure and unusual vantage point. He knows things. I understand he's a philosopher. I should look up his stuff.

As it turned out, we didn't find any Roerichs on Monhegan. It was just this great trip. I thought about it as I stared at my fish and tried to block out the ongoing disagreement from downstairs. I couldn't believe that the family from that time, from that vacation, was on the brink of disaster. How could it be? I remember this nice man we met there who was staying in a nearby cabin with some friends. He was a painter. He wore a beret and lightly tinted sunglasses. One day we were all out on Manchester Crimp's fishing boat. We had just pulled out when I noticed a large seagull moving backwards along the deck in our direction. He was dragging what appeared to be an enormous piece of old cheese. When he got closer I could see it was some indiscernible type of discarded melon. Mom and Dad noticed him, too, and we started laughing. The gull was so serious, so intent on some inner plan for the unappetizing melon. It was a simple thing, but it got to us. Soon Mom and Dad were doubled up with laughter, holding on to each other, laughing. I dropped my fishing line, I was so crazed with hysterical laughter. First, it was the backing up and the seriousness of the gull's expression, coupled with the unappealing nature of the rotten melon, that made us laugh. Then it was the sound of each other's laughter, especially my dad's. He has this very distinctive and contagious laugh with loud, unexpected hooting noises in it. They can always get me going, or let's say they used to. I haven't heard a good hoot in years.

Anyway, we were all hysterical with laughter. Jenny was playing with Bunny, and we were laughing and so was this nice man with the beret and the lightly tinted glasses. I remember when we were getting off the boat later he said, "You have a beautiful family, really beautiful." I never forgot that. Or how it rained for three days straight. We stayed inside and played cards and sang songs. My dad played the guitar (another item gone by the wayside). My mom sang great harmony. Other things: Mom and I collecting shells on long, exploring walks; Dad and I on picture-taking expeditions, taking color slides to show my grampa; a church carnival with a tiny Ferris wheel that Jenny loved incredibly (Dad took her on it something like ten times); the four of us swimming, holding hands (could Jenny swim? how old was she, two?); lobster dinners where we all had ridiculous-looking matching bibs that we wore back to the cabin after dinner. Jenny got this thing one of those nights where she made friends with her lobster shell and refused to leave it at the restaurant. My parents let her take it to the cabin. She slept with it for two nights.

There was a knock on the door.

"Who is it?"

"It's me."

"Come in."

It was Jenny. When she opened the door I noticed

that my parents had stopped fighting. There was no sound at all from downstairs. Jenny moved into the room. She was still covered with mud. With her right hand she held Bunny by the ears. "I'm starving to the point of death."

"What time is it?"

"*The Flintstones* stopped, and it's only news."

"Take a shower."

No response.

"It becomes unhealthy."

"Can you make me a grilled cheese?"

"After your shower."

Jenny approached the fish. She leaned on her elbows, staring into the tank. "Hello, fish," she said. "You're verrrrry quiet."

Does she remember Monhegan? I thought. Does she have the slightest conception of family life? What does it mean to her? Is it all grilled-cheese sandwiches and parents too busy fighting and being unhappy to tell her to take a shower?

"Fish, fish, fish," she said. She was making faces at the fish as they swam past.

"Do you remember Monhegan?"

"What's that?"

"Monhegan. It's an island."

"Nope."

"We went on this very big boat and you got to stand in front and get splashed?"

"Not me."

"You don't remember the boat?"

"Nope."

"Or the lobster shell?"

"Nope."

"Or the ocean?"

"Nope."

"You must remember something."

She looked up from the fish. "Oh, yes."

"What do you remember?"

"Bunny got wedged."

"What do you mean, 'Bunny got wedged'?"

"Wedged and stuck."

"On the boat?"

"That's right, 'cause there was this seat like a bench and he got caught down behind it and this big fishing man got him out with tools."

"I don't remember that."

"Well, he did. Didn't you, Bunny?"

"Yes." Jenny made this high-pitched voice for Bunny's reply.

"That's all you remember?"

"That's it," she said. "The rest is locked in my computer brain."

CHAPTER 4

School on Monday was typically boring, although Marion, this friend of Amy's, livened things up by telling me about how her boyfriend, Zeus Pitkin, had just spent the night in jail because he punched somebody in the head in Detroit and knocked a bone into this person's brain, thereby killing him. Marion comes up with a lot of weird stories, so you have to take her comments with a grain of salt, as they say, but when Marion told me that, I told her that if she was serious, Zeus (I love that name) was going to be spending a lot more than one night in jail. Try life! Marion said she'd thought of that, which was why she was looking for a new boyfriend. Amy told me later that the whole thing was Marion's way of flirting with me, telling me the story, that is. Amy maintains that Zeus really did knock a bone into somebody's brain in Detroit, thereby killing him, but I'm not so sure. There's always this enormous intrigue thing with those girls. It's hard to sort things out.

In any event, after school some of my friends came over, Ben and Ronald and Haverman to be exact, and we hung out in the backyard. Ben and Haverman are in my class and Ronald is Ben's little brother. Well, not little in actuality, but smaller than the rest of us. Ronald is twelve. Jenny was inside. I couldn't go anywhere because my mother was at Slimnastics (an unappealing term for an exercise class) and my father was at work. Helen, who cleans our house, always leaves at four—and who would take care of Jenny? You guessed it.

I remember I was carving a medieval dagger with my new Eddie Bauer survival knife. It's a great knife. It's got all this survival stuff stored in the handle: string, a compass, matches, a fishhook. You name it, it's in there. It has an amazing and handy assortment of items stored away in comparative secrecy. It's totally black and sharp as hell. My dad ordered it from the Eddie Bauer catalogue by calling them one Saturday night at something like eleven-thirty. It was nice of him. He loves calling their twenty-four-hour call service, but still, he didn't have to get it for me.

Anyway, I was carving, and Ben and Ronald were arm wrestling (an uneven match if I ever saw one), when Haverman started going into this whole thing about The Old Fish People. Haverman (that's his last name) is my best friend. He's tiny and energetic and also brilliant, with some incredibly high IQ, I would imagine. He's also a little crazy because of all the divorces in his family. Both his parents have been married twice already since they got divorced from each other three years ago, and that's got to have an effect on Haverman, which it does. He's pretty hyper.

"It's terrible," he was saying. "I thought they were gone."

"Explain yourself, or change the subject," I said, carving away. You have to bring Haverman down to earth a lot of times.

"The Old Fish People," said Haverman, his eyes burning with intensity.

"Can you be more specific?"

"They were always there when I was a kid, but they went away. Last night they came back."

"Where's there?"

"Under my bed. I would always have to take this running leap and lunge into my bed because they were waiting underneath to grab my ankles. They wanted to pull me underneath."

"Who did?" said Ronald.

I was waiting for that. With Ronald everything is cause for concern—rain, the Fourth of July, whatever can happen. I knew he wasn't going to go for The Old Fish People.

"They're dying," continued Haverman. "They want to get your life force."

"Who's dying?" said Ronald. He had stopped arm wrestling and was staring at Haverman in abject terror.

"The Old Fish People," I explained.

"They come at you from the back," said Haverman. "I don't turn around."

"Why not?" said Ronald.

"I don't want to see them, their dried lips, their mournful eyes, their scaly skin."

"Why do they have dried lips?" said Ronald.

"It doesn't matter," I said.

"Do they have bodies, or only heads?"

"Oh, they have bodies all right," said Haverman. "They live in the swamps, but they never get to go there so they're all dried out and clammy."

"Maybe you're seeing into another dimension," said Ben. He was lying on his back, staring up at the tip of his boot, lining it up in some relative perspective to the leaves of this big oak tree we were sitting under.

"Don't tell me that," said Haverman. "Jesus. Give me a break."

"What do you mean, 'another dimension'?" said Ronald. "You mean they're real, and there might be other real things like Fish People or something, and they're around us all the time, like around here, under this tree, but we can't see them?"

"Probably," I said, "but I wouldn't worry about it. They haven't gotten us so far."

"There's always a first time," said Ben.

Just then I heard Jenny scream from inside the house. Then she started crying, so I hurried inside. When I got into the living room I found her in a heap on the floor. She had her dancing stuff on. The Muppets were singing on the stereo. There was this mess on the floor of torn fabric and stuffing.

"What happened?" I asked.

"I was on the chair and throwing Bunny up and spinning and jumping down to catch him," she said. She was crying a lot so it was pretty hard to understand her. "He went too far and I couldn't catch him and he hit the bookcase and I fell down."

"This whole thing was not a good idea."

"It was ballet."

"Well, it was too rough."

I noticed this cut on her knee. It didn't look bad, but it was bleeding so I went to get the first-aid kit. "You're all right," I said on my way to the bathroom.

She screamed again. "Bunny's all ripped!"

"We can fix him," I tried to reassure her.

I got the first-aid kit from the cupboard and headed back into the living room. Jenny was collecting sections of Bunny from around the floor. "He hurts so much," she was saying. "Is he gonna get back to regular?"

"He'll be fine." I opened the first-aid kit and took out the peroxide, the Merthiolate, and some Band-Aids.

"Fix him," said Jenny.

"In a minute." I opened the peroxide, then poured some on her knee. It fizzed like crazy.

"Fix Bunny."

"In a minute." It was hard to manage everything without spilling the peroxide all over the rug. Then Jenny started squirming and it became impossible.

"Bunny first," she said. She banged into my arm, nearly demolishing the rug by sending the Merthiolate bottle flying through the air. Thank God the top was on and also that I caught it before it hit the stone fireplace.

I should have known Bunny would have to be fixed first. She could have been on the point of death. It wouldn't have mattered. Bunny first. I also should have known kids by this time. I wasn't so far away from having been a kid myself.

We collected all the stuffing and various sections of the poor, nearly demised rabbit and restuffed him. Jenny got the ears from over by the bookcase. We sort of held the parts together while I wrapped him around with adhesive tape. The effect was pathetic.

"He looks awful," said Jenny.

"I'll sew him later."

When later? I thought. Tonight? When tonight?

I had so much homework I couldn't even afford to think about it and maintain my sanity, not to mention the possibility of preparing another round of grilled-cheese sandwiches. And what? Hunter's soup, or chicken with wild rice?

"It won't hurt him," said Jenny.

"What won't?"

"When you sew him."

"No."

"He doesn't have feelings, 'cause he doesn't have skin."

"Right," I said. "This'll sting." I was about to apply the Merthiolate to Jenny's knee when Haverman poked his head in through the kitchen door. Ben and Ronald were behind him.

"What's the story?" said Haverman.

"Jenny cut herself."

Jenny held up Bunny. "He's not gonna always be taped funny like this."

"Good," said Haverman.

"Is he all right?" said Ronald.

"He's getting stitched," said Jenny.

"Good," said Haverman.

"He doesn't have feelings, 'cause he doesn't have skin."

"That would do it," said Haverman. "Listen, Chris, we're going over to Ben's. Want to come?"

"I have Jenny." I was applying the Band-Aid, or trying to. I often have trouble with that. The two ends always seem to stick to each other and I can't pull them apart.

"I'm too young to be alone," said Jenny. "It could be dangerous."

"We see that," said Haverman.

The guys said good-bye and left.

"Bad day for Bunny," said Jenny.

She was right there. She just didn't know how bad.

CHAPTER
5

I find it ironic that this night, of all nights, we had a conventional, sit-down, family dinner. My mother cooked it and the four of us sat down together at the same time and ate. I don't think we'd done that for weeks, but THIS NIGHT we had a family dinner. The food was not great, or thought out at all, but who could blame my mother? At least after finding out the extent of the pressure she was under that night, who could blame her? Not me.

Nobody said a word throughout the entire meal. Jenny had taped Funny Bunny Richardson to a high kitchen stool, and he sat, or stood, there next to her at the table. I remember staring at him with this incredible knot building in my stomach and nobody speaking. I still hadn't sewn Bunny, and the adhesive tape made him look like a mummy. The expression of alarm and fear on his face was totally grotesque coupled with the bandaging. Jenny periodically fed him her peas, which sort of dribbled down onto his plate and lay there, forgotten. The whole scene was too depressing. I could tell that my mom had been crying because it was all swollen in the area around her eyes and they were bloodshot. She ate less than Bunny. My dad ate, but he didn't look at any of us. He didn't even notice Jenny wasting her peas. He finished the last of his overdone hamburger and set down his fork. "Your mother and I have something to tell you," he said. "I'll start and then your mother will pick up with what she wants to say."

I went totally numb. Jenny served Bunny some more peas.

"First, before I say anything else, I want to say this. Your mother and I love you both very much. You must remember that."

My mother was staring at the tablecloth. Her eyes were starting to cloud up and I knew she was going to cry again. My father folded his napkin in consecutive geometric layers and set it under the side of his plate. "Your mother and I are getting a divorce."

It was like my whole insides gave away. There was this sense of falling. I wanted to grab on to something, but everything was evaporating and there was nothing there. Then the phone rang.

Oh, God, I thought, not the phone. Isn't the news enough, the announcement of the end of our world? Isn't that enough to bear without having to deal with a person on the phone? Somebody should answer it, I thought, but I couldn't move.

My father just went on. "I know you understand what this means, Chris, so I'm going to address myself to Jenny, but everything I say goes for you, too."

The phone rang again.

"The phone's ringing," said Jenny.

"I know," said Dad. "For a long time now Mommy and I haven't been getting along very well. There have been a lot of fights. Have you noticed that?"

"Bunny has."

"Bunny has. Yes, well, right. He's right. There have been a lot of fights. Too many, and it's not good."

The phone rang again. My dad got up to answer it. My mother kept staring at the tablecloth. I could hear my dad on the phone—business. "Tell him it's now or never," he was saying. "We can't wait around."

I started feeling dizzy.

"Can I call you back in ten minutes?"

TEN MINUTES? Our lives are at stake and he gives it TEN MINUTES?

Dad hung up and returned to the table. Jenny was removing the tape that attached Funny Bunny Richardson to the stool. "Bunny's leaving," she said.

"Let Daddy finish," said my dad. "Sit down now and don't fiddle with the tape."

Jenny sat down. Then my dad went into this speech about divorce and what it means. I swear (and I don't do that often) but I swear it was the stupidest and most nonsensical speech I had ever heard. It was like I was in the midst of a black comedy, some bizarre, unwanted satire on the reasonableness of the insane. I wanted to scream, but I felt somehow paralyzed.

"Now, as I said earlier," my dad continued, "we love you both very much and that will never change. But sometimes the person you marry changes and sometimes you change."

Don't say "change" again, I remember thinking. I felt that if he said "change" one more time I would go for his throat.

"Mommy and I have both changed in the sixteen years since we've been married."

There it is, I thought. He said it. The past tense does not get him off the hook.

"We don't make each other happy anymore, so we have to make a change. And that change will be a divorce."

Why? Aren't there other kinds of changes? Can't people change for the better, bring out the best in each other?

"We're going to be getting a divorce and what that means, Jenny, is that we won't be living in the same house anymore. You and I will be living in the same house sometimes, and you and Mommy will be living in the same house sometimes, but Mommy and I will be living in different houses."

He was trying to make it sound like a nice idea, but it wasn't working. I felt this wave of total lack of respect for him, which scared the hell out of me. This was my dad who I loved and who had taught me so much and taken care of me and been my friend and ordered presents for me from Eddie Bauer in the middle of the night and held my hand when I had nightmares from the measles.

My mother reached out her arms to Jenny. "Come here, sweetheart," she said.

Jenny got off her chair and climbed into my mom's lap. She curled up into a kind of ball.

My dad kept going. "So, Jenny, you and Chris will live with Mommy part of the time and with me part of the time, the time you're not living with Mommy. But Mommy and I won't be living in the same house, not anymore. Mommy will stay in this house, for a while at least, and I will have an apartment in the city, so when you live with me you'll be in the city and when you live with Mommy you'll be here, for a while, at least."

The room started to spin and I felt I was either

going to pass out or throw up. My mother was stroking Jenny's hair. Then the phone rang and I totally freaked out.

"NO!" I screamed. I jumped up and ran to the phone, ready to rip it out of the wall.

Coward, I thought.

I simply lifted the receiver. "WE CAN'T TALK NOW!" I shouted into the phone. Then I slammed the phone down and turned to my dad. "YOU CAN'T DO THIS!"

"You're upset," he said. "Let's talk about it."

"I DON'T WANT TO TALK ABOUT IT!"

"Please, Chris," said my mother.

"YOU'RE NOT GOING TO DO THIS!"

"It's not up to you, Chris," said my dad.

The phone rang and I turned and left the house. I slammed the front door and found myself in the front yard in the dark. I had to pace, to move. I started wildly circling the large oak tree, ready to pull it out by its roots. Now who was going crazy? Inside I could see Mom holding Jenny, and my dad on the phone. That was almost the worst part of the whole thing to me, at that moment anyway. How could he be on the phone at a time like this? I kept circling the tree, then pacing back and forth, the energy building and building inside of me.

WHERE IS MY FAMILY?

Just then I spotted our Halloween pumpkins on the front steps, Jenny's and mine, a gift to the children of Bedford from the Bixler Real Estate Company. They had grotesque and jagged smiles (the pumpkins, not the Bixler Real Estate Company), and were rotting, with dark patches and green mold beginning to grow. I felt this immense hatred for those pumpkins. They took on this whole meaning for me, the fact that they would rot and turn ugly like that.

Everything rots, I thought. Everything changes. WHY?

The pumpkins symbolized my family to me. I grabbed my pumpkin, leaving Jenny's to rot in peace, and carried it to the back of our house. It was truly disintegrating. My fingers went into layers of soft mush and green, slimy fur. I had to destroy the pumpkin, stamp out the rot (The Demise of the Bixler Pumpkin). Somewhere there was a twisted logic to it, but how it would help my family I'm not sure. Behind our house is a bird sanctuary. It's down a hill, forty acres of woods. I ran toward the hill and the woods and hurled the rotted pumpkin over the side. It hit some rocks and truly exploded. A cataclysmic array of exploding pumpkin. I stood there, breathing heavily for a few minutes, and then just sat down on the grass and cried.

I wish I had a dog, I thought. I could hold on to him and cry. You can't hold on to fish.

CHAPTER
6

I don't know how long I was out there. It seemed like hours. And it was freezing. November gets cold, but I wasn't thinking about coats when I left the house. After about an hour, I guess, I perceived a presence moving toward me. It was my mother. She sat down next to me and we just held on to each other. We didn't say anything, just held on, and then we let go and just sat there on the grass. Two lost souls. That was the thought I had at the time. She had her jeans on and over her sweater she wore a large man's shirt. My father's? I remember being glad she wasn't wearing her warm-up suit. Both my parents continually wear them. Do they do it because it's the thing that a lot of other people are doing? My mind went off on this whole train of thought about warm-up suits, and then I remember wondering, Why? Why am I thinking about warm-up suits at a time like this? Avoiding the contemplation of disaster? Probably. But it was also my father's shirt. Maybe that was a good sign. Why would she wear his shirt if she really hated him? I wouldn't do a thing like that.

These thoughts were running through my traumatized brain as we sat on the grass, freezing in the moonlight. I started shivering. My teeth were chattering. My mother was holding her head in her hands. "We'll get through this, Chris," she said. "I promise."

Speak for yourself, I thought, but I didn't say anything.

Then Mom turned up her collar and hugged her knees. She looked like a little kid almost. "I need your help," she said.

"In what way?"

"This is going to be roughest on Jenny. You can help her in ways nobody else can."

"I don't know about that."

"You can."

"Right now I'm just trying to get through this night."

"I understand." She looked over at me, shivering and chattering there by her side. "Aren't you cold?"

"I'm freezing."

"Come inside."

"I'm not ready for that. I'd rather sit here and freeze."

We sat there quietly for another several minutes, shivering and watching the moonlight slanting through the trees in the woods. Mom was crying. "Better luck next time," she said.

"What do you mean?"

"Nothing. Listen, Chris, if you're not ready to come in for the night, could you come in for a few minutes?"

"What for?"

"Jenny got really upset after you left. She shut herself in her toy chest and she won't come out. I tried to pull her out, but she just got more upset. She's mad at me. Maybe you could help. It's cold and it's late and I want her to get some sleep."

The thought of Jenny crumpled up and confused in her toy chest really got to me. "All right," I said.

We stood up and brushed the grass and stuff off our clothes and started toward the house. "I'm not going to let it happen," I said. I surprised myself. I hadn't expected to say it.

I didn't see Dad when we went back inside. I didn't know where he was and I didn't much care. I went upstairs to Jenny's room, which appeared to be empty, of people that is. There were toys all around and stuffed animals, but no sign of Jenny, or Bunny.

"Jenny?" I said.

There was no answer.

"Jenny."

"I'm not here."

"Yes, you are. You're in your toy chest."

"Bunny's in the toy chest. I'm disappeared."

"You can't be disappeared," I said. "I hear you talking."

"So you think in your mind."

I approached the toy chest and opened the lid. Jenny was staring up at me. Of course she was holding Bunny. "I have a stomachache," she said.

"Come out and I'll get you some bicarbonate."

"No."

"You and Bunny come out and I'll give you both some bicarbonate."

"Bunny doesn't need bicarbonate."

"Lucky for him," I said.

"He has other problems."

"Listen, Jenny, I know you're upset about what Dad told us."

"I'm not."

"You are. I can tell. Why would you be hiding in your toy chest?"

"I have my reasons."

"Such as?"

"Such as never mind." She slammed shut the lid of the chest.

"I think it would be good if I explained a few things," I said.

"I don't want to know anything about anything."

"You can't take that attitude."

"I can if I want to."

When Jenny gets stubborn like that there's practically nothing you can do. I figured I was going to be there for a while so I sat down on the floor next to the toy chest in the middle of all the toys and stuffed animals. I usually leave her alone when she gets like that because she can drive you crazy, but this was a special circumstance. I sat there for a minute or two, waiting for her to soften up. A stuffed donkey stared pathetically up at me. So many stuffed toys have sad expressions. This particular donkey was an old one of mine, Rusticales. How did he get that name? I couldn't remember. I sat there smoothing the fur back away from Rusticales' eyes. Then I had an idea. I addressed the toy chest. "Could Bunny come out now?"

"I doubt it."

"It's time to stitch him."

There was a pause. Then the lid of the toy chest opened very slowly. A hand appeared, holding Bunny, still grotesquely taped with adhesive.

"You have to come out, too," I said. "You have to hold him. He might be nervous."

She climbed out of the toy chest, letting the lid drop shut and sat down next to me on the floor, holding Bunny.

"What will happen?" she said.

"In what sense?"

"Who will take care of Bunny?"

"You mean if Mom and Dad get divorced?"

Jenny nodded her head, a tiny nod, like she didn't want to admit the whole thing was even a possibility, but she needed information.

"They won't," I said. "I'm not going to let it happen."

What did I mean by that? I didn't know. I only knew I had to do something, shock them back to their senses.

"What can you do?" said Jenny.

"I don't know."

"Nothing, that's what."

"I wouldn't be so sure."

"But what? What if you can't do anything? What if you can't stop it, because it's in their minds and they decide and they're grown-up and big? Maybe they made their minds up to a stupid way, but that's it. They're parents."

"I don't care who they are," I said. "If something's wrong, it's wrong."

"You're wrong," said Jenny. She was twisting the lace of her sneaker around her index finger, virtually to the point of cutting off the circulation. "What if it happens anyway? You're not Superman."

She had me there.

"What then? Who will take care of Bunny?"

"You will," I said. "Just like you always do."

"But I won't be anyplace."

"Of course you will."

"But no. If Mommy goes away from Daddy and Daddy goes away from Mommy, then I'm on the side-walk."

"You're not on the sidewalk. Why do you say that?"

"Because."

"Don't just say because. Tell me what you mean."

"Don't be mad."

"I'm not mad. I'm trying to help you."

"You're not doing a very good job."

That did make me mad, but I tried to control myself.

"Listen, Jenny, if Mom and Dad got divorced, you'd be okay. They'd remember you and so would I. You wouldn't be left on any sidewalk. You have to believe me. It would be hard, but you'd be okay, and you could take care of Bunny."

"Well, see, I have to," she blurted out. Then she started crying. "Funny Bunny Richardson is the best bunny in the whole world," she said, tears pouring down. "He needs me. He's the best and helpless bunny."

CHAPTER
7

          I didn't sleep well that night. My feeling is that I didn't sleep at all, but that's probably an exaggeration. I remember lying in bed, staring at my fish, going over and over again what had happened. At first I tried to forget about it. I tried to concentrate on something else, but when I succeeded in doing that, invariably I would suddenly remember what I was trying to forget. Divorce! It was as if I were hearing the news for the first time, torn apart once more. I discovered it was better to keep thinking about it. That way I couldn't be taken off guard. I was already in the midst of disaster and still alive. Small comfort.

In thinking back, I must have slept that night because my clock went off as usual, tearing me from another world. (Where do we go when we sleep?) Anyway, I have a nice thing, which is a clock radio with a cassette-tape set-up. The sound quality is not great, but you can set up a tape to wake you up. I usually awake to the score of *Raiders of the Lost Ark*, which is a favorite of mine and also has a rousing score. If there's one thing I need at six o'clock in the morning, it's a little rousing. *Raiders* summoned me to a new day, and it was only moments before I remembered THE NEWS. It came crashing down on me once more.

I fed my fish, washed, brushed my teeth, made a protein drink for myself, drank it, collected my books, and left. Everyone else was still asleep. My mom and dad usually get up just after I leave and I don't know when Jenny gets up. She doesn't leave until eight forty-five.

Nothing is colder, or more horrendously depressing than walking to the bus stop at six forty-five on a dark November morning. I should have worn my down vest, I thought as I trudged down the hill toward the main road. I had my jean jacket on, definitely a mistake. It was as if I had never warmed up from the night before. In actuality, I hadn't. Would I ever?

When I got halfway down Elm Ledge (the road that leads to the main street, Main Street) Amy came out of her house. She had this humongous stack of books, plus a totally crammed book bag. Sometimes she stays up all night to study—not my idea of a good time.

"Hi, Chris," she said.

"Hello, Amy."

That's about as much as we usually say in the morning, any of us, except maybe Haverman. Who can think at that hour, in the cold, in the dark?

When we reached the bus stop Haverman was already there. He doesn't live on our road, but on the days he stays with his father (he has a split-week situation, three days with his dad, four days with his mom) he comes over from Commodore to ride with us. He cuts through the woods.

"Hi," said Haverman.

"Hi," said Amy.

I put my books down on the ground and leaned

my back against this big tree that's down there. That's my usual position.

"Remember me?" said Haverman. He was peering directly into my face, two inches away from my nose.

"Why wouldn't I remember you?"

"Things change."

"It's not a good day, Haverman."

"What's wrong?"

"Nothing."

"Something's wrong," said Amy. She was still holding her humongous book bag. I wondered why she didn't set it down. "I thought you were in one of your moods when we walked down the hill."

"What's that supposed to mean?"

"What?"

"One of my moods."

"One of your moods. You know. How you are. Prevailing grouchiness!"

"You haven't seen anything yet. If it's prevailing grouchiness you want, watch out."

"I don't want it. I just noticed it was there."

I adjusted my position against the tree. Some rough and spiny bark sections were sticking into my back. Then I noticed a strange thing. It was Ben, sort of stumbling down the hill. He looked, without exaggeration, like he was literally still asleep. His eyes were closed and his hair was rigid and stiff. I guess the way he had been resting on his pillow had mashed it that way and he needed a shampoo, so his hair was unpliable and kind of stayed where it had been mashed.

"That you, Ben?" asked Haverman.

Ben mumbled something in response, but it was indiscernible. He lay down on the cold ground and continued to sleep.

"They're all out today," said Haverman.

"Don't start," I said.

"What's wrong?" said Haverman. He dropped his spiral notebook (he never carries textbooks, I don't think he studies) and got down on his knees, staring up at me. "I plead with you on bended knees."

"Don't bother."

The group at the bus stop was growing. Alison was there and Bruce and Wendy, but they were off to one side in a kind of clump of their own. Haverman was still on his knees. "Answer me, my lord, my liege."

"Get up, Haverman. Don't make a whole big thing now."

"Pardon me for living."

"Just get up."

He got up and brushed the dried leaves off his survival pants. "What is it, Mills?" he said. "I won't kid around, okay? Maybe I can help."

"My parents are getting a divorce."

"No."

"Yes. Or so they say."

"I can't believe it."

"That's two of us."

"Bummer," said Amy.

"It's a bummer, all right. I'm not gonna let it happen."

"I went through that, too," said Haverman. "All three times."

"Through what?"

"Thinking I could stop it. You always figure that way. Pretty soon you realize you can't do a damn thing about it."

"I will."

"Good luck."

"Whose side are you on, Haverman? For God's sake."

"He's only trying to help," said Amy. She was still holding her twelve tons of books. "You have to face reality."

"And what is that?" I asked.

"You know."

"I'm asking you."

"It's . . . facts."

"What facts?"

"All facts."

"All what facts?"

"All the facts there are."

"As who sees them?"

"As they are."

"And how is that?"

"It's just . . . as they are."

"And who decides?"

"Who decides what?"

"How they are."

"Nobody decides. It's just the way they are. They exist. Reality is there. It's just a matter of opening your eyes."

"I see one thing, you see another."

Amy put her book bag down on the ground by her feet. She pushed up the sleeves of her rose-colored CB jacket and gave me a stare, like I was being difficult or something.

"You don't believe in reality?" she asked.

"Of course I do. I just think we get confused a lot of times and we can't see it."

"And you think your parents are confused?"

"Yes, I do. If you want to put it that way, I think they're confused."

"And you're not."

"Not about this."

"What are those peaches called?" said Haverman.

He was sitting on the ground not far from Ben, who was snoring away in his morning sleep.

"Don't interrupt," said Amy.

"It's driving me crazy," said Haverman. "It's on the tip of my mind."

"What peaches?" said Amy.

"The ones without any hair."

"Nectarines."

"Nectarines! Jesus, that's it! I couldn't think of what the hell they were called. You know how that can drive you crazy?"

"You drive me crazy!" I said. "My parents are getting a divorce and all you can think of is nectarines? What the hell is wrong with you?"

"I'm sorry," he said. "It was just, you know, I couldn't think. It was jamming my brain."

The large orange bus pulled to a stop and wheezed. Its door groaned open. Amy retrieved her book bag.

"Up, Ben," said Haverman. He nudged him hard in the side. "Abandon ship. All hands on deck. Rise with haste, or forever face your briny death."

"What?" said Ben.

"The bus is here," said Amy. She stepped over Ben and started up the stairs.

Inside the bus, as usual, it was mayhem. Ben slept, sitting up, and Haverman and I found a seat near the back. Amy sat behind us with her books, peering over our shoulders.

"I'm sorry about the nectarines," said Haverman.

"Forget it."

"I get crazy sometimes."

"Tell me about it."

"Listen, it's not so bad. You're going to get more attention and presents and stuff than you ever had. I'm telling you. It's called guilt and they're both gonna get it. They're gonna get it and you're gonna reap the benefits."

"There's no benefits, Haverman. It stinks."

"You can't fight it," said Amy.

"What am I supposed to do, sit around and watch it happen?"

"Everybody feels like that," said Amy. "Like, you know, you just don't want to accept it, but then you do."

"Not me."

"What are you going to do," said Haverman, "round 'em up and give 'em a talking to? 'Ah, listen folks, I've thought this divorce thing through and it's just not feasible. What's happened here is you've briefly lost your minds. What I want you to do is return to your room, both of you, and remain there until you regain your sanity.' "

"I don't want to talk about it, Haverman. If you can't be serious, I don't want to hear from you."

"Don't get testy."

"I'm not testy."

I was testy, but who could blame me?

CHAPTER
8

Of all days Mr. Story chose this one to pressure me about the homecoming float. Mr. Story is this overly enthusiastic guy, a nice person, actually, but he can get on your nerves. He keeps coming at you from around corners in the hall and questioning your school spirit. He teaches "Ancient Myths and Their Meaning in Contemporary Life," or something in that general order. I understand from certain seniors, the only ones who can take the course, that he loves his subject. He also loves science fiction, and beyond all, it seems, he loves dear old Wallace Beeley.

"Going to the prom?" he'll say, popping out of J building and scaring you half to death as you're madly dashing to incomprehensible chemistry. (Does Doc Merns understand his subject not at all, or is he so brilliant that no other mortal can get a foothold?)

Anyway, this morning Mr. Story popped out of the faculty lounge, wearing a muffler, as is his custom, and went into this entire thing about the homecoming float. I was totally in a world of my own, just trying to get through the day, unable to assimilate the horrendous news of the night before, so it was hard to get a grip on what he was saying. The gist was, wouldn't

I love to give up my weekend to immerse myself in the construction of two big dummies, or enormous, stuffed, doll-like figures, they were planning, of a Wallace Beeley football player demolishing one of our friends and neighbors from Fox Lane on the back of a disguised truck.

"I don't think so," I said. It was an appealing offer, but it didn't feel timely.

"Oh, come on, Chris. It'll be a ball. What do you say?"

"I can't. I'm sorry."

"Where's your school spirit?"

"I don't know, Mr. Story," I said.

"What kind of an answer is that?"

"It's . . . ah . . . my answer. You'll have to forgive me, Mr. Story. It's not a good morning."

"Want to talk?"

"No thanks."

"A little work on the float might be just the thing."

"I don't think so."

"Get out there with the other kids, breathe the fresh air, do something for your school . . ."

I couldn't stand listening to him anymore. I felt bad about that because I like him in a funny way, but I had a splitting headache and I was exhausted and depressed and SCARED. I had to think, but nobody was giving me any time. Class bells, announcements in the halls, locker combinations, homework assignments, noisy kids, over-enthusiastic teachers. It was all too much. I had this impulse to shout, "MY PARENTS ARE GETTING DIVORCED! THERE'S NO TIME FOR FLOATS, OR SCHOOL SPIRIT, OR MUFFLERS, OR FOOTBALL! I HAVE TO DO SOME-THING!"

"I have to go," I said. I moved off in a daze to K building.

What happened next was a kind of miracle. If I had to pick a turning point in my life, a point when everything shifted, I would, without question, pick my social studies class on that very morning. At first I was really out of it. I just sat in a depressed sort of stupor, or state of reduced sensibility, sketching our beloved teacher, Mr. Marrone. He's a great teacher, my favorite, I would say, even before the whole rest of my life was changed as a result of his tutelage. I was trying to keep my mind on what he was saying and having no luck at all. My sketch was pretty good, though, as I remember. Mr. Marrone is this vaguely macho-looking guy, about thirty-five, with a beard and very straight hair. He wears these kind of rayon shirts, somewhat shiny, with the buttons open in front and a lot of gold chains. What he mostly looks like is a hairdresser/disco-dancer combination. He's nice, though. I like him a lot. And he's very smart.

Near the end of the class C.J. (his name is Charles, but I never call him that) got kicked out for mooing. C.J. has a certain dubious talent whereby he can make authentic-sounding cow noises without moving his facial muscles to any discernible degree. Most teachers don't send him out when he does it, because he always denies it. He's a great actor and they never know for sure if it's him. He also gets incredibly high marks so they start out by being on his side. Mr. Marrone always sends C.J. out whenever there's any untraceable disturbance because he knows what a troublemaker C.J. is in general and how he gets away with murder.

After C.J. got kicked out I was drawing away and

trying to quiet this fear and anger inside myself. I was half hearing what was going on in class. Mr. Marrone had just asked Ben a question that had gone right by me to which I heard Ben answer, "It's got ten things."

"Amendments," said Mr. Marrone.

"Amendments, right," said Ben.

"What else?"

"I liked it."

"What did you like about it?"

I drew a fourth chain around Mr. Marrone's neck. Then I filled in the beard.

"It had a lot of stuff to say about freedom," said Ben.

"Such as?"

"What?"

Ben's bluffing, I thought, stalling for time.

"What did it have to say about freedom?"

"I'm a little hazy on the specifics."

"Read it," said Mr. Marrone. Then he started asking some more questions and I drifted off again.

I have to do something, I thought. And it's not for me. I can survive it. I've had a family life. I know what it's like. It gave me roots, something to live on. In a few years I'll be away at college, or working somewhere, or at art school. But what about Jenny? They make a stupid, selfish mistake and she pays for it for the rest of her life. Haverman's sister's only five and she rides the bus to kindergarten with a tag telling the bus driver which house to take her to. I can't let that happen to Jenny! It's inhuman! It's not fair! Doesn't she have any rights?

At that point Lorraine's voice started drifting across my consciousness. She sounded smug as usual. "The purpose of the Bill of Rights is to safeguard the people's rights to life, liberty, and the pursuit of happiness."

I got these intense shivers throughout my body. My heart made this kind of surge and then I had this feeling as if my heart had flipped on end and was thumping into the front bones there. What are they? Ribs. I knew we were studying the Bill of Rights. We had been for several days, but in my traumatized state it didn't click in. I was too busy worrying about THE DIVORCE. I went back over the last days' homework in my mind as Lorraine continued her dissertation in her tidy, egotistical way.

Think back.

I forced myself.

There is a Bill of Rights for people who live in this country. This country. What is that? A step at a time here. This country is the United States of America. That's my country! I am in that country now, as I sit here at my desk. What does that mean? That means there is a Bill of Rights here, in this school, in this town, right where I am now! Not just in the past, not ancient history, not just for people with wigs and tights and buttons on their coats and quill pens, not only for them, but for all people in this country, then, since then, and now. Did they revoke it? Think back. Was the Bill of Rights revoked? No. Nobody revoked the Bill of Rights. If they did, I never heard about it. I would have heard. Think back. The little blue pamphlet. "The Bill of Rights consists of the first ten amendments to the Constitution." Okay. And what is the Constitution? The cornerstone of our country. That's what the book said. Thursday's homework. I did it while watching *Magnum, P.I.* Tom Selleck nearly drowned. "The Constitution of the United States of

America is the cornerstone of our country." Okay! So, if the Constitution is the cornerstone of our country and the Bill of Rights is part of the Constitution, then the Bill of Rights is also the cornerstone of our country, being, as it is, part of the Constitution. It has to be true now, today! Just because it's in a textbook, that doesn't make it obsolete. Boring maybe, but not obsolete. Think, brain. Slow and steady. "The purpose of the Bill of Rights is to safeguard the people's rights to life, liberty, and the pursuit of happiness." WHAT ABOUT JENNY'S PURSUIT OF HAPPINESS? ISN'T THAT BEING TAKEN AWAY FROM HER? IT CAN'T BE. THAT'S NOT LEGAL!

My mind raced on and on, like some incredible time machine. Underneath I became aware of Mr. Marrone questioning Haverman and then Haverman's answer.

"How do we safeguard these rights?" was the question.

"Well, that gets into our judicial system," said Haverman. "Trial by jury."

My heart was thundering in my chest. The bell rang. You know how it happens sometimes when you're concentrating hard on something and the phone rings and you jump with the sensation of literally going out of your skin? It's terrifying. Well, that's what happened here.

I raced up to Mr. Marrone's desk, nearly demolishing Haverman who was bent over just in front of me, tying his sneakers. "Sorry," I said.

"It's only my body," said Haverman.

I reached Mr. Marrone's desk as he was collecting his stuff, keys, papers, and a container of cottage cheese. That's all I ever see him eat.

"When does it start?" I asked. In my insane state I was being totally incomprehensible.

"Rephrase your question," said Mr. Marrone. You couldn't blame him.

"The Bill of Rights," I said. I breathed in deeply, trying to get some air. I had shortness of breath. "Is there an age you can be when you don't have them?"

Mr. Marrone took a plastic spoon from the top right-hand drawer of his desk and rested it precariously on top of his cottage-cheese container. "You mean do kids have rights?" he asked.

"Yeah."

"Big subject."

CHAPTER
9

Mr. Marrone had to go somewhere and eat his cottage cheese so we didn't have time to talk. He did, however, recommend that I get a paperback book called *The Rights of Young People*. He said I could probably find out what I wanted to know by reading it, but, if not, he'd be happy to talk with me and answer what he could, or suggest other reading. I thanked him, grabbed my books, and literally ran through the halls to the library. Not only did they not have *The Rights of Young People*, but our librarian, Mrs. Stintman (the smallest mature woman on earth), had never heard of it.

"I'm sorry," she whispered from over her stack of books. Only her eyes were showing and the uppermost top of her head. They ought to requisition her a stool.

Haverman's father is a lawyer! The thought struck me suddenly and without warning. I had just locked up my locker (16–9–22) and was heading for the bus. That's it! My God! Haverman's father is a lawyer! Talk to him. Get legal advice. Trial by jury. There has to be a trial in a court. But how do you do that? What are the steps?

I boarded the bus, searching desperately for Haverman. No luck. Not a trace of him anywhere. I sat down by a window near the back.

Why can't things go right for once? I thought. I was feeling sorry for myself. Things often went right, but at that moment I didn't remember.

After a couple of minutes Amy approached with her famous book sack. She sat down in front of me, adjusted her sack, then twisted around in her seat and started complaining about her unspeakably horrible day. It seems she had failed a math test.

"I'm sorry," I said.

"Thanks a lot."

"I mean it. I'm sorry."

"You don't sound like you mean it."

"I mean it. It's just my life is falling apart. I need a little peace and quiet."

"On the bus?"

"Forget I spoke."

"I'm sorry about your parents. Really."

"Thanks. Have you seen Haverman?"

"I think he has rehearsal."

"Oh, no!" I jumped up and headed for the front of the bus.

"What's wrong?" said Amy.

I didn't answer. I was just about to jump off the bus when Haverman popped out of the theater. He was dressed totally in black and wore a cape. He was rehearsing *The Fantasticks*.

"Haverman!" I shouted.

The bus driver pulled the lever to close the door.

"No! No! Wait!" I shouted.

Haverman stopped in front of the theater. "A Spanish rape!" he sang at the top of his lungs, arms outstretched. That's a line from one of his songs in the show. Then he noticed the bus. "Wait up! Oh,

God!" he shrieked. "Don't do this to me!" He started running toward the bus.

The driver heaved a big sort of groanlike sigh, then opened the door. She's used to Haverman's lateness. I returned to my seat as Haverman boarded the bus. He moved back and sat down next to me, staring at the driver.

"She's got no patience," he said. Then he started rummaging in his half-empty lunch bag.

"I have to talk to you," I said.

"Shoot."

"Not here. It's too noisy."

"Wherever."

"When we get off."

"Okay." Haverman was pulling things out of his lunch bag. Napkins, Saran Wrap, a Hostess Twinkie wrapper, a half-eaten sandwich. "I hate it when cheese sweats," he said. "Look at this. A perfectly decent sandwich, decimated in the heat of my locker."

"Life is hard."

"I'm starving."

"If you were starving, you'd eat the sandwich."

"No, I wouldn't. Sweaty cheese makes me want to puke."

"Fine," I said. "Why don't you just put the sandwich away for now before you start throwing up on innocent passengers."

"What?"

The noise level was reaching monumental proportions.

"Never mind." I turned and stared out the window, praying that we wouldn't get stuck behind a garbage truck and that I could somehow save my sister's life and that Haverman would put away the sweaty cheese sandwich before throwing up on my only pair of wide-wale cords.

Finally we stopped at Elm Ledge. It's always a relief to step off the bus, to hear the blessed quiet, a bird chirping, a dog barking, anything sane. As we started up the hill I pointed to a grassy area off to the side where we sometimes sit. "Let's sit down, okay?"

"You got it," said Haverman.

"Private?" said Amy.

"Not really," I said.

I knew she wanted to join us in the worst way. She can always sense intrigue.

Haverman hurled himself on the ground and stretched out, cape and all, staring at the sky. "Infinity is large," he said.

"Can I quote you on that?" said Amy. She sat down on one side of Haverman. I sat down on the other. Ben hovered nearby, examining a rather alarming rip in his jacket.

"I have to talk to your father," I said.

"What for?" said Haverman.

"You with him tonight?"

"What day is it?"

"Tuesday," said Amy.

"Yup," said Haverman. "Sundays, Mondays, and Tuesdays it's me, my dad, and Sherry."

Sherry is Haverman's father's third wife. Haverman likes her pretty well, but she drives too fast and she doesn't know how to cook. (Could that explain the sweating cheese?)

"Can I come over?" I said. "It's important."

"What do you want with my old man?"

"I need some legal advice."

"What for?"

Just then Ronald approached with his sister, Melanie. They must have walked from Bell, the junior high.

"Does he die instantly, or does he sense his body parts dispersing?" asked Ronald.

"How would I know?" said Melanie. They stopped when they reached us, but they didn't sit down.

"What did it look like?" said Ronald.

"Parts of him went in different directions."

"Parts of who?" said Haverman. He was still lying on his back, his arms and legs stretched out, cape asunder.

"This crocodile," said Melanie. Although younger than Ronald, she looks older. In a certain way she looks entirely grown up, except for her braces. "It's from this stupid movie," she added. "It's so gross. These guys creep up and they're gonna like catch this crocodile and take him to the zoo for research or something, but these other guys plant dynamite in him so he explodes and blows up these two research guys like at the same moment."

"I'm not gonna see it," said Ronald.

"Who asked you?" Melanie reached into her shoulder bag and took out these type of candies placed evenly on a paper strip. She bit at them, removing them with her teeth.

I, on the other hand, was going privately insane. I like a good special effect as well as the next guy or girl, better even, but at this point I felt on the verge of hallucinating. The whole crocodile thing seemed surrealistic, like some twisted nightmare.

What's happening? I thought. Had we not been involved in a serious conversation? Why the crocodiles? Am I dreaming? Will I wake up and find my mother standing by the side of my bed with a cup of hot chocolate like she used to do sometimes when I was small? Will I hear strains of Beethoven's Sixth wafting into my bedroom from the living room stereo? Cozy weekends in a life gone by. What happened?

"Do they really explode him?" said Ronald.

"Special effects," said Ben. "It's tricks."

Ronald sat down.

"Why do you want legal advice?" said Haverman.

Thank God, I thought. If he hadn't spoken I might have sat there for eternity, in a strange and twisted time warp, reviewing the destiny of crocodiles.

"I have to stop it," I said.

"The divorce?" said Amy.

"You're crazy," said Haverman.

"Your parents are getting divorced?" said Melanie.

"They told him last night," said Amy.

Haverman was sitting up now, staring into my face as if he thought I should be locked up for several lifetimes. "You're gonna sue your parents?" he asked.

"If that's what it takes."

"They'll kill you." Haverman reached out for a strip of Melanie's candies. "You expect to go on living with them when they find out?"

"I can't worry about that. There's no family now. It can't get much worse."

"Famous last words. What are you gonna sue them for?"

"I don't know. That's why I have to talk to your father."

"You know what he charges?"

"What?"

"A hundred an hour."

"Dollars?" said Amy.

"Give that girl a Kewpie doll."

That's impossible, I thought. It must take hours

of work, thousands of dollars. Where would I get the money?

"That's even for phone calls," continued Haverman. "The phone rings, he picks up, on goes a timer, and as the minutes tick by, there goes your life savings, right down the toilet."

"My life savings would be gone in three and a half hours."

"My cousin's a lawyer," said Amy.

"A dollar fifty a minute," said Haverman.

"He doesn't practice," said Amy.

"Why doesn't he practice?" said Haverman.

"He's kind of weird."

At that precise moment, and I'll never forget it, I had this flash, a premonition, you would say. I saw the whole thing. This weird guy who didn't practice was the one. He would be my lawyer. We'd be inexorably linked, for better or worse. And I was feeling a lot of the "worse."

CHAPTER
10

Haverman would not let up. "Why doesn't he practice?" he repeated. He had taken off his cape and was rolling it into varying sausagelike shapes.

"He does sometimes," said Amy. "Like a couple of years ago there was an old man, like a hermit or something? He was living in Armonk in a shack and they wanted to take this tree away from him. It was on some land or something. He took that case."

"Is he any good?"

"I don't know," said Amy. "He fixes cars."

"Cars?" I said.

"You know. Cars? Trucks? Motors? He's got a garage."

"Where?"

"In Millwood."

"He sounds crazy," said Melanie. She had finished her candies and was leaning back on her elbows, her legs stretched out, sneakers off, exercising her toes.

"You want to meet him?" asked Amy. "I could like take you over."

"I don't know," I said. I was getting a weak feeling in the pit of my stomach. Fear, I guess, is what it was.

"If he doesn't practice, he might be cheap," said Haverman.

"Want to go?" said Amy.

"How would we get there?"

"My mom could drive us."

"I don't think so."

"Why not?"

"It would be strange, her standing around while I talk about suing my parents."

"She could sit in the car."

"It's not right."

"She could go shopping."

"Maybe she doesn't want to go shopping."

"I'll find out."

Amy went to talk to her mother and I went home to check on Jenny. I couldn't remember where she was supposed to be. Was it Trudy's? I sincerely hoped not. What a day to ship her off to Trudy's. Had my mom asked me to take care of her? I couldn't remember, so I stopped off at the house. There was no sign of her, no sign of anyone, not even Helen. "A house deserted cannot stand." Or was that divided? Both were true. Deserted and divided. That was our house, all right.

I had a banana with some peanut butter on it (it tastes better than it sounds) and then headed over to Amy's. Amy's mother was nowhere to be found either. Amy figured she was probably having her hair done, which she does every two or three days. How much can you do to hair?

"I'm calling Marion," Amy announced. She had just pulled a package of Oreo cookies out of a high kitchen cupboard. She moved toward the phone. "Marion'll take us."

Marion is sixteen, a junior, and has a car of her

own. It's basically a piece of junk, but it runs, a lot of the time, anyway. Marion's father may be divorcing her stepmother soon. If that happens, he's promised to buy Marion a Toyota, a type of consolation prize, I would expect. Marion loves her stepmother.

Amy called Marion while we both ate some Oreos. I wasn't hungry, but who can turn down an Oreo? Marion, as we had expected, was totally excited about the entire idea and promised to pick us up in ten minutes. She was early.

On the ride to Millwood Amy filled Marion in on all the details of my personal existence, which, of course, Marion loved. I mean she was sympathetic, but you could sense the excitement. INTRIGUE. As I think I mentioned earlier, both girls love it.

So there we were, wending our way along Route 22, sharing the remains of the Oreos, with Amy filling Marion in and Marion asking me all types of questions.

"Do your parents still sleep together?"

"How would I know?"

"Well, like does one of them sleep on the couch or something?"

"I don't know."

"It's not indicative anyway."

"Really," Amy added knowingly.

Marion reached for an Oreo. "My parents got separated and then they started sleeping together a lot and then they got separated again and then they got divorced and then they started sleeping together."

"How did your stepmother deal with that?" asked Amy.

"I don't think she knew."

I was feeling carsick. At first I blamed the Oreos, but I think what was really behind it was fear. My whole life seemed uncertain. Suddenly I was on my own. Nobody had asked me if I was ready.

Maybe it's not so serious, I thought. It could have been just another fight. I could go home tonight and they'd be friends again, like it never happened. I'm rushing this whole lawyer thing.

"Here we are," said Amy.

Marion turned into the driveway area and stopped the car. I had no desire to get out. I was still feeling carsick and generally vague and weird.

Maybe I'll sit here forever, I thought. I'll just sit in the car and nothing else will ever happen.

I was in a strange frame of mind.

"He's probably inside," said Amy. She took a huge comb out of her purse and started combing her hair.

The garage itself was a small, wooden, houselike building with what looked like an apartment above, the garage area below. A few cars were around, some half apart, hoods open, motor parts strewn here and there, stacks of tires, but not a soul. I take that back. There was a dog. He stood over by a gas pump, staring at us as if he'd never seen people before.

"That's Bozo," said Amy. "He's a sweetheart."

He looked sweet, I had to admit, a typical garage dog, slow, medium-sized, a little fat, puffed out in the rear quarters, stiff-legged, with a tiny pinhead and sad eyes. I later learned that he has flat teeth from carrying rocks around, his hobby, but I didn't notice that at first. I did, however, notice a sign above the door to the garage. "CORELLI BROS.—FOREIGN CAR SERVICE" it said.

"Let's go in," said Amy.

We got out of the car, Marion carrying the Oreos, as a VW Rabbit pulled up and stopped by the tire air-pressure thing. A sharp-looking young guy in a three-piece, pin-striped suit got out of the Rabbit, took the air hose off the hook, and started filling his tires. He held the hose with only two fingers and kept it far away from his body.

He doesn't want to get his suit dirty, I thought. Then I wondered why, once again, I was thinking about other people's suits when my life was falling apart. The mind has intricate ways.

"Does he bite?" said Marion. She had stopped somewhere between the car and Bozo, who was staring at her, unmoving, eyes steady.

"It's the Oreos," said Amy.

Marion dropped an Oreo on the ground just in front of Bozo, who moved forward and ate it without gratitude. We moved into the garage. Just inside, a young mechanic was working on a small BMW that was up on a rack. He was very tall, over six feet, with dark hair, very handsome. What I would like to look like if I could make a selection. "Hi, Ames," he said.

"Hi," said Amy.

Is this him? I thought. He looks too young. Twenty-four, maybe. How old do you have to be to be a lawyer?

"This is Chris and this is Marion," said Amy. "This is Joey."

"Glad to meet you," said Joey. He wiped his forehead with the sleeve of his dark-green mechanic's suit.

"Same here," I said.

"I'll say," said Marion. She appeared to be nearly collapsing from his general attractiveness. (Take a backseat, Zeus.)

"Where's Archie?" said Amy.

"In the office," said Joey. "So how's your love life?"

"Poor," said Amy. "How's yours?"

"You really want to know?"

"Yes," said Marion.

"We have to talk to Archie," said Amy. She grabbed Marion by the arm and practically dragged her along as we headed for the tiny garage office.

CHAPTER
11

       The office was pretty much a shambles. Car parts, stacks of papers, and magazines littered the place. A picture of a pretty girl wearing a large man's jacket and a muffler was in a frame on the counter between the cash register and a metal spike that impaled a stack of receipts. On the wall behind the register was tacked up a list of upcoming classical concerts at Carnegie Hall, some checked off, others crossed out, and next to it, in a cheap dime-store frame, was what appeared to be a law degree. The whole thing was bizarre, verging on a painting by Salvador Dali—not that twisted or creepy, but the assemblage of things that didn't go together, that was the same. Across from the door where we stood was a shelf next to an ice-cream cooler, and by the shelf, on the wall, was a phone. Sitting on the shelf was another mechanic. He was older than Joey, in his early forties, I would say, with basically similar looks, but more rough, a little craggy. His hair was dark, like Joey's, but curly, not straight. He had the same dark-brown eyes, but more intense. He also wore the same drab green mechanic's work suit. With his free hand he was rummaging around inside the ice-cream cooler.

That's him, I thought.

I knew it instantly. A kind of déjà vu tripped my mind, swept through my body, and was gone. I tried to get it back, to no avail.

"Check your belts, Mrs. Winderman," he was saying into the phone. "If they're not hooked up, the car won't start." He rummaged somewhat violently in the ice-cream cooler with his free hand and came up with a chocolate ice-cream sandwich.

"That's him," whispered Amy.

God help me, I thought.

"Think back, Mrs. Winderman." He tore at the ice-cream wrapper with his teeth, ripping it free of the sandwich, and continued speaking through the ice cream as he chewed. "We went through this last year, remember? Joey picked you up in Hawthorne with the frozen meat?"

He was not my idea of a typical lawyer.

Not typical, I thought, but that might be good. Typical has its drawbacks, a hundred dollars an hour, for one. Keep an open mind.

He looked over at Amy. "Hi," he said. Then, with his ice-cream sandwich hand, he covered the mouthpiece of the phone. "I'm on the phone."

"Right," said Amy.

"Take some ice cream." He removed his hand and spoke back into the phone. "Try it, Mrs. Winderman." He took another bite of ice cream. "If it's not the belts, call me. I'll send my guy." He hung up and jumped down off the counter. "Take some," he said. He meant the ice cream.

"We just had cookies," said Amy.

"So what?"

I was trying to keep an open mind, to give this guy the benefit of the doubt. It wasn't easy. I became aware that my hands were going deeper and deeper into my pockets. I do that when I'm nervous. I thrust my hands down in there to somewhere vaguely within the vicinity of my knees.

"This is Chris and this is Marion," said Amy. "This is my cousin, Archie, or Corelli as he's sometimes called."

"Hello, Mr. Corelli," I said.

"Drop the mister."

"Okay."

"You want some ice cream?"

"No thanks."

Isn't he going to say hello? I thought.

He turned to Marion. "You?"

"Me?"

"Ice cream?"

"No thanks, really. We had a lot of cookies."

"So what?" He turned to Amy. "What's up?" he asked.

"Chris needs a lawyer."

"Oh yeah?" He took the final bite of his ice-cream sandwich, threw the wrapper into the wastebasket, and walked out.

"Don't worry," said Amy. "I told you he was a little weird."

"You weren't kidding."

"You have to get to know him."

"Where's he going?"

"The garage, I guess."

My uneasy feeling about this guy was building. He not only seemed to be totally disinterested in my situation, but more importantly, perhaps, I could not conceive of his really being a lawyer. Not in any way, shape, form, or universe.

Amy led us out of the tiny office. We followed Cor-

elli, as I later came to call him ("drop the mister"), as
he passed Joey and headed for a white Fiat convert-
ible, parked with its hood up. Corelli grabbed a rag
and some tools, bent over the hood, and began working on the engine.

"Could he talk to you?" asked Amy.

"About what?"

"About needing a lawyer."

Corelli turned and shouted over his shoulder in
the general direction of where Joey was working.
"Where's a damn wrench?"

He doesn't want to talk to me, I thought. What am
I doing here?

Joey brought over the wrench, winked at Marion,
much to her delight, and returned to the under-
workings of the small BMW.

"He's busy," I said to Amy.

Corelli bent over the Fiat engine, speaking into its
various inner parts. "What do you need a lawyer for?"

I could hardly make out what he was saying.

"Is this a good time to talk?"

"Why not?"

"You seem busy."

"I'm always busy."

"Maybe some other time."

"This is good." He bent farther under the hood. I
doubted he could hear me.

"Can you hear me under there?"

"Yeah."

I could be dying on the spot for all this guy cares,
I thought. I was beginning to get angry.

"Why do you need a lawyer?"

"My parents are planning a divorce." I nearly
shouted. I felt sure he couldn't hear me.

"So?"

"I want to stop them."

"What for?" He grabbed the wrench and began tapping on something under the hood.

"It's a mistake."

"How do you know?"

"I know."

"How?"

"I'm involved. I know."

"How do you know?"

I felt this anger building.

Why is he fighting me? Why won't he look me in the face?

"Is that what holds the wheels on?" Marion had inched her way over to where Joey was working on the BMW. She was staring up at the rear axle.

"Better believe it," said Joey. "That and a few other things."

"Wow," said Marion. She doesn't know a lot about cars.

"Look, Mr. Corelli," I said.

"Drop the mister."

"This seems like a bad time to talk."

"Why is it your business?"

"It's my family."

"It's their marriage."

More noises from underneath the hood, tinkering, scraping, tapping.

"They're breaking up my family," I said. "I call that my business."

"Really," said Amy.

"So you want to sue them."

"I don't know if I want to sue them. I want to stop them. I need legal advice."

"Forget it," said Corelli. He wiped a large bolt with his rag, then put the rag back in his pocket.

"You think it's not my business?"

"It could be."

"But you don't care." I was surprised at my pushiness. Normally when I first meet people I'm somewhat reserved, but I was in a semihysterical state and he wasn't helping. My life was falling apart. The least he could do was look at me.

"You'd never win," he said.

"How do you know?"

He ignored my question. "But that's not the main thing."

"What's that?"

"What?"

"The main thing? What is that?"

Just then the guy in the three-piece suit with the Rabbit (the car, not the Easter favorite) poked his head through the front door. "Six months to go!" he announced.

Corelli looked up briefly, then back to the engine. "Great," he said. He was removing the battery caps.

"Less than a year, you got yourself a partner."

"Right."

The young guy nodded to Amy, then reached out to shake my hand. "Jerry Ritzer," he said. "How ya doin'?"

"Chris Mills," I said. "And this is Amy."

"How's it goin'?"

"Good," said Amy. She was impressed, I could tell. How can I get his phone number, was her major train of thought.

"Catch you guys later," said Ritzer. Then he left.

Corelli continued working. "Poor bastard," he muttered.

"Why's that?"

"He's in his third year of law school."

"You don't seem particularly in favor of the law."

"I'm not."

"Maybe we should forget this."

"Why?"

"You don't seem particularly interested."

"I'm too interested."

"I see."

I didn't, but I was beginning to search for the easiest way out of the place.

I'll plead with Haverman's father, I thought, beg for free advice. Anything!

"You wanna know my main objection?"

For some reason, at that moment I noticed he had a slight Italian accent.

"All right," I said.

He stopped working for the first time and stared at me with intense eyes. "Pain," he said.

"What pain is that?"

"You fight for something you think is right . . ."

"I know it's right."

"That's worse." He was looking right at me, through me almost. "You fight for something you know is right and you lose. It doesn't change a thing. Pointless torture."

"But if I'm right, why wouldn't I win?"

"You tell me." He went back to the engine.

"Listen, Mr. Corelli . . ."

"Drop the mister."

"Corelli! Listen. I don't know what your story is, but I don't understand you at all."

He stopped working and stared at me while I went through this entire thing. I don't know where it came from. As I said, I'm usually reserved with new people, but for some reason all this just poured out. It was unlike me. I really let him have it.

"I'm going to tell you something, okay? You talk about pain? Well, I've got a six-year-old sister. If this divorce goes through, what about her pain?"

No answer.

"How do you know we couldn't win? We've been studying this stuff in school. People are supposed to have rights! It says so in the Constitution! Justice for all should mean justice for all, wouldn't you say?"

I felt so angry. It wasn't so much at him, although that was part of it. It was basically at the whole situation. I was out of control. I was a hairsbreadth away from crying in front of two girls I go to school with and one total fruitcake auto mechanic/ex-lawyer I had only minutes before been introduced to, but I couldn't stop. I had been told by a supposed lawyer that being right had nothing to do with winning a case, that justice was a thing of the past, an idea that maybe never even had been put into practice. I couldn't accept that. I kept going at him, all this stuff just pouring out. "What about my sister? If a little six-year-old person is too young to do anything about anything, well then, to hell with her! Well, I don't like that way of thinking. I think it stinks!"

"You're right."

"WHAT AM I SUPPOSED TO DO?"

Corelli stared at me for a long time. Then he wiped his hands on his rag, stared blankly at the car engine, then back at me. I was breathing hard. I remember trying to steady myself, trying to settle down enough to leave without stumbling over cables, hoses, and random car parts. I became aware of Amy and Marion staring at me. I remember wishing the ground would open up underneath me and quietly suck me in, or that I would just disappear without anyone realizing, or remembering, forgotten for all time and eternity.

Corelli was staring at the engine, deep in thought. Or was it no thought, his mind a blank? Moments taken to postpone the inevitable. He looked defeated, beaten. He breathed in deep, then let the air out in one great sigh. "Come back tonight," he said. "We'll talk."

CHAPTER
12

I had a lot to think about. I told Corelli that I would come back at eight o'clock, but simultaneously I was thinking I could always cancel. The guy had me totally confused. He was a virtual enigma. Something in me liked him. A lot. But I couldn't get a foothold. I couldn't tell where he was coming from. I needed time to think.

The ride home was uneventful. I pleaded with the girls to be quiet and they were, God bless them. I tuned out. My mind was on overload.

When we reached the house, Mom's Honda was in the garage so I knew she was home. No lights were on, though, or so it appeared. That was puzzling because it was already dark. I thanked the girls and went inside.

"Hello," I called out into the inner reaches of my once cozy and comfortable home, but there was no answer. I turned on the hall light, dropped my books on the marble-topped, wooden table, and took off my coat. "Hello?"

I moved into the living room and turned on the light. No one there. There was no one in the kitchen either. I checked my watch. Five-fifteen. I remembered five-fifteens in years past, Jenny watching *Sesame Street* in her bunny suit, Mom in the kitchen washing lettuce or putting something tasty into the oven. Enchilada pie. I used to love her enchilada pie. We hadn't had it in months. Even a baked potato would have been nice. She often used to put four potatoes into the toaster oven around this time. They'd be ready at six-thirty.

WHERE IS EVERYBODY?

"Hello?" I called.

No answer.

I went upstairs and noticed the door to Mom's room was slightly ajar. It was dark inside.

Did she kill herself?

I honestly had that thought at that moment. I'm not sure why. I peered in through the crack in her door. There was light coming through the window from the streetlamp, or the moon. Mom was on the bed.

Dead?

She still had her clothes on, a suit. She even wore the jacket. I stood there a minute or two, making a somewhat halfhearted attempt to determine whether or not she was breathing. I couldn't tell. After another minute she turned over and faced the other way on her pillow. My heart flipped over. I felt dizzy. There was a kind of rush of relief.

She's not dead, I thought. That's good. It's nice to know these things.

Still feeling a little dizzy, I shut her door and switched on the hall light. Then I headed for my room, ready to collapse in a heap on my bed, stare at my fish, and ease my traumatized soul. On my way down the hall I noticed that Jenny's light was on. Her door was closed, but I could see the light underneath the door. Her room is at the back of the house, which is why I hadn't seen the light from the car.

I knocked on her door.

"Come in!" she said. She sounded cheery. I couldn't understand that.

I opened the door and there she was on the floor of her room, playing with Mr. Muscle Man. Mr. Muscle Man is a body-builder type of doll, or figure, about a foot or so tall, made of this stretchable rubberlike plastic. By pulling on him and stretching him in different ways you can change the contour of his muscles. At that time Jenny was pulling on his left arm, totally disfiguring the poor unsuspecting guy. "Better get stretched," she was telling him.

"Hello," I said.

"Hello."

"How are you?"

She didn't respond. "Now, puff 'em up!" she said. She bashed Mr. Muscle Man's arm back into his shoulder socket. His muscles swelled visibly. "Turnip muscles!" she said. "Big and gigantic!"

I closed the door, wanting to keep things quiet for Mom's nap. "Has Mom been asleep long?"

"Mom would know."

"Of course Mom would know, but she's asleep. I wouldn't want to wake her up to ask her, now, would I?"

Be nice, I thought. This is no time to be tough on her. I wonder if she's worried about Mom being dead, too.

I sat down next to her on the floor. She pulled both Mr. Muscle Man's arms simultaneously. His muscles shifted, then diminished before my eyes. I noticed that Funny Bunny Richardson stared down at us from the edge of the bed. I had stitched him the night before, and the combination of the stitches and his general look of alarm made him look like a Frankenstein rabbit experiencing severe pain.

"Where'd you go after school?" I asked.

"Only Trudy's."

What a day to send her off to Trudy's, I thought. Mom knows better than that, or she should, at least. DID SHE OR DID SHE NOT MAJOR IN CHILD PSYCHOLOGY? This was an afternoon to spend with Jenny, to draw fish pictures with her, or do some coloring books, to drink hot chocolate, to read her a story, to listen to her fears, to reassure her. My mind searched rapidly over all the places my mother could have been that afternoon. What could possibly have been so important? A game of tennis? A trip to Bloomingdale's? An exercise class? A haircut? Was she reading to other people's children at the library? I sincerely hoped not. My respect for my parents was in serious jeopardy. I've later become aware of some of what it must have been like for them, their private tortures, their attempts to survive in a time of crisis. It wasn't easy for them, either. I know that now, but at that time all I could see was Jenny's pain. And, let's be honest, mine, too. Why didn't my dad take off from work for once and pick Jenny up at school, take her to Gedney Park, show her some continuity, some tinge of ongoing father-daughter experience? At that point I was enraged by both my parents, the ones I loved with all my heart. It was not a comfortable way to feel.

"How did things go at Trudy's?" I asked.

Jenny had pushed Mr. Muscle Man's arms back

into place and was squeezing his calf muscles, causing his upper thighs to puff to bizarre dimensions.
"Benjamin bit me on the nose."

"Let me see."

She tipped over in my general direction, thrusting
her face toward mine. "He was quite a baby, but then
he bit me on the nose. You see?"

"I see."

"How terrible?"

"Well, it's not terrible. I mean, he didn't break the
skin."

"There's a terrible mark."

"That's true."

There was a reddish-blue, rather thin line of a
bruise on one side of her nose.

"I better not lose it."

"Lose what?"

"My nose."

"You won't lose your nose. Don't worry about it."

"I better not."

"How was school?"

"You know."

"Were you upset?"

"Nope."

"Was it hard to do different stuff?"

"Not for me."

"You weren't upset?"

"Why's that?"

"About the divorce."

"There's none."

"What?"

"No divorce."

"Well, I'm going to try and stop it, but . . ."

"TURNIP MUSCLES!" She pushed down on Mr.

Muscle Man's head, causing him to bulge out every-where.

"I'm trying to talk to you."

"Pretty soon his skin is going to pop!"

"Put Mr. Muscle Man down, okay? Put him down for a minute."

"His muscles get bigger and bigger, but not his skin!"

"Right."

"Someday it's gonna pop!" She bashed down hard on Mr. Muscle Man's head, presumably to see if his skin would pop, but it didn't. She was obviously vent-ing her anger on poor Mr. Muscle Man, attempting to deny the entire divorce problem altogether. It made me think of a nine-year-old kid I read about in this book on kids adjusting, or not adjusting, to divorce. He said: "The big problem with joint custody is that you have to remember where the spoons are." I can't forget that. All this anxiety built up and shut off and all he can talk about is spoons. It's really sad.

Jenny was stretching Mr. Muscle Man's legs now, attempting to tie them in a large, unwieldy knot.

"I just want you to know that I'm working on it," I said. "I've got some ideas on how to stop it. I met a lawyer this afternoon. I think he's going to help us."

"Trudy buried her cat in the backyard."

"Did she die?"

"Yup."

"That's too bad."

"Yup. She used to snore."

"Trudy's cat?"

"Yup."

"I never heard of a cat that snored."

"You did now."

"I guess I did."

"She was a snoring thing. Just like Dad."

"Did Dad come home yet?"

"Not to my eyes."

"Listen, I don't want you to worry, okay?"

"Not me."

"You seem a little worried."

"You're a stupid one."

"Don't be mean now. There's some hard stuff going on and we have to stick together."

"I know."

"Okay."

"I have a trapdoor mind."

"What's that?"

"It's what you need to figure and I've got it."

"You mean a steel trap. A mind like a steel trap."

"It could be steel."

She was doing that thing I can't stand—when she's wrong or she makes a mistake, and she knows it but will not admit it. It drives me up the wall. I didn't want to challenge her at that moment, so I let it pass. I took a deep breath and stared at the moon, which was visible out her window. It was just a sliver. After a moment or two of cool-down I returned my attention to Mr. Muscle Man, who was all knotted up and bulging from the strain of being tied in knots. He now had what looked like muscles, or maybe more like tumors, on his skull. I thought of my mother napping in the other room. Tumors, death, mother napping. It made a kind of twisted sense. Bunny stared down at us from the edge of the bed. His pain seemed to be mounting.

Those stitches should have been covered, I thought. I shouldn't have left them like that.

"Bunny should have a shirt," I said.

Jenny looked over at Bunny. "He should."

"Do you have one he could wear?"

She shook her head.

"Why not?"

"They're too big."

"I don't mean a shirt of yours, I mean a doll shirt or something."

"No." She dropped Mr. Muscle Man, all gnarled up and bulging, and pulled Bunny off the bed.

"The stitches should be covered."

"I was thinking that before."

I could see the handwriting on the wall. There was no way out of it and I wasn't even sure I wanted there to be.

"I'll make him a shirt," I said.

"Have you seen a vest?"

"Where?"

"Anywhere."

"Sure. "

"They have buttons in the front, but they don't have the sleeve parts."

"Right."

"Daddy has one."

"Right."

"So that's what Bunny wants."

CHAPTER
13

I left Jenny's room and went to lie down for a while with my fish. I do that when I need time to think. I lie on my bed with the room lighted only by my fish tank and watch my fish in their fish ways, doing their fish things, existing there for better or worse in the water with the minimal marine plant life and occasional rocks. I watch them in their simplicity, just letting my mind go, no thoughts imposed, no plans. I gather it's really a form of meditation, which is something that interests me. I'd like to find out more about it. I read a couple of chapters in this book called *Autobiography of a Yogi* that was at Haverman's house for a while. God knows why it was there. I know Haverman never read it. Maybe one of his parents did. Anyway, stuff in that book is so extraordinarily like the basic material in the *Star Wars* movies, which I totally love. I have this inner sense that THE FORCE is real, that what they talk about in those movies is not only exciting and fantastic and incredible, but that it's based on utter fact. I get the sense that my inner desire to be a Jedi warrior is not symbolic, but rather a tangible and practical thing to aspire to. Sometimes when I think about it in a certain way I think it's just brilliant filmmaking, but then at other times I feel like I have my own Obi-Wan Kenobi just waiting somewhere for me to wake up.

Anyway, I lay there watching my fish and listening to my Walkman, *The Empire Strikes Back* it was, and just let my mind go. After a short time I remember thinking I should make a plan.

Okay, now what will I do when I get off this bed? The first thing is to find out if they're still serious. Mom's nap may not have meant anything more than that she was tired. It's unusual for her to take a nap, but it doesn't necessarily mean disaster. Maybe she'll get up soon, hug Dad, smile at him, and head for the kitchen. She may open up the toaster oven and put in those four (key number, four) famous potatoes. She might start broiling a nice chicken. Dad might start setting the table. Maybe he'll be wearing the slipper moccasins that I got him for his birthday. He might have put on a Mozart piano concerto. That might be calmly playing in the background. Let's hope for the best. But let's be prepared! WHAT IF HE DOESN'T COME HOME AT ALL? WHAT IF MOM'S NAP RUNS THROUGH TOMORROW MORNING? I HAVE TO DO SOMETHING! What about this Corelli! I wonder if he's related to the composer. And more important, is he sane? Could he really help me, or would he drive me hopelessly into the ground in confusion?

I figured the only way to find out was to pursue it—him. Go back once more and see what he had in mind. He might be crazy, but I needed someone a little crazy.

A little, I thought. There's the nub of it. A little, I need. A lot, I can do without.

I decided to take Bedford Taxi. Marion had offered

to take me, but since the meeting didn't start until eight, it was conceivable that it wouldn't be over in time for us to get back home by nine. Being sixteen, Marion could be arrested for driving after nine. This thought in no way bothered Marion (intrigue!) but I didn't like it. I insisted. I'd take a taxi.

"Leia's Theme" was just building to a soulful pitch on my Walkman when there was a knock on my door.

"Who is it?"

"It's me."

It was my dad.

"Come in." I turned off my Walkman, pulled the headphones from my ears, and sat up.

My father opened the door. "Am I disturbing you?"

"Not at all. Come in." I switched on the little blue lamp at the end of my bed.

"I brought you something," said my father, moving farther into the room. He was carrying an irregular-shaped package, wrapped in art-store wrapping paper. "The Art Emporium," it said repeatedly on its surface.

"What's this?" I asked.

"Open it."

He handed me the package. It was heavier than I thought it would be and had what felt like metal poles inside.

An easel? I thought. I had been wanting one.

It was an easel, a beautiful, sturdy, bright-red metal easel!

"Thank you!" I said. "Thank you so much!"

"You're welcome. I know you wanted one."

"I did."

I remember thinking how formal we sounded, like we didn't know each other very well. It was strange.

I was really touched, but I only sounded polite. Was it because I really wanted to hold on to him and cry like a baby and beg him never to leave me?

"It's portable," he said.

"I know."

"I thought you might like to take it to the Met."

"I would."

I had always wanted to copy some of the great paintings at the Metropolitan Museum. Dad and I used to go there together a lot, in earlier times when we did things like that. He started taking me when I was real little, like five or six. He loved the paintings so much it never occurred to him that I would be bored. And I never was. I bet I caught my love of art right there with him, relaxing among the Monets.

"We'll go," he said. "Just the two of us."

"Great."

"When all this quiets down."

WHEN ALL THIS QUIETS DOWN! The phrase struck me like a knife, ripped through me, and tore with it all the possibilities of life continuing as I knew it. No turning back. Was this my first consolation prize?

"You could copy the Kunji."

"No, I couldn't."

I was instantly aware of having a headache. I also felt, oddly, that I was made of stone.

"Sure you could. Why not? You love that painting."

"It's beyond me, Dad. It's in another realm."

Kunji is a Russian painter, the teacher of Nicholas Roerich, whom I talked about earlier. They both have this otherworldly quality in regards to light, but Kunji's work is more intricate. His painting at the Met is maybe my favorite painting, a blazing sunset over a river. I would never presume to copy it.

"It wouldn't have to be perfect," Dad continued. "You know. Just an exercise."

"No."

"Well, copy something else."

"Okay."

"We'll go sometime."

"Whenever you say."

"When all this quiets down."

"You said that."

Mom woke up after an hour or so and boiled some hot dogs. They were chicken dogs to be precise, hot dogs made of chicken. I love them, actually, but once more, I wasn't hungry. Mom and Jenny and I sat in the dining room and ate. Well, Mom and I didn't eat very much. Mom drank white wine and stared at her hot dogs and I didn't drink anything and stared at mine. Jenny seemed pleased with the menu. She ate everything on her plate. She had definitely tuned out on the current trend of events. She held Bunny in her lap, but she didn't feed him. That was unusual. She hummed, but she didn't talk, which was even more unusual.

The most and primary disconcerting thing about the supper was, of course, the number three at the table, the EMPTY place. And then to top it all off, my dad was hurrying through the house, PACKING TO LEAVE. How could Jenny have eaten if she had admitted to herself what was going on? With her trapdoor mind and all, you think she would have figured out what he was doing, but no. She couldn't face it.

After dinner I helped Mom clean up. We didn't say anything to each other, or even look at each other, really. I had an uneasy feeling when I dumped our uneaten chicken dogs into the garbage. I felt sorry for them, the chicken dogs, that is, or the chickens that made them. Their existence had had no meaning. (As my dad used to say when he thought he was sounding crazy, "Get the net!")

After Windexing the counter I went upstairs to get organized for my meeting with Corelli. I called Bedford Taxi and told them to pick me up at Elm Ledge and Main Street (my famous pick-up spot) at seven-thirty. I didn't want to have to explain taxis picking me up at the house in the dark, not that anyone would have noticed, the way things were going. I changed my shirt, put on a sweater, took the fifty dollar bill I kept in my desk drawer, put it in my wallet, fed my fish, and headed back downstairs. My homework would have to go untouched for the night. I could probably do everything except my sketchbook assignment in study hall tomorrow. If not, I couldn't worry about it.

When I got downstairs, my mom was on the desk phone, phoning people about her whales. Jenny was in the middle of the living room floor making towers out of these plastic food tubs, Tupperware, I think they're called. She was pulling them out of a large shopping bag. I hadn't remembered seeing the tubs before, or the shopping bag. Was that what had occupied Mom's afternoon, the acquisition of plastic food tubs? It seemed untimely.

" 'Save the Whales' in caps," my mom was saying as I reached the middle of the stairs. " 'Stop the Killing' in small letters underneath."

Save the whales? I thought. What about us?

"I don't care," she continued. She seemed angry. "Just tell him if they're not ready Friday, he can forget the whole thing."

I moved to the hall table to search for my New York Yankees hat. It wasn't there.

"Tupperware, Tupperware," chanted Jenny, mindlessly stacking the tubs. "Get yourself some Tupperware."

"Quiet, Jenny," said my mother. "I can't hear."

Jenny pulled back her right arm and swung it full force, knocking into the tower and sending tubs and lids in all directions. "BASH!" she yelled.

"JENNY!" shouted my mother.

I looked in the closet for my hat, found it on the top shelf among a tumble of gloves and scarves, put it on, along with my jacket, and shut the closet door. Just then my dad came down the stairs. He was still dressed in his suit from work. He carried his tennis racket and a large suitcase.

"Where are you going?" he asked.

"You're the one with the suitcase."

"I asked you a question."

"Out," I said.

"What?"

"Out. I'm going out."

"Where?"

"I'm going to see a friend."

"What friend?"

"What's the sudden interest?"

"I asked you a question."

"What difference does it make?"

I knew I was being grossly disrespectful, but I had no power to stop. I was like a dead person, no feelings of any kind. I take that back. I was furious. I think what got me most was the tennis racket. How could he think of games at a time like that? How cold-blooded. I felt betrayed. The easel meant nothing. I'd throw it out.

"Where are you going?" He had come down to the foot of the stairs. We were standing nose to nose. "Where?"

"I'm going to see my lawyer."

He assumed I was kidding. "Don't get smart," he said.

"Okay. I'm going for a walk."

"CRASH AND DEATH!" shouted Jenny from the living room. She had just knocked down another tower of tubs.

"Can a person make a phone call in this house?" screamed my mother. "For God's sake!"

Things were ganging up.

My father moved into the living room with his stuff. "Your mother's on the phone," he said to Jenny. He set down his suitcase. Still carrying his famous tennis racket, he moved to the coffee table and picked up a pack of his cigarettes.

"You'd better stop smoking," said Jenny, "or terrible things will happen."

My dad put the cigarettes in his pocket.

"Smoke, smoke, smoke, smoke, smoke. You're big and stupid."

"Don't talk to your father like that."

"It's a warning," said my mother. She was still on the phone. "It reads, 'Warning. These pictures of baby seals being slaughtered may be highly disturbing.' "

"You'll die," continued Jenny. "You'll smoke all those terrible many cigarettes and your lungs will turn into brown things and shrink up and get crusted and disgusting and they won't work."

"I CAN'T HEAR!" shouted my mother.

"Take the phone in another room!" said my father. "For God's sake! What a time to make phone calls!"

"You'll die and then will be the terrible thing."

"Can I go now?" I said.

My father didn't answer me. "Let's talk, Jenny," he said. "Stop building with those, ah, plastic containers and come into the dining room."

"I'm busy,"said Jenny, but she didn't move.

"I understand you're upset," said my dad. He still held the tennis racket. That killed me. It was so bizarre and out of place.

"Do you know what the terrible thing is?" said Jenny.

"No," he said. "What is the terrible thing?"

"The terrible thing is that if you die from too much disgusting smoke and crusted up and stuffed lungs they're gonna bury you in Trudy's backyard with her dead cat and that will be very creepy."

"I'm not going to die," said my dad.

"Never?"

"Not now. Not from too much smoking. I don't smoke enough to do any real damage."

"So you think in your mind."

CHAPTER
14

When I got to Corelli's I made arrangements with the Bedford Taxi Man (small, morose, eyes close together) to come back in an hour. I figured that would be about right, although it was hard to know for sure. We said our fond farewells and he pulled off, leaving me to stand alone, a solitary figure in the dimly lit service area amid the gas pumps.

What am I doing here? I thought.

There was not a soul to be seen, not even Bozo. All the lights were out in the garage, but there were lights on in the apartment, or what looked to be an apartment, above the garage.

Maybe he's up there, I thought.

The whole area was pretty dark and deserted. I was getting a little creeped out, to tell the truth. I tried the garage door, which was locked. I was about to panic when I noticed a flight of stairs on the side of the building, leading to a door up there. I climbed the stairs and knocked on the door. No answer. Bozo, or some dog anyway, began to bark. I knocked again. More barking. I was aware of battle noises coming from inside, which I took to mean that someone was watching TV.

I hope it's him, I thought.

I hate to knock on strange doors, especially at night. For some inexplicable reason I had this image of the door opening and there's this enormous lumberjack type of guy with a plaid shirt and suspenders, work boots, and an axe, ready to kill me before speaking.

The battle noises were building, lots of shooting, rocket sounds, and explosions, more barking, and then, "Come in!"

I opened the door to be greeted by Bozo. He stopped barking when he saw me and moved to about a foot from where I stood. Then he just stared at me. It was unusual. Mostly, dogs either stand off at a distance and bark at you, or else they jump all over you and act friendly. Sometimes they sniff, but Bozo just stared with his very sweet and sad eyes, set firmly in his scruffy pinhead. I love that dog.

Corelli was seated at a card table on the far side of the room, playing this electronic game called Vectrex. That explained the battle noises. It's a good game, actually. I have one at home, but it annoyed me that he would be playing then, with my life in the balance and all. I moved into the room and shut the door.

"Shut the door," said Corelli. He was engrossed in the game. The explosions were reaching climactic proportions. I remembered how Dad and I used to play a lot of Vectrex. I don't play anymore.

"I'll be two seconds," he said, violently working the control buttons. "Sit down."

Bozo followed me over to the couch where I sat down. He sat at my feet and continued staring. He seemed to want something, but I couldn't figure out what. I looked around. The apartment was cluttered with pieces of machines, a dismantled bicycle, records, plants, and various other stuff strewn about.

There were some nice prints on the wall. One of my favorite Monets was among the group. In a sense it was cozy. The plants looked well cared for.

Does he take care of them? I thought.

He didn't seem the type. Plants, like animals, need constancy. He seemed too scattered.

There was an enormous bookcase near the card table, filled with legal-looking books. Other law books were stacked randomly in that area. Off to the side was a small kitchen. There was a nice stereo setup. A plastic alto recorder was lying on the coffee table, and some recorder music was on the table also. The table was one of those types that are made out of an old ship's door. I also noticed a picture of that same girl whose picture was downstairs in the office. In this picture she was sitting on the grass with her arms around Bozo. She looked like a nice person.

Maybe she takes care of the plants, I thought.

Corelli was shouting now as the explosions reached their peak. "NO, NO, NO!" he shouted. And then "OKAY!"

The noises abruptly stopped.

"That's it," he said. "I'm quitting." He flicked off the machine, got up, and moved toward the couch. "I got into the second level of spacedust."

"Great," I said. I was unimpressed.

"You ever play that thing?"

"I used to."

"Got any secrets?"

"Not really."

"You let your men die off until the last one. Then you keep redoing things."

"I know."

"Wanna play?"

"No thanks."

He flopped down next to me on the couch. He wore a dark blue sweatshirt and jeans, no socks or shoes. "Listen, kid," he said. "I owe you an apology."

"What for?"

"I was kinda rough on you today. You're in a tough spot. I wasn't much help."

"That's all right," I said.

"See, I got kinda complicated feelings about the law. I won't go into it, but—" He stopped mid-sentence. Another thought seemed to have intruded on his mind. "What did you say your name was?"

"Chris."

"Chris what?"

"Mills."

"You live in Bedford?"

"Yes."

"Your father own a BMW?"

"Yes."

"With an oil leak?"

"Yes."

"It figures."

"You're my dad's mechanic?"

"You're lookin' at him."

Leave it to me, I thought. Fifty thousand lawyers in the state of New York and I pick my dad's mechanic.

I remembered having heard my dad talk about this really good mechanic he had recently found in Millwood. In a small and twisted way it was encouraging. If he was a good mechanic, maybe he was also a good lawyer.

Probably not, I thought. Anyway, why would he help me? He'd lose my dad's business. People don't like to lose business.

"Does that mean you're not interested?" I asked.

"Screw it."

What does he mean by that? I wondered. Screw it in the sense of screw helping me? Screw it in the sense of screw the fact that he worked for my dad?

As so often happened in my early days with Corelli, I didn't know what the hell he meant.

"He's a nice guy, your dad. I like him."

"So do I. Or I used to."

"OH, JESUS!"

"What?"

Corelli jumped up suddenly, alarming Bozo, and ran into the kitchen as if he'd been shot out of a cannon. He pulled open the oven and removed a pair of socks, checking to see if they were dry. "My socks!" he shouted.

"Oh."

He shut the oven door and returned to the couch. Then he sat down and put his socks on. At that specific moment I seriously doubted his sanity.

"I don't have a lot of time," I said.

"Shoot."

"What?"

"Tell me what's going on."

"I don't get the feeling you're all that interested."

"I am. I'm telling you. If I wasn't interested I wouldn't have told you to come back. See, basically, I've given up the law."

"Why's that?"

"You really want to know?"

"Yeah."

"I've always been interested in the truth. The law doesn't get into that much."

"I don't understand."

"Me either. I had some disappointing experiences—disillusioning would be the word. You ever think about disillusionment?"

"In what way?"

"What it means. It's a positive thing when you think about it. The taking away of illusion. Brings you closer to truth. You understand what I'm saying?"

"I think so."

"So I was disillusioned with the law. There were a couple of instances where I knew my client was right, but we lost anyway. The other guy argued it better. I couldn't come to terms with that. I also couldn't stand arguing for things I didn't believe in. It was a mess. I had always wanted to be a lawyer. See, I cared too much. I don't know. I went through maybe three, four months trying to decide what to do, you know, whether to give it up, chuck the whole thing. Then one night I was in this Chinese restaurant with my girlfriend."

"Is that your girlfriend in the picture?"

"Yeah. So we were at the Chinese restaurant and we finished eating and the waiter brought us these cookies, these fortune cookies. I open mine up and it says: 'Oratory is persuasion, not the truth.' That did it. I dropped the law that night and never went back. That was six years ago."

It was strange sitting there, listening to his life story. It made me forget about myself, which was nice. I was getting caught up in his whole problem, and then the story was over and I remembered my life. It was a bad shock.

"So that's my story," he said. "I fix cars. But every once in a while something happens, somebody comes to me, and I gotta do something."

"Is that how you feel about me?"

"How?"

"That you have to do something?"

"I think so. Maybe. Tell me what's going on." Socks in place, he stretched back on the couch and gave me his full attention. For the first time. I noticed at that moment that when he gives you his full attention it's incredibly intense. It's like nothing else exists. It's a great feeling.

CHAPTER
15

I figured I'd start at the beginning.

"Well, last night my dad told me and my sister about the divorce. He said he and Mom had tried everything and it wasn't working. But I don't think that's right. I don't think they have tried everything."

Corelli adjusted a small pillow behind his head at the end of the couch. He folded it double, then laid his head back on it and folded his arms. "Go on," he said.

"I think it's a mistake. We have a wonderful family and we belong together. They can't see that now because for some strange and twisted reason they've become very selfish."

"Why's that?"

"I don't know. It's been driving me crazy trying to figure it out."

"Maybe they don't love each other."

"They do."

"How do you know?"

"I know! They just don't try. It's not the family that's wrong, it's the way they're acting."

"How are they acting?"

"Different."

"How?"

"When I was Jenny's age, they used to do stuff together. We all did."

"Like what?"

"Like picnics, or playing music, or hiking in the woods. We planted a tree. We painted the house. We did that. Just the three of us. We painted all the rooms."

Bozo got up and rested his head on Corelli's chest.

"Good dog," said Corelli. "Lie down."

Bozo obeyed, but he was careful about it. He seemed to be feeling very stiff in his joints.

"Now they're never home," I said. "They're putting all their time and energy into other stuff."

"Such as?"

"Such as making money and whales and shopping and going to the gym and jogging and I don't know what all. They're going to blatantly destroy, or seriously damage, at the very least, the life of my sister, and it's not fair. She has a right to life, liberty, and the pursuit of happiness, and because of their selfishness they're going to deny her that. It's not fair and it seems to me that it's also unconstitutional."

"You'll never win."

"Why not?"

"You're interfering in the personal life of others. Their relationship is their business. And so far as the Constitution is concerned you can forget about that. This is the twentieth century. Nobody takes those things literally."

"I do."

"Good luck."

I was getting that desperate feeling. I knew I was right, but I didn't know how to make him understand.

"Look," I said, "I know it seems crazy, but I can't worry about that. I know what people will think, but that's not a good enough reason to drop the whole thing and say to hell with what I know! I don't think *nobody* should get divorced. Probably some people should. But with my folks, it's a mistake! I know it! Maybe I'll look like a total jerk, but if I feel something is true, I don't think it's right to lie about it, or just shut up. Everybody's getting divorced these days and it's getting totally out of hand. If a family is breaking up and one of the people in that family knows it's a mistake and sees another person in that family being ruthlessly and needlessly damaged, then I think they have to do something!"

"Is there peace in your house?"

"No."

"You want that to continue?"

"What?"

"The lack of peace. You want that to go on?"

"No."

"Don't you think if you forced them to live to-gether—let's say you could do that—don't you think they'd continue to be unhappy? Wouldn't it be worse? They'd have no option of living apart, no choice about it, see? That's a tough spot to put them in."

"It wouldn't be like that!" I felt helpless and over-whelmingly stupid, inarticulate, to make matters worse.

Keep going! I told myself. Forget what you sound like! He has to understand!

"It's a mistake" was all I could say. The word had jammed my mind. It was all I could think of. Like Haverman and the hairless peach. Mistake, mistake, mistake! The rest of this just poured out. I don't re-member the exact words, but this was the gist.

"They don't really want it, not deep down. I know that. I can't tell you how, but I know it! Sooner or later, they'll realize. It's timing. They're going to come back to their senses. But when? That's the thing! They don't know their own mind. Minds! Haven't you ever had that happen? You get caught in something. Some strange, alien motor is driving you, like you're maintaining a direction and it's not good for you at all. It's not what you want even. Like when you're exhausted and you just don't go to bed? You sit, reading magazines or something, or watching TV, or playing ten extra rounds of solitaire, and all you really want to do is sleep? That's what's happening to them. I don't know why, but it is. It's the same thing. They don't know their own minds and I do and I have to help them! They'll see the mistake. I know they will. But what if they're already divorced when they see it? Or worse yet, what if they're both already married to other people? What are they going to do then? How will they fix it? It'll be too late! And what about Jenny? I have to stop them! They're good people and they love each other and they want the family to work. You have to believe me! I wouldn't be saying all this if that wasn't true. They're just confused. That happens to people. It's just like the worst parts of them come out and run things and it's bad, but then it passes. It passes, and when it passes, it shouldn't be too late! Not for my mom and dad! They deserve better than that. They want to do the right thing. Under all the craziness, they do! They have to have a chance! Please, Mr. Corelli! Corelli! Help me! I don't know what else to do!"

I sat there on the couch, limp, spent, totally depleted. I felt this wave of embarrassment. I didn't really know what I had said, but I knew it had been foolish. My lower arms felt numb. Corelli was staring at me very hard. I couldn't tell what he was thinking. I looked at Bozo, asleep through the whole thing.

Dogs are simple. I thought.

I wished I was him.

"Okay," said Corelli.

The sound of his voice startled me, intruding on my dog thoughts.

"What?"

"Okay."

Okay what? Does he want me to go? Does Bozo need a walk? More socks in the oven? Another game of Vectrex?

The farthest thing from my mind was that he meant what I wanted him to mean more than anything else in the world.

"It's always the same damn thing," he said.

"What's that?"

"Someone who's telling the truth. Somebody nobody else is gonna listen to. No money."

I knew what he meant. In an instant my life made a one-eighty turn before my eyes. Energy surged back into my body. "I have money," I said.

"I don't want it."

"I have three hundred dollars."

"Give me a dollar."

"A dollar?"

"Make it official."

"Thank you!" I said. I wanted to jump up and run around the room, but I didn't. I just sat there, trying to be mature.

Corelli sat up. He pulled down on his sweatshirt, which had ridden up to show a wedge of his stomach. He leaned forward, very serious. "I gotta tell you in front, I don't think you'll win. I don't think you've got a chance in hell, to be blunt about it, but I like you and you're honest and you've got a point. Nobody thinks about what the hell they're doing in this damn world anymore. They're all out for themselves and it stinks. I'd like to make some people think. I don't mean your parents exclusively. I mean judges and lawyers, people, whoever might hear about it. Who the hell knows? You want some Grape-Nuts?"

Nothing could have been farther from my mind. "I don't think so," I said.

He got up, arousing Bozo, and headed for the kitchen. "Reconsider. I'll bring you a bowl."

Bozo stretched and moaned, heaved a sigh, and settled in for additional sleep in a different position, on his side, legs straight out in front of him.

I wouldn't mind a bowl of Grape-Nuts, I thought. I was suddenly hungry. No wonder, considering the size of my dinner. Cereal is comforting, especially at night.

"Here we go," said Corelli, returning from the kitchen. He had the Grape-Nuts, milk, sugar, spoons, and bowls. He didn't use a tray, but hugged everything to his chest. He held the box of Grape-Nuts between his chest and chin. "You ever think about Grape-Nuts?" he said. He bent over and set the things on the coffee table next to the recorder.

"Sometimes," I said. I didn't know what he was driving at.

"Grape-Nuts," he repeated. "There's no grapes or nuts in them anywhere. Think about it."

I didn't really want to.

"Change your mind?" he asked.

"What?"

"About the Grape-Nuts?"

"Oh. Yes. Thank you."

He began dumping Grape-Nuts into the bowls. This woke Bozo, who stared, totally alert, with death-defying attention, at the innocent cereal box.

"That got you, huh?" said Corelli. "He's always hungry. He wants Grape-Nuts, but he CAN'T HAVE THEM." (These last three words were said with extra volume and were directed precisely at Bozo, who continued to stare.) Corelli handed me my bowl. I added sugar as he did. We sat there eating for a minute or two in silence.

"First thing," said Corelli.

"Yes?"

"You need a guardian."

"Okay."

"A grandmother, a relative, somebody you like. You're underage."

"Right."

"How old are you?"

"Fifteen."

"You're underage. Technically, the guardian has to bring the suit." He poured some more Grape-Nuts into my bowl. "NOT FOR YOU," he told Bozo.

Bozo stared at me as if I were eating his best friend.

"You know anybody?"

I thought right away of my grandfather. He's a great guy. He's a little vague sometimes, but he doesn't miss a trick. There's just some things he doesn't care about and he won't pay any attention. He doesn't care what anybody thinks. Anyway, I've never minded his vagueness. Underneath he has a big heart. He lives in this place called Heritage Village that he hates because it's so far away from us. Well, not horrendously far. It's in Connecticut, but he would like to be closer. I wondered if he even knew about the whole DIVORCE PLAN. Probably not. My parents didn't pay much attention to him, a further symptom of their ruthless self-involvement.

"My grandfather might do it."

"Great."

"What would it entail?"

"Not much. Sympathy to your situation, a willingness and availability to appear in court. He'll have to sign papers saying he's bringing the suit."

"I think that could be arranged."

"Ask him." Corelli got up, picked up the box of Grape-Nuts and the milk, and headed for the kitchen.

I was aware of this uneasy feeling ranging around in the pit of my stomach, despite the calming influence of the Grape-Nuts. What was it? I caught myself looking at the stacks of law books gathering dust in the far corner of the apartment. Dust. That was it.

This man will help me, but does he know what he's doing? Has he read any of those books in the last six years? Am I joining up with disaster?

I watched him in the kitchen, rinsing out a metal bowl.

I have to say something, I thought. Clear this up, get it out in the open.

I tried to sound casual. "This isn't going to be a strain for you, or anything, is it?"

"What?"

"Well, you know. Going back into this whole big law thing after all these years? Do you have to remember a lot of stuff? You know, reread a lot of books?"

"No."

No, what? It wouldn't be a strain? He wouldn't have to reread anything? He wouldn't bother? What?

I don't understand what he means, I thought. This is not a great quality for a lawyer.

Corelli set the bowl on the counter, poured in the

Grape-Nuts, and added the milk. He seemed so decent, a good quality for a lawyer, for anybody for that matter. My brain was swimming, overloaded.

Let go, I told myself. You have to relax. Enough for tonight. Time for digestion.

Corelli came back from the kitchen. He bent over and set the bowl of Grape-Nuts down on the floor. "Time for Bozo," he said.

Bozo made a beeline for the bowl. Corelli sat back down on the couch. "Okay," he said. "Your father's gonna have to find himself another mechanic."

We just sat there on the couch, watching Bozo devour the Grape-Nuts. He lapped the milk with his tongue, snapped at the bits of cereal, and when he was finished he stuck his nose in the bowl and nosed it around, bashing it repeatedly into the wall.

CHAPTER
16

When I got home the house was totally dark once again, except for one tiny light that had been left on in the kitchen. It almost doesn't count for a light. It's more of a night light, really. It plugs directly into the wall and is decorated with colored-glass overlays, like stained glass. A friend of my cousin's makes them. Anyway, the one we have in the kitchen was the only light on in the entire house. I have to take that back. The upstairs hall light is always left on at night so Jenny doesn't get scared. When the hall is dark she always says the nunus are back. I'm not sure who they are exactly, but they're not good.

I closed the door. I could vaguely discern my mom sitting alone in the darkened living room with these odd shadows and extraterrestrial colors falling on her from the glow of the tiny kitchen light.

Are we going to be living in the dark ages forever? I thought. The dark ages. It seemed to apply.

"Hello," I said. I took off my baseball cap and jacket and put them in the closet.

"Medicinal," said my mom.

"What?"

"Medicinal."

By that time my eyes had adjusted to the light, or lack of it. I could see the bottle of brandy on the end table and the glass in her hand. She was holding the glass high up in the air by way of description.

"Did Dad leave?"

"Gone," she said.

"I'm going to bed."

"Jenny won't speak to me."

"She doesn't like this whole divorce thing."

Mom just stared at her brandy. I stopped at the bottom of the stairs. "Was it Dad's idea?"

"Not really."

"Was it yours?"

"It just evolved."

"I'm going to bed."

"Good night, sweetheart," she said.

"Good night, Mom."

Normally, I would have given her a hug, but I just didn't feel like it.

The next morning I called Grampa from school. I had a short break after typing, which was my first opportunity to call. Actually, I should have been in the listening center, listening to Spanish (¿Te gusta jugar al volibol?) but I wasn't up to it. I had to contact Grampa. I needed his answer right away.

There are a couple of phones across from the cafeteria, which is where I stationed myself. Both my little fingers were cramping to a horrendous degree from typing class. It was my first semester of typing and I always got terrible cramps when I typed certain letters. A, Z, Q, and P mostly. Sometimes, my whole hand would cramp up. Despite the discomfort, I dialed the operator and gave her our credit card number. It's a handy thing to have, although since Dad pays the bills I probably shouldn't have used it in connection with the business of suing him.

"Hello," said Grampa.

I could picture him in his bathrobe, Duke Ellington playing in the background, hot water heating on the stove for his second cup of coffee.

"Hi, Grampa. It's me."

"Chris?"

"Yeah. It's me."

"Hello, Chris. How are you? Wait a minute. Let me turn down the music." A pause and then, "I was just thinking about you. Isn't that the darnedest thing?"

"Yeah. Listen, Grampa . . ."

"When am I going to see you?"

"Soon, I hope."

"I haven't seen you in months."

"I know, Grampa."

"What am I supposed to do here? Walk the dog and listen to the phono? If I could drive I'd come down there."

Grampa had had an eye operation a little while before that so he wasn't able to drive. He still can't, as a matter of fact. I really miss him. We've had some of the best times together. The circus, the airport, the beach, exploring in the woods, playing Indians, making models. I don't see him now. My dad bought him this condominium in Heritage Village about three and a half years ago, around the time, come to think of it, when everything within the family was beginning to fall apart. Grampa hates it, as I mentioned earlier, because it's so far away. He wanted to be in Bedford, near us. Dad says he picked Heritage Village because it's somewhat set up for older people. I don't think of Grampa as an older person, but I guess my dad does. Anyway, this place has beautiful surroundings, a shopping mall, restaurants, a bank, you name it. It even has a bar with jazz—a self-contained world, easy to maneuver in, but boring. Grampa's got too much going for him to be confined to a place like that. I think Dad just didn't want to be bothered with him, Grampa and all the rest of the people he loves.

"Listen, Grampa," I said.

There was a loud, whistling noise in the background.

"Let me get my coffee."

The hall started getting really crowded. Ben passed with his Walkman 'phones on and waved. C.J. was right behind him with a couple of seniors. "I told you he broke his nose," said C.J.

I wondered who he meant.

"I'm back," said Grampa, returning to the phone.

"I have something important to ask you," I said.

"What's that?"

"Do you know about the divorce?"

"What divorce?"

"Mom and Dad."

"What?"

"They want to get divorced."

"No."

"Yes."

"I don't believe it."

"It's true."

"Oh, no. What do they want to get divorced for?"

"I don't know, Grampa."

"What the hell's the matter with them?"

"I don't know. I don't have time to talk now. I'm at school, but I have to know if you'll help me."

"Of course I will. Anything. You know that. Why do they want to get divorced?"

"I can't explain it now, Grampa, but it's a mistake and I'm trying to stop it. There's this lawyer who's going to help me, but I need a guardian. That's like you have to sign some papers 'cause I'm too young. It might mean appearing in court."

"Name the time."

"You'll do it?"

"Of course I will."

The bell rang for my next class.

"Listen, Grampa, I have to go now. I'll call you back as soon as I get more details, okay?"

"Sure."

"Thanks, Grampa. Thanks so much."

"I'd do anything for you. You know that, don't you?"

"Thanks, Grampa."

"How's my Jenny?"

"She's having a rough time right now, but she'll be all right."

"I love you both."

"I love you, Grampa."

"Why the hell do they want to get divorced?"

I hurried off to art, a breath of fresh air, and then to English. Mrs. Moonsman was being her typical intense and over-intellectual self. She's tall, with large glasses and a frightened way of speaking. We were reading *The Grapes of Wrath* and she went into this whole thing about the corn being a metaphor for people. She kept stressing how Steinbeck loves people—which he does, he's incredible—but you want to think about the people and she goes into this whole corn thing. It's depressing.

After English it was time for lunch. Haverman and I lined up with our plastic trays on the lunch line and perused the available food. It was pitiful, as usual. We had just passed what appeared to be beanless chili and were trying to figure out what the next thing was. It had an orange-brown color. It was coming out of a sliced, hard French bread wedge.

"Oh, God," said Haverman. He had stopped suddenly and was looking off into mid-space with a tortured look of impending doom.

"What's wrong?"

"I'm aware of my tongue."

"Fine. Let's move ahead."

"Have you ever had that happen?"

"Not that I recall."

"It's like your entire inner tongue is swelling."

"We're holding up the line."

"You never had that happen?"

"No."

"Oh, God, I hate it! No room in your mouth!" He was verging on unintelligibility. "No speech! The teeth will slice the tongue!"

"Tell me about it."

From behind us on the line, "Let's go! Move it! For God's sake!"

I shoved Haverman down toward the potato chips. "There's people behind us."

"Too crowded in the mouth!" He had started to lisp. "HOW DO YOU KEEP YOUR TONGUE AWAY FROM YOUR TEETH?"

"You'll have to work it out." I took a bag of potato chips and looked around for Amy. I had to talk to her about Corelli. She was nowhere to be seen.

"Sandwich?" said the overweight serving lady.

"Ugggghhhh," stammered Haverman, pointing to his tongue.

"Give him one," I said. "He's retarded."

She plopped a totally greased grilled-cheese sandwich on Haverman's tray. "You?" she inquired.

"Please."

I hate the grease, but the cheese was appealing and I was starving. Mom had given up making my lunch.

We moved ahead to the salad area. I put one on my tray. It was basically an excuse for a salad. It was almost too small to notice.

"You call that a salad?" said Haverman. He spoke in his normal voice. I could only presume his tongue had suddenly shrunken. "That's no salad. Where's the sense to it?"

"Where's the lettuce?"

"Starve your way through Wallace Beeley." Haverman threw himself across the serving counter. His head was virtually millimeters away from a large tub of luminous-orange French dressing. "Oh, please!" he begged. "Another shred of lettuce! A morsel more, a tad!"

"Next," said the serving lady.

"Your mercy knows no bounds!"

"Shut up, Haverman," I said. "It's pointless."

Haverman picked himself up, took the tiny cup of lettuce bits, scooped out a blob of orange dressing, and we headed off to get our milk and straws and ice cream.

CHAPTER
17

Nothing in this universe is as loud or disgusting as the Wallace Beeley cafeteria at lunchtime. It defies description. I looked around amid the noise and craziness for some sign of Amy, but I didn't see her.

"Over there," said Haverman, nudging me in the ribs with his elbow. He had spotted some empty seats at a table near the door. Ronald virtually had the table to himself. He was probably the only human person in the entire room who wasn't shouting. I followed Haverman over to the table with my tray and we sat down next to Ronald, who was eating his grease sandwich with this immensely serious expression on his face.

"Hi, Ronald," I said. I opened my milk container and took a long drink. I get so thirsty sometimes.

"Do you inhale cigars?" asked Ronald.

"No," said Haverman.

"Probably because you'd choke to death."

"That could be it," said Haverman. He bit into his sandwich, nearly swallowing half of it in one bite. "God, this is disgusting."

"Tiny and disgusting," I added.

"Minuscule and gross." Haverman continued eating his sandwich. He seemed to be enjoying it, disgusting or not. "So who the hell is this lawyer? I can't get a picture."

"Neither can I," I said. "I have to talk to Amy. I like him, but I think he might be nuts. He wants to help me."

"He's nuts."

"You're a special friend, you know that?"

"Just my opinion."

"Forget it."

"He's one pickle short of a barrel."

"I don't want your opinion."

"The elevator doesn't go all the way up to the roof. What's he charging?"

"A dollar."

"The price is right."

Ronald stood up. "I'm going to get some more food."

"I wouldn't," said Haverman.

Ronald ignored the comment and left with his tray. Just then I noticed Amy and Marion approaching the table.

Thank God, I thought.

They didn't sit right next to us, but sat, as is their custom, off to one side in a minute cluster of their own. You never can tell if they're with you or not.

"I have to talk to you," I said as Amy sat down with her tray. Her entire lunch consisted of a single, microscopic salad.

"Expect to live on that?" asked Haverman.

"I have a better chance than you do." Amy eyed the uneaten section of Haverman's grilled-cheese sandwich. "I hate to think what that was fried in."

"Don't think," said Marion. "It's the only way to survive." Her tone suggested she was speaking in the broadest terms. She seemed depressed. Had she not heard from Zeus? Did her aunt's sister have a cold? Who could know?

"How'd it go with Archie?" asked Amy. She had started in on her lettuce shreds, no dressing.

"I have to ask you something," I said.

"What's that?"

"Is he nuts?"

"I don't think so."

"Now she tells you," said Haverman.

"He's not nuts. I mean he's not crazy. He's just, I don't know, weird."

"The lights are on, but there's nobody home."

"You think he can handle this thing?"

"I guess."

"That's not definitive."

"For God's sake, Haverman!"

"He's a nice guy, really," said Amy.

"Is he at all responsible?"

"Oh, yeah. Sure."

"You sound vague," said Haverman. "You want some potato chips?"

"No," said Amy.

"You may have brain damage from lack of food."

Amy pushed her half-empty salad cup off to the far end of her tray. "Something just crossed my mind."

"Short trip," said Haverman.

"Would you mind?" said Amy.

"I mind not."

"One time my mom had like a problem with my brother and stuff, like, he was maybe in some trouble? I don't remember. It was a long time ago, but Archie really helped him. Like, he knew what would be legal and all and my mom was always really grateful. I don't know the details."

"We see that," said Haverman.

"But, like— Will you let me finish? Like, he really helped her and my brother and, like, my mom said he was really understanding. I've heard her say that a few times. Like, he was really understanding. I'd say give him a chance."

"The price is right," said Haverman.

At that point Ronald approached with a bowl of beanless chili. Haverman looked up with alarm. "Oh, God, Ronald!" he said. "You didn't get the chili?"

"Why not?"

"Throw it out! Out! Into the basket!"

"Why?"

"Don't you know what they put in there?"

"Not while we're eating," said Amy.

"You're not eating," said Haverman. "Miss Closet Anorexic."

"What do they put in there?" said Ronald.

"I can't say it. It's too terrible."

"What?"

"Remember that dog that was in the art lab this morning?"

"Don't start," said Amy.

"Poor thing," I said. "I liked that dog." Sometimes I can't resist teasing Ronald. He's virtually the perfect person to tease.

"I don't believe you," said Ronald, but he said it in such a way that you knew he wasn't sure.

"I kid you not," said Haverman. "They ran low on dead cows so they— Oh, God! It's too terrible!"

"Shut up," said Amy.

Marion looked over at Haverman with mild disinterest. She had more pressing matters to contend with.

"In the basket, Ronald!" shouted Haverman.

"I don't believe you," said Ronald. "They wouldn't do a thing like that." He sat down.

"Up! Up on your feet! Put not your plastic spoon twixt hungry lips."

Ronald started to eat. "There's no dog in here," he said. You could tell he was worried.

Haverman stood up and started shouting. "He's eating the chili!"

"He's eating the chili!" The word spread from table to table. "He's eating the chili!"

"Help!" shrieked Haverman. "Ambulance! First aid! Knowledgeable people! Healers of all nations!"

From there it went from bad to worse, with total screaming and hysteria throughout the lunchroom, throwing of food, the works. C.J. rushed over from a nearby table, grabbed Ronald's spoon from his hand, pulled him from his chair, and threw him to the ground. "Get the stomach pump!" he shrieked. Then a lot of other people started running around and acting generally insane. It was worse than usual. Right at the peak of the hysteria I noticed Mr. Sivalo, my math teacher from last year, standing in the doorway, his glasses halfway down his nose, his hair kind of standing out at the sides the way it does, the picture of seriousness and wasted dreams. I don't think he wanted to be a teacher, or he doesn't like math. He was obviously displeased with the noise level and stood there watching things and waiting for a trace of sanity to return to the area. Other kids noticed him, too, slowly at first, and then the noise began to quiet down.

"All right now," he said. He was standing right

next to me in the doorway. I could see the chalk marks on his pants. "What's all the screaming?"

"Mr. Sivalo," I said. "I scream, you scream. We all scream for ice cream."

He didn't think it was funny.

CHAPTER
18

Mr. Marrone did the nicest thing. Immediately following the great bean-less-chili riot, I had social studies. After class Mr. Marrone stopped me on my way out and gave me a copy of *The Rights of Young People.* He had no way of knowing how desperately important the book was to me at the time, but since I had expressed an interest, he made it available. I think that's a sign of a good teacher. If a kid is interested in something, help them find out about it and don't waste time. The whole thing could be lost forever. In this case Mr. Marrone probably thought I was interested in the book purely as extraterrestrial reading. (I call it that. The literal term is extracurricular, as you may or may not have guessed.) Still, he got it for me, and right away. I like the guy.

I wanted to read the book immediately, but I had not one free mod for the entire afternoon. It never pleases me when that happens, but this day it nearly drove me crazy. There was no way I could concentrate. I would have read on the bus, but I get carsick (bus sick) from reading on any type of moving vehicle. Haverman was not on the bus. It was a "mother night," and she lives on the other side of town. Amy had stayed late for band practice so it was just me and Ronald, of my close friends, that is. Ronald was morose and didn't speak. He may have had a stomachache. Although the chili had no dogs or beans in it, it may have contained other indigestible ingredients.

When I reached my house I got a surprise. My dad's BMW was parked in the driveway. I felt this wave of excitement.

Is he home? I thought. Is it over?

I hurried to the car as he rolled down the window. "Hello, Chris," he said.

"Hi."

Something in his mood told me he wasn't home to stay.

"Get in," he said.

Is he going to kidnap me? I thought.

I'd heard about parents doing that type of thing. I had seen a whole thing about it on TV the week before. It was on one of those magazine-type of shows with the cohosts who always make fun of each other.

I rounded the car, shifted my books to my left hand, and opened the door. *The Rights of Young People* was on the top of the stack. Somehow I hoped my dad wouldn't notice it. It made me feel like a traitor. It shouldn't have. He was the traitor, not me. I got into the car and closed the door.

"How was school?"

"All right."

He started wrestling with the ashtray. "You pay thirty thousand dollars for a car, you'd think the damn ashtrays would open. Wouldn't you?"

"You would."

"The hell with it." He took a cigarette from his pack and lit up. Then he opened the window about two inches and thew out the match.

"Aren't you supposed to be at work?"

"I took the afternoon off."

"How come?"

"I needed to."

There was a pause.

What do I say? I thought. There was so much I wanted to say, to ask, to find out. Too much. I just sat there.

He took another drag on his cigarette. "Anything good on cable this week?"

"Not that I know of."

Another pause. It was getting uncomfortable.

"Listen," he said at last. "I'm sorry about last night."

"You mean leaving?"

"No. Ah, well, yes. I am. But what I meant was about snapping at you. I was gruff."

That made me think of a goat.

"I was not in a good mood."

"Neither was I."

The car was filling up with smoke.

"Listen, Dad, would you mind not smoking?"

"It bothers you?"

"It makes me sick."

He threw the cigarette out the window. I felt so blunt. I had hurt his feelings. I hate to do that. But what about my feelings? What about Jenny's? We sat in silence for a minute or so. Then he started. "I want to level with you."

"Okay."

"This isn't easy."

"What's easy?"

"I badly don't want you to think I don't care about you. I do care. You matter deeply to me. One of the best things, something I hold . . . this is the truth."

He was getting emotional. I was relieved, in a way. I could tell he loved me, but I hated to see him like that. Normally, he was so organized. Now he could hardly form a sentence.

"One of the best times I had in my life, and I mean this, Chris, one of the best times, a time when things made more sense to me than at any other time, I often think about it, was our trip up the Nose." (The Nose is short for Anthony's Nose, a mountain over by the Bear Mountain Bridge.) "You remember?"

"I remember."

It was a wonderful trip, a special favorite of mine.

"We took that hunk of cheese and your broken scout knife?"

"With the blue, kind of scraped-off handle."

"Right. And the army blanket with the holes?"

"And the leaking canteen."

"Right. And the pomegranate."

"Oh, Jesus!"

"What a mess."

"Oh, God."

"And we just climbed that mountain. What a mountain."

"It's not very big."

"It's big enough."

"That's true."

He closed the window. "The air was clear and still. The birds were happy. You remarked about that."

"And those army guys came?"

"Oh, right. I'd forgotten about that."

"In those jeeps and we thought they were going to arrest us?"

"That's right. We did. But they just waved."

"Right."

"And when we got to the top we sat back and had our cheese and the pomegranate and we were just there. There was nothing to question."

"I know what you mean."

"I look forward to more times like that."

"Doesn't seem likely."

"Why not?"

"That was five years ago."

"Was it that long?"

"Why didn't we do it again?"

"We will, Chris. This divorce thing isn't going to change what we have."

"What do we have? I never see you! You're always working, or jogging, or playing tennis."

"I've been busy, Chris. Life is complicated."

"No, it's not."

"It is for me."

"Whose fault is that?" I was starting to get claustrophobic. My legs were cramping up. It felt like my pants were putting needles into me. I wanted to open the door and run screaming from the car.

"You act like I'm doing this on purpose."

"Who's forcing you?"

"Chris, I'm lost. I'm forty-one years old and I don't know who I am."

I felt suddenly cold. I didn't want him to be saying this.

He went on. "I feel like I'm drowning. I need time to be alone. I'm not happy about leaving, but I don't know what else to do."

Stay.

"Your mother and I are just . . . we're not . . . I don't know."

"Why don't you stay until you find out?"

"Find out what?"

"What you and Mom are or aren't. You just said you don't know. I think you should stay around until you find out."

"I've tried."

"Try harder."

"Your mother's not interested. We both have to work at this thing. She has other things on her mind."

"Like what?"

"You tell me. It's hard to explain, Chris. You just have to trust me. I don't want to lose you, but I have to find myself. I have to breathe."

Open the window.

"Say something."

"Open the window."

"Please, Chris, talk to me. Don't be smart. I'm a person. I have problems, too."

"I don't want to hear that! You're my dad. You're supposed to take care of me. And Jenny! What about Jenny?"

No answer.

I was furious. "What am I supposed to say? Okay, terrific? Go leave me and Mom and Jenny and go find yourself? I don't give a damn if you find yourself. I don't care if you go and find yourself and have a terrific life without us! I don't care! Are you gonna come back? If you learn how to get happy, are you gonna come back?"

"I don't know."

"See? Why can't we learn that together?"

"Daddy, Daddy, Daddy!" Jenny was running toward the car, her arms outstretched, as happy as I'd ever seen her. I couldn't stand it. What would happen when he told her? Nice knowing you. See you around.

He rolled down the window. "Hello, Pumpkin Face."

"Hello!"

He opened the door and Jenny leaped onto his lap. I stared at my *Rights of Young People*. It has a green cover.

"Back, back, back!" said Jenny. "I knew it so much!"

"How was school, sweetheart?"

"Stupid, as you would expect." She began playing with his face, pushing it into different forms, like playing with dough, a living Mr. Muscle Man. It was a game they often used to play. This time she was being rougher than usual. "I love your face!"

Dad grimaced. She was hurting him, you could tell. "Don't do that, honey."

"But why?"

"It hurts Daddy."

"It doesn't."

"It does."

"But no!"

"Daddy has something for you. Wait. Look."

"What?"

Dad twisted around and got a plastic shopping bag out of the backseat. "Let's close the door, sweetheart. It's cold."

"What's it?"

Dad slammed the door. Then he gave Jenny the bag. "Open it."

I watched as Jenny opened the bag. Inside was a box. She threw the bag on the floor of the car and opened the box. Inside was a pair of slippers. They were the furry animal type with enormous cat faces where the toes would be. Jenny had been wanting a pair like that for the last couple of months, ever since she saw Trudy's. "Daddy, Daddy, Daddy! My slippers!"

"I knew you wanted them."

"So much! My furry, furry, kitty slippers with faces!"
She pulled off her sneakers.

"Why don't you wait, sweetheart? Wait till you get
in the house. You don't want to wear them outside."

"I do."

"It's cold."

"Never mind it."

"It's not a good idea."

"It's good." She put the slippers on and wiggled
her toes. The cat faces stared up at her. They even
had whiskers. "Inside now," said Jenny.

Here it comes, I thought.

I stared at my *Rights of Young People*. The title
was written in large white letters.

"Daddy's not coming inside, sweetheart."

"He is."

"No, he's not, sweetheart. Not now."

"But why?"

I looked up. Her lower lip had started to quiver.

"Daddy's staying at the hotel. You remember."

"But no."

"This weekend you can come and visit me. They
have a big machine that makes ice cubes."

Now the tears. They came quickly, silently, rolling
down her cheeks. She stared at her slipper faces.

"It's only a few days. We'll go to the movies."

Jenny shook her head.

"Chris will come, too. We'll eat in the restaurant
and use the soda machine. We'll do fun things."

Very slowly, Jenny reached down and took off her
slippers. She was still crying.

"That's a good girl," said my dad. "We'll put the
slippers in the box and put your sneakers back on
and you can carry your slippers back into the house
and when you get inside you can put them back on."

She doesn't want them, I thought.

"Shall we put them back in the box?"

Jenny opened the car door and got out of the car. The tears were coming quicker now.

"Put your sneakers on, sweetheart. It's cold out there."

Jenny started walking toward the house.

"Sweetheart? Come back. Put your sneakers on. Get your slippers."

"She doesn't want them, Dad."

"Jenny?"

She just kept walking, a tiny figure in her snow jacket and socks.

"Jenny!"

She didn't turn around. She just opened the door of the house and went inside. My father and I sat for a couple of minutes, not saying anything. I felt such extreme sadness, sadness for Jenny, sadness for my mother, and sadness for myself. I also felt sorry for my dad. I knew he had been excited about getting Jenny the slippers and now she didn't want them.

CHAPTER
19

That night Mom sent me out to Mario's to pick up a pizza. It's a pretty long walk to Mario's, but I didn't mind. I needed the quiet and the fresh air and the simple, straightforward task. We had called ahead to order, one large pizza with mushrooms, peppers, and anchovies. Jenny doesn't like anchovies ("disgusting, salty fish strings," she calls them), but I always get them for me and Mom, Dad, too, when he's in the neighborhood. We clear them off Jenny's slice before she eats it.

The afternoon had been pretty depressing. Jenny had stayed in her room and Mom had been God knows where. I remember the house felt enormous. I sat alone in the living room for a while, eating a cucumber and wondering about the meaning and purpose of life. I couldn't come up with anything. Finally, I forced myself to take action and began to read *The Rights of Young People*. I found some interesting information. For instance, you can only sue your parents in twenty-nine states. Thank God, New York was one of them.

I was thinking about all of this and ruminating over the afternoon as I stood in line for the pizza. Number twelve. They never take the order by name.

God help you if you forget your number. The video games were loudly in action behind me. I was remembering how I had taken Jenny's slippers up to her room and how she had refused to let me in. She professed to be sleeping. How a sleeping person can tell another person they're sleeping is more than I can figure, but there was no convincing Jenny. I finally left the slipper box outside her door.

"Number twelve," said the sweating pizza man.

"That's me."

"Ten dollars."

I paid the man and left. I was glad I had remembered the number. I was too hungry to wait to reorder. They run a tight ship at Mario's. No number, no pizza.

When I got home Mom had somehow gotten Jenny to come out of her room. I'm not sure how she did it, but I came into the kitchen and found Jenny on the floor. She was sitting on her quilt, facing the wall, surrounded by about ten of her stuffed animals and other various toys and things. Mr. Muscle Man was there and so were a couple of trucks, a mechanical bathroom frog with one eye, and some tiny plastic dishes from her Tea Time Fun Set. She held Bunny, stitched and vestless. Mom was wearing her warm-up suit. She sat at the table, drinking her famous medicinal brandy from one of Jenny's *Flintstones* jelly tumblers. She got up when I came in with the pizza, got the plates, napkins, and glasses, then sat down.

"How many pieces?" I asked Jenny as I opened the box.

She didn't answer.

"I'll give you one, okay?"

Still no answer. I reached into the box, pulled the anchovies off her slice, cut cleanly along the sides, and set it on a plate. "Are you going to eat on the floor?"

No answer.

"It's all right," said Mom. "Let her eat on the quilt there."

I put the plate down next to Jenny on the quilt, poured her some milk, then sat down to eat. Mom wasn't eating and neither was Jenny, Bunny either, for that matter.

I have to make him a vest, I thought. He's too pathetic.

Jenny was still facing the wall, motionless, silent.

"Jenny, sweetheart," said Mom. "Don't you want your pizza?"

No answer.

"Jenny? Why won't you answer?"

"Gorillas ripped my tongue out."

"If gorillas ripped your tongue out you wouldn't be able to speak," I said.

"They left a stub."

"You couldn't talk with a stub."

She turned suddenly and made her angry monster face. She does that when she wants to scare you into leaving her alone. She bares her teeth, slits her eyes, makes claw hands, and pants heavily through her clenched jaw. It's an awesome sight.

I stayed up that night until almost two o'clock, reading *The Rights of Young People*. I was exhausted, but I knew it was one of those times when you're too tired to sleep. My brain was racing, overloaded, anxious, scared, you name it. My shoulders were all gnarled up and tight, too. I get that sometimes with severe stress, like pains in my shoulders and this severe knot under my left shoulder blade. There I lay. Two

o'clock, three o'clock, three-thirty. My fish swam silently, glowing in their simple fish world. I watched
them, counted them. (There weren't any sheep.) I tried
to name all the states in the greater United States,
all the kids in my English class, all the cities I had
ever been to, all the breeds of dogs I'd ever heard of
—nothing helped. No amount of boredom or catalog-
ing of obscure and repetitious information could ease
me into sleep. Suddenly, I heard Jenny scream. I
jumped up, grabbed my robe, and dashed into the
room.

"Too many! Too many!" she screamed.

Mom came into the room. "What is it?" she asked.
She went to Jenny's bed. "Baby. Sweetheart."

"Too many!"

"It's all right, sweetheart. You're dreaming."

"Don't take them! Don't take them!"

"What, sweetheart?"

Jenny opened her eyes. She looked right at Mom.
Then she pushed her away. "No," she said. She didn't
seem to recognize her.

"It's all right. Mama's here."

"No!" Jenny was looking right at Mom. It was like
she was scared of her. "No!" she screamed.

Mom seemed confused, like she didn't know what
to do. I didn't either. Jenny sat up. She kept looking
at us like she didn't know who we were.

"Turn on the desk light," said Mom.

I went over and turned it on. It wasn't very bright,
which was good. It just allowed Jenny to get a sense
of where she was.

"It's all right," said Mom. "Chris turned on your
light."

Jenny blinked her eyes, getting her bearings. Mom
picked up Bunny. "Here's Bunny, okay?"

Jenny looked at Bunny.

"Here. Take Bunny. Take Bunny and cozy up now."

Jenny took Bunny.

"You want to go back to sleep?"

Jenny lay back down.

"You want some milk?"

No answer. Mom leaned over and looked at Jenny's face. "Her eyes are closed," she whispered. "Jenny? I think she went back to sleep." Mom kissed her, then got up off the bed. "Put the light out, Chris, okay?"

"Okay."

Mom left the room. I stood there for a minute looking at Jenny. She was such a tiny, pitiful sight lying there, clutching her injured Bunny, surrounded by all her stuffed animals. I suppose I was remembering in general what it was like to be so young and helpless and dependent on stuffed toys and a parent to rescue you from terrors in the night. I turned out the light and started out of the room when I was struck by the thought that she was not asleep. "You okay?" I whispered. I had stopped by the door.

"Maybe not."

"What's wrong?"

"Too many cats."

"In your dream?"

"Yes."

"What did they do?"

"Bad things." She sat up, clutching Bunny, and leaned back up against a large stuffed bear.

"Like what?" I asked.

"They needed parts."

I was starting to feel very tired, but I couldn't leave her. I had this strange, irrational thought that if I didn't listen to her at that precise moment she might never speak again. I'm sure that wasn't true. I'm sure it wasn't all that crucial, but I knew it was important. I came back into the room and sat down. I didn't turn the light back on. I could see pretty well by the light coming in from the hall. "What parts did they need?"

"There was this witch and she was mean with needle fingers and there was this giant man with underwear and we were in this woods place with vines and they were mad and screaming and then all these cats came and they were needing parts."

"What parts?"

"They were taking parts to different trees."

"What kind of parts?"

"My arms and my toes. It was all mixed up."

"Dreams are like that."

"I know."

"It's over now."

"I hope."

"You want some milk?"

"Yes."

"Why didn't you tell Mom?"

"About the cats?"

"Well, yes, about the cats, but also about the milk. She asked you."

"My voice got stuck."

"I'll get the milk." I stood up and started out of the room.

"Like before."

She wants to talk, I thought. Why now? Why not earlier with the pizza, or after that when I was counting fish, suffering acute insomnia? Why now?

I was totally exhausted. It was like I had sandpaper in my eyes. My body was a dead weight. I would have given anything for the feel of a cool, soft pillow beneath my heavy head. I adjusted my bathrobe and tightened the sash.

You have to stay, I thought. Nobody else will listen. Mom's in dreamland and Dad's at the Holiday Inn. (A good song title?)

I took a deep breath and sat back down on the bed. "So when was that?" I asked.

"What?" Jenny was rubbing Bunny's face and twisting his ears.

"When was it before that your voice got stuck?"

"I don't know."

"When I asked you about the pizza?"

"No."

"When?"

"When they said about the divorce."

"Oh."

"I wanted to tell them it was a stupid thing, but I was all ripping inside and my voice got stuck."

"I know the feeling."

She stopped twisting Bunny's ears. A thought had crossed her mind, a troublesome one, you could tell. Her eyes had that look of focusing inward, like she didn't see anything outside her head, like her mind had turned in on itself. "I don't know," she said.

"What?"

She started to cry.

"What don't you know?"

"I was knowing something."

"What's that?"

"It was stupid."

"What was it?"

"I was knowing that Daddy wouldn't go."

"He might come back. I'm working on it."

"But he went. See, I was knowing he wouldn't."

"What do you mean?"

"It was a stupid reason."

"Tell me."

She was crying harder now. I wanted to hug her. Then I did. She's really small.

"Don't cry. Come on. Tell me your reason."

"It was stupid."

"Stop saying that now. What was it?"

"It was only that if Mommy loved me so much like I thought and Daddy loved me so much like I thought then we were in the safety zone."

"What safety zone?"

"We would always be in this bunch."

"How would that work?"

She pulled away from our hug and roughly rubbed her face. It was all wet from the tears. "Well, see, I would be someplace . . ."

"You would be here."

"I would be here. Right. So, I would be here and Mommy would be loving me so much that she would only have to be here, too, because she couldn't simply stand it if she wasn't with me and I would be here. And then Daddy would be from his side also loving me so much that he would only have to stay here, too, because he couldn't stand it if he wasn't with me and I would be here so he would be here. You see how that would be."

"I see."

"In my reason Mommy would stick to me like glue and Daddy would stick to me like glue and I would be in only one place so they would both be in that place and that would make them be together for always."

"It doesn't work that way."

"But why?"

"It just doesn't. They love you."

"Not so much."

"They do."

"Daddy went."

"It's not because of you."

"It doesn't match."

"To what?"

"To my way."

"Dad loves you."

"If he loved me so much, then he would only stay."

"I don't think that's true."

"It could be."

"I don't think so."

"I'm cold."

"Get back under the covers."

She lay back down, settling in, with her arm around Bunny. "I have bush pellets."

"What?"

"Those bush pellets."

"What bush pellets?"

She pulled her free arm out from under the covers and with her other hand, her arm still wrapped around Bunny, she pushed up the sleeve of her nightgown. "Can you see? The bumps?"

"Goose bumps."

"Bush pellets."

"Right. I'll get you some milk."

"Chris?"

"What?"

"You're good for a brother."

"You're good for a sister."

"I know."

CHAPTER
20

The next morning I called Corelli from school. I had tried to reach him the day before, but hadn't been able to. It was during E mod and the halls were fairly quiet.

"Hello," I said. "This is Chris."

"Chris?"

"Chris Mills."

"Oh, yeah. Hi, Chris. How's it going?"

"Good. I talked to my grampa and he'll do it."

"Do what?"

"Be my guardian."

"Oh, right. Great." I expected him to say more, but he didn't.

"What do we do now?" I asked.

"I gotta figure." Then he shouted. "Open the hood and take a look!"

"What?"

"Excuse me."

"Is there something I can do?"

"When?"

"Now. While you're figuring things out."

"Yeah." He sounded vague.

Keep after him, I told myself. Keep calm.

"What can I do?"

Again he shouted, "She was down a quart last month!"

"Tell me what to do."

"Find stuff out."

"Like what?"

"Like when they plan the divorce. Do you know?"

"No."

"Okay. So find out when, what kind, contested, uncontested, things like that."

"Contested, uncontested."

"Right."

"Is that it?"

"For now."

Push him, I thought. Be daring.

"Shouldn't we have another meeting?"

"Sure." He didn't seem to care.

"I don't want to force you, or anything."

"No. Let's meet."

"When?"

"What's today?"

"Thursday."

"How about tomorrow?"

"Tomorrow night?"

"Yeah."

"Same time?"

"That's good." It didn't seem to matter.

"Okay. I'll see you then."

I hung up feeling uneasy. I liked the guy, but he sounded so VAGUE. It would be an uphill battle with even the best of lawyers. I knew that. I couldn't get a grip on this guy. Was he scared? Was he bored? Did he hate me?

The bell rang. Noise. Craziness. I gathered my books from the ledge beneath the phone.

I need this man, I thought, as I made my way down

the long and suddenly crowded hallway. He can't be vague. He has to save my life. At that same moment a little voice inside was telling me that only I could do that.

My next class was art. I love that course. Mr. Pucci is so enthusiastic. That particular day, as I remember, he went into this whole thing about the drawing I had done for that week's sketchbook assignment. It was of a sneaker with a candle behind it that was lighted and dripping wax. He liked the rendering, as I recall, but was particularly taken with my placement of the sneaker. It was way down in the lower left hand corner and not totally visible, part of it being off the page. Mr. Pucci liked that. He hates it when you place things in the center of the paper. He's very into negative space.

Contested, uncontested. After art I wrote the words repeatedly in my notebook among my notes for film study class. I couldn't concentrate. I was so nervous about questioning Mom.

Contested, uncontested. I wrote the words again, this time in three-dimensional block letters beside the detailed sketch I had done the week before of our beloved film study teacher, Ms. Costa-Gravas. (Isn't that almost a director?) She was in the middle of a lecture that I could not follow. Something about the camera being tipped to show disorientation. If I ever make a film of my life I must remember to tip the camera. I had Ms. Costa-Gravas last year for English (pre-Moonsman), but that was before she got married so she had a different name. Last year she was Ms. Costa, Minnie Costa to be exact. She's short, so it all kind of worked. Anyway, last summer, to everyone's shock and amazement, she married Mr. Gravas, the ceramics teacher, so now her name is Minnie Costa-

Gravas, or Ms. Costa-Gravas, as we call her. Haverman insists that she married Mr. Gravas for his name, but I don't think so. It might have been a contributing factor, but the entire motivating reason? I doubt it. She's a very sincere person, in her own way, and passionate about film. Unlike me, she likes to dissect meanings. I just love film, but that's not enough for her. She likes to EXPLORE. Oh, well. God bless Minnie Costa-Gravas.

For some inexplicable reason, Mom was home that afternoon when I got back from school. The familiar Honda was parked right where I wanted it to be, in our very garage. Not Bloomingdale's parking lot, not behind the Vanity Box Beauty Salon, not in front of Slimfit—The Exercise Place in Scarsdale, not behind The Bistro on Route 22, or even in Evelyn Beckner's driveway, but here, home, the very base and center of our existence. What could it mean?

When I went inside I found Mom stretched out on the living room couch with a blanket over her and a mug of herb tea (Almond Sunset, I believe) on the coffee table at her side. I dropped my Spanish book with a thud on the dependable marble-topped table.

"Hello, sweetheart," she said.

"Hi, Mom."

Contested, uncontested.

I moved into the living room. "Are you okay?"

"I guess so. Why do you ask?"

"You're home."

"What's that supposed to mean?"

"Nothing. Just you're home and you're usually not, so I thought something might be wrong."

"I'm not usually home?"

"Not usually. I thought maybe you didn't feel well, or something."

"Oh."

"Maybe it's the blanket."

"The blanket?"

"I connect people being covered with blankets during the day with being sick."

"Oh."

I moved over to the couch and sat down. Mom was staring at her hands.

Contested, uncontested.

"Are you okay?"

She started to cry.

"Come on, Mom. What's going on?"

"It's a hard time."

"Tell me about it. Mom. Please. Don't cry." I handed her the napkin that was next to her mug of tea. She blew her nose. "Thank you," she said.

We sat in silence for a while.

Contested. Uncontested.

"Mom?"

"Yes?" She blew her nose again.

"Do you want this divorce?"

"Oh, I don't know."

"Well, don't you think you should figure that out? It's a big step."

"It's not that simple." She reached out for her Almond Sunset and took a small, ungratifying sip. There was no steam coming from the cup. It must have been cold.

Contested. Uncontested.

"When is it supposed to happen?"

"In about a month."

Contested. Uncontested.

"Joint custody?"

"Yes."

Contested. Uncontested.

"Is it contested?"

"What?"

"Is it contested, or uncontested? I heard there were different kinds."

"It's uncontested."

"What does that mean?"

"It means one person brings the suit, and the other doesn't contest it."

"Is Dad bringing the suit?"

"I am."

"But you don't know if you want the divorce."

"I want to get it over with."

"But you don't know if you want it in the first place. You just said that thirty seconds ago. Did you change your mind?"

"No."

"Then why do you want to get it over with?"

"I just do."

"But why?"

"I can't explain it."

"Try."

"It's just the way it is."

She was making no sense. I wanted to tell her that, but I couldn't. I felt disrespectful as it was.

She took another sip of tea. "It's cold," she said.

"Want me to make you some more?"

"No thanks."

"You sure?"

"All right."

I took the mug.

She doesn't even know if she wants tea, I thought. How can she decide if she wants to be married? Who's the child here? Who needs taking care of? Parental Guidance Suggested.

I thought of the old familiar movie rating, Parental

Guidance Suggested. I had always taken it to mean
that it was suggested that parents should guide their
children. It could also mean that parents should be
guided, I thought. They didn't make that clear.

Jenny came down the stairs. She wore large, furry
earmuffs. I also noticed that her clothes were on inside out. She carried Bunny.

"Hi, Jenny," I said.

"I can't hear you."

I raised my voice. "I said hi."

"I can't hear you. I'm wearing earmuffs."

"I see that."

"You better not talk to me. You'll waste your tongue."
She moved into the den area and switched on the TV.
Roadrunner was making a beeline for somewhere or
other.

"Can you hear the TV?" I asked.

"No."

"That's nice."

Dad called that night. He said he was at the Mt.
Kisco Holiday Inn and the air in his room was dry
and the ice machine was just outside his door and
was very noisy and room service forgot his potato and
he was very tired. I didn't say much. When it was
Jenny's turn to talk she wouldn't take off her earmuffs.

CHAPTER
21

           I tried to talk her out of it, but on Friday night, risking arrest and bodily imprisonment, Marion drove me over to Corelli's. She picked me up at seven-thirty, wearing her standard outfit, sweatpants, a turtleneck, and a jean jacket. It wouldn't matter if it was twenty below zero. Sweatpants and a jean jacket. That's it. A lot of the girls were wearing sweatpants around that time. I'm not sure why. I find them rather strange, funny-looking to be precise.

Marion honked from outside. Mom was taking a nap, so I left her a note. I told her I was going for a short drive with Marion. I didn't get into the lawyer part.

"Is the other guy going to be there?" asked Marion as I climbed into the car.

"You mean Joey?"

"I think that's his name."

"You know that's his name."

"Is he gonna be there?"

"I don't think so. Want me to hitch?"

"Sure." She didn't mean it. She doesn't mean nine-tenths of what she says.

We pulled onto Route 22.

"I'm going to the mall," she said.

"Tonight?"

"No." She didn't mean it.

"Is anything open?"

"No." She didn't mean it. "I'm going for my health."
She didn't mean that either.

"Well. So, how's Zeus?"

"Don't ask." She definitely did not mean that. For
the whole, entire ride I heard about Zeus and how
he hadn't really killed the person in Detroit when he
knocked the bone into the person's brain, but they
just thought the person was dead because he was
paralyzed and in a coma for seventy-three hours. He
was awake now, it seemed, though unable to speak
or move his fingers. The biggest news was that Zeus
was due east for a visit at Christmas. The whole thing
sounded questionable, to say the least. I made a
mental note that if Zeus did show up for any reason, questionable or not, I had better keep my distance.

Marion let me off by the gas pumps and departed
for the Great Sweatpants Search at the Denim Mine.
I headed up the long and somewhat unstable flight
of stairs that led to Corelli's apartment.

Pin him down, I told myself. Don't be afraid.

It was cold. I held my blue, puffed Eddie Bauer
jacket closed with my right hand. My left hand clutched
The Rights of Young People. I carried it everywhere
at that time. It was somehow the only concrete thing
in my life. That's what it felt like, anyway. A paper
book. It wasn't concrete, or even close to it, but I felt
it held the answers. If I could master the information
it contained, perhaps I could save my life and the life
of my sister. It sounds silly as I write it now, overly

dramatic, but that's the way I felt. It was, at the very least, a comfort, like cereal at midnight, or my old, torn, yellow blanket. My very own Funny Bunny Richardson.

When I reached the top of the stairs Bozo started to bark. I could also hear recorder music. It was pretty, although somehow strange to hear at a garage. At first I thought it was a record, but then one of the players made a mistake. I knocked on the door.

"Come in!"

The music continued and so did the barking. I opened the door. The moment Bozo saw me he stopped barking and came over and nuzzled my hand. He has the saddest eyes. I shut the door. The music continued. Corelli was sitting in a straightbacked chair with his feet up on the card table by the Vectrex machine. He was playing a plastic alto recorder. Next to him sat the pretty girl from the picture, the one who took such good care of the plants. I liked her instantly. She was playing a recorder, too, a soprano. Hers was wooden. She sat up very straight. I later learned her name was Carol. She looked about twenty, but she's really in her thirties. She has straight, brown, kind of thin hair. That night she wore it in braids. She reminded me in looks of this recorder player I love called Michala Petri. She's Danish, I think. Mom and Dad took me once to hear her at Lincoln Center. She was so amazing, all alone on this enormous stage with this tiny instrument. She played so easily. After the concert Mom and Dad and I went to the Russian Tea Room. We all had blintzes. Mom's ongoing diet was momentarily held in abeyance. Blintzes and hermit cookies are the only things that do it. Anyway,

Mom and Dad were so inspired they decided to buy recorders and learn some duets. They did, too. They sounded really nice. WHAT HAPPENED?

These thoughts rushed through my mind as I stood there, clutching my *Rights of Young People*. I realized the piece they were playing was by Corelli. I thought about the name. Corelli. Were they related? The piece ended.

"Hi, Chris," said Corelli. He got up, carrying his recorder and moved to me at the door. He patted me on the back. "How's it going?"

"Okay."

"This is Carol."

"Hello."

"Hi," she said. "Sorry we didn't stop."

"That's okay."

"We'd never gotten that far without terrible mistakes," she said. "We couldn't stop."

"It sounded good."

"I wouldn't go that far."

"It wasn't bad," said Corelli. He flopped down on the couch, socks, no shoes, wearing his famous jeans and dark blue sweatshirt.

Carol began to clean her recorder. Corelli set his down on the coffee table. Bozo moved over and sniffed it.

"Get away!" said Corelli.

Bozo backed up, head lowered, shoulders hunched in guilt.

"He'll eat anything," said Corelli. "WON'T YOU?"

"Oh, don't," said Carol. "He thinks you're mad."

"I am mad."

Carol took her recorder, now in three separate sections, and put it carefully into its box. She wore blue jeans, too, and a large work shirt and sneakers. The more I looked at her, the younger she looked. Nineteen? Eighteen? She could easily have passed for a senior at Beeley.

"Sit down," said Corelli.

"Thanks." I sat down on the end of the couch.

Corelli adjusted his feet so there was room. "Take your coat off."

"Okay." I took it off and set it down on the floor by the side of the couch. "Was that Corelli?" I asked.

"What?"

"That piece you were playing."

"You know Corelli?"

"He's my favorite. Well, him and Beethoven."

"Oh, Beethoven."

"Yeah."

"They don't get any better."

"That's true."

"What's a kid your age doing with classical music?"

"I like it."

"Me too."

"Are you related?"

"To what?"

"To Corelli."

"I don't think so."

"Oh."

"I was named after him though."

"That's not your real name?"

"Sure it's my real name. Corelli I was born with, Archangelo they gave me."

"Your name is Archangelo?"

"You're lookin' at him."

Get to it, I thought. It's time. Marion will be back

with twenty pairs of sweatpants and we'll still be reviewing the lineage of baroque composers. Intriguing
perhaps, but hardly timely.

I glanced down at my *Rights of Young People.*

"Whatcha got?" he asked.

"It's a book on kids' rights."

"You got any?"

"Ah . . . yeah."

Doesn't he know? What am I here for?

"Tell me one," he said.

There were many I could quote. "A child has the
right to work." "A child has the right to fringe benefits." "A child has the right to be supported by his
parents." I could go on until the fish swam in, but
the most important?

"A child has the right to sue his or her parents in
the state of New York," I said.

"That's right. How many states let you do that?"

"Twenty-nine, currently."

"That's right. Want some popcorn?"

"No thanks."

I like popcorn, but I wasn't ready for a whole big
production over making it.

Corelli got up. Bozo stared. He was getting the
drift, or trend as it were.

"That's a whole big thing," said Carol. She was
folding up her music stand. "Why don't you have some
ice cream?"

"No, it's not," said Corelli. His mind was made up.
"Chris wants some, don't you, Chris?"

"Not necessarily."

"Yeah, you do." Corelli headed for the kitchen. "We
got any corn?"

"I don't know," said Carol.

Corelli looked through the kitchen cupboards under Bozo's intent and steady gaze. Carol put her now folded music stand and her recorder, in its case, on a nearby shelf. She returned to the card table, pulled up her chair, and sat down. "I admire what you're doing," she said.

"You do?"

"You can make a lot of people think."

"I hope I make my parents think."

"I hope so, too."

CHAPTER
22

Corelli came out of the kitchen carrying a glass jar of popping corn. "Where's the thing?" he asked.

"In the closet behind the bicycle," said Carol. She bent down and picked up a piece of heavy green construction paper that was on the floor by the table. Then she reached into a large canvas bag by her chair, took out some scissors, and began cutting turtlelike fragments, or sections, from out of the paper. "Turtles," she said. "I teach nursery school."

Corelli approached the closet, stepping over bicycle parts. "I'll tell you about books," he said.

Did anybody ask?

He pulled a yellow and white plastic popcorn popper from the closet and set it down on the coffee table.

"Close the door," said Carol.

Corelli kicked the door shut with his foot. Then he plugged in the popcorn popper. Bozo sat down. His ears were pulling forward, making added folds of skin above his eyes.

"When I was in law school, second year, Fordham," said Corelli, "I had to pick up books for two courses, tax and ethical responsibility. It should have been a tip-off."

"What happened?"

"So I go down to pick up my books, right?"

"Right."

"So what do you think?"

"I don't know."

"The book on tax is enormous. It's this thick." He demonstrated with his thumb and index finger about five inches apart. "What's that, five inches?"

"I guess."

"Yeah, it's five inches and it cost sixty bucks."

"That's expensive."

"Damn right. And ethical responsibility? What would you say?"

"I don't know."

"A pamphlet! A lousy two-dollar pamphlet! It tells you something, doesn't it?"

"I guess it does."

"It stinks. You wanna get the butter?"

I didn't really, but it seemed like a practical move.

If I don't do it, then he'll have to do it, I thought, and the whole popcorn thing will elongate into tomorrow.

"It's in the fridge," he said. He opened the jar of corn and dumped some into the popcorn popper.

I went into the kitchen. My stomach had gone back into its familiar knot. Everything seemed too much, unreal, impossible. I wanted to be home, in bed asleep, my trusty fish maintaining a silent guard.

I can't do this, I thought. It's wrong. The whole thing is wrong. He can't help me. No one can help me. Let go to that fact. Go home.

"It's in the door."

What's in the door? The butter. The butter is in the door. The butter for the popcorn. I don't want popcorn. I WANT MY DAD. We used to make popcorn.

We'd make it together before we went to the movies. (Parental Guidance Suggested.) We'd make the popcorn in a whole great rush to get to the movies on time. We'd leave the kitchen looking like it had been raided by enemies. We'd dump the popcorn into a big white plastic bag, put the bag in my duffle, and smuggle it into the theater. We'd have enough popcorn to last the entire film. I WANT MY DAD.

I opened the refrigerator, took out the butter, closed the door, then brought the butter in to Corelli. I felt numb, a specimen of the living dead, an inhabited body from *Invasion of the Body Snatchers.* (One of me and my dad's favorite movies, the original, that is.) Bozo could contain himself no longer. He got up and started barking at the popcorn machine.

"Quiet," said Corelli.

"My mom said the divorce is supposed to be in about a month." My own voice surprised me. It sounded strong, almost like it was coming from somewhere else. "Joint custody. It's uncontested."

"Can't be no fault."

"What's that?"

"No grounds."

"Why not?"

"In New York it takes a year."

"My mom says she wants to get it over with."

"There you go."

"But she doesn't know if she wants it."

"Go figure it."

"I can't. She says she's bringing a suit."

"What grounds?"

I tried to imagine. As far as I could tell, there was nothing terrible going on, aside from senseless arguing, but that could hardly be grounds for divorce. Corelli thought she'd probably go for intentional infliction of emotional distress, a subheading under the main heading of cruelty. He said a lot of people do that. They collect a lot of gripes and construe them to meet certain degrees of badness in order to get the divorce. Like the simple Beckner Tennis Court Incident could be stretched to meet the requirements of "ridicule in public" or "hostile and rude conduct specifically calculated to upset spouse."

The popcorn was making loud popping noises as it exploded, hitting the see-through plastic lid.

"Almost ready," Corelli told Bozo.

"So Mom will accuse Dad of all these things, and Dad won't contest it?" I asked.

"Why should he? He wants to get it over with. As long as it's joint custody, he's got what he wants."

I thought of Dad's car.

For some strange and totally incomprehensible reason Corelli lifted the see-through lid of the popcorn maker. The corn started spinning out, flying in all directions, landing in all corners of the room. Corelli slammed shut the lid.

Bozo lunged from one corner of the room to the other, snapping at the unpopped corn, nosing about for hidden remnants.

He waits years for a thing like that, I thought.

Carol reached into her canvas bag and pulled out some kernels that had landed there. She ate them while gluing on the turtle feet (paws?).

"We'll give it another couple of minutes," said Corelli.

"What's our procedure?" I asked.

"Okay." Corelli held the lid tight on top of the popcorn maker. He seemed in gear suddenly, energized, enthused.

Why now? I thought. What happened? What changed?

Did the popcorn explosion give outer form to his inner fears? The mess, the mistake. Was the worst behind us now? Who knows.

"Normally," he continued, "when you take a case, in theory, you want to prove something. You're party A and you want to prove that party B did something that caused you injury, deprived you of your legal rights. Drop that in there." He handed me the butter, nodding in the direction of a large metal bowl that was on the card table, next to the popcorn maker. The bowl looked a lot like the one Bozo had eaten the Grape-Nuts from earlier on in the week. I dropped in the butter.

"Okay," he continued. "So what do you do?"

"You look up past cases?"

"Right. That's what a lot of these books are for." He pointed to the stack of dusty books in the corner. "What you're looking for is a past case which is the same as your case."

"Are there any?"

"No."

"So what do we do?"

"It gets tricky."

"What do we do?"

"The whole thing hangs on precedent, right?"

"Right."

"You know what I'm saying?"

"I do. You have to prove that your case is the same as another case they already had and since that case was decided in a certain way, then your case has to go the same."

"Right. Okay. So if there's no case like yours, there's no precedent, right?"

"Right."

"So what do you do?"

"You set one?"

"Right. You got a feel for this." He pulled the plug on the popcorn maker and removed the lid. Bozo watched with an intensity unparalleled in modern existence.

"LATER FOR DOGS," Corelli told Bozo. He dumped the popcorn into the metal bowl, then stirred it around with his hand to mix it with the butter. "Have some," he said, pushing the bowl in my direction.

I took a handful. "How do we do that?" I asked.

"Do what?"

"How do we set a precedent?"

He took a fistful of popcorn, then shoved the bowl over to Carol. "Take some," he said. He turned to me. "We gotta prove that your parents' divorce is in violation of your rights. It's gotta be something like dissolution of the marriage would do irreparable harm and the only restitution would be to keep the family intact. See, we gotta talk legal here. You can't just walk in there and say, 'I'm not getting my rights because my parents are making a mistake.' What's that? It's nothing. We gotta translate that stuff into grounds."

"Like what?"

"Any number of things. We gotta prove that your parents' behavior is in fact synonymous with certain established grounds proved to be unlawful, thereby making their behavior unlawful. See what I'm saying?"

"That's precedent on another level."

"Sure. Nobody likes change. It scares them to death. So they stick to the past."

"But isn't it like safeguards? They don't want somebody bad coming in and making bad changes. There have to be ground rules."

"Ground rules, sure. I mean, in essence that's why

it was set up like that. To protect people's rights. But, see, other things come in to it. Economics, stepping on people's toes, fear. You gotta leave room for new ideas, positive growth, change. That's what life is. You know what I mean?"

"I know."

"Right." He took a fistful of popcorn, moved over to the couch, and flopped down on his back.

"So what are the grounds?"

"A lot of possibilities." He was getting vague.

"Which one do we use?"

"Who the hell knows?"

I had lost him. It happened in a hairline instant. One minute he was with me, ideas coming a mile a minute, and the next, nothing, a blank.

I had that old, too familiar, sinking feeling. You thought you could handle this, didn't you? Well, think again. I felt this wave of discouragement. I felt foolish, naive, stupid, helpless, defeated. I also noticed that my right sock was wet. My whole foot felt clammy. Bozo was sitting next to me, drooling all over my ankle. I gave him the rest of my popcorn.

CHAPTER
23

The following week was oddly uneventful. Life is like that. You're in the midst of some whole big thing and you think there should be nothing but action, and it's QUIET. The eye of the hurricane? Who knows? Anyway, this week was boring, heavy, thick, uneventful.

Corelli had promised to "work on it" and "see what he could come up with." It sounded vague, but I could see no choice at the moment but to go along with him. I told him I would call him in a few days to see how things were going.

Jenny and I ended up not seeing Dad on the weekend. He had a sudden business trip to Denver, so that was that. In a way it was probably a good thing. I don't think Jenny wanted to see him anyway. She probably wouldn't have taken off her earmuffs and Dad would have gotten guilty and upset and it would have been a whole unpleasant thing. Instead, Jenny watched television, earmuffs and all. Twenty-six hours of television. It was pitiful and depressing.

From what I could tell, Mom slept through the entire weekend. Before the Whole Divorce Thing came up I never knew her to take a nap, but suddenly it seemed like she was always asleep. Either that, or in the tub. She always used to take showers before the Divorce Thing, but now it was baths. I remembered worrying on occasion that she would nap in the tub and drown, or "drown to death," as Jenny likes to phrase it. I've told her many times that the "to death" part is unnecessary; that if you drown, you're dead and you don't need to explain it any further, but she gets stubborn.

One thing I did on the weekend was make a vest for Bunny. I found some red felt that was left over from an art project I had done of a circus puppet. I made the vest out of that. It turned out amazingly well. I found three tiny white buttons in Mom's button box and sewed them on the front. I also made tiny slits for buttonholes. Jenny was pleased. It took me over an hour to make it. She watched the whole time, wearing her earmuffs, not saying a word. At one point I suggested she take off her earmuffs. She didn't like the idea and pretended not to hear me.

"You shouldn't wear them inside," I said.

She shrugged her shoulders.

"Your ears will sweat."

She shrugged again.

"I'm telling you. It's not healthy. You need ventilation."

Another shrug.

"Suit yourself." I tied off the final stitch and buttoned up the buttons. Then I handed Bunny to her.

She stared for a long time. "It's excellent," she said. "This is the one he wanted." She spoke in her most serious voice, which was funny coming from such a small person wearing earmuffs.

The rest of the weekend was taken up with cleaning my fish tank, writing a ten-page report on invertebrates (animals that lack a backbone, or spinal column, but may have an exoskeleton; an example would be a sponge), and studying *The Rights of Young People*. I had, by this time, begun to take notes. ("Judges are bound in virtually every state to make custody decisions based on the best interests of the child." Is there a way in here? "While a child's wishes are not controlling, the current direction of the law is for courts to attach some weight to their preferences." How about this? How about the position taken by the Supreme Court of Washington? "Children . . . are to be treated as interested and affected parties whose welfare should be the prime concern of the court in its custody determination." Could this apply in New York? How far can we take this?) I had actually started to keep a notebook, with notes and thoughts and info to share with Corelli. I had to do my best here. This was no simple test in geometry. No test that I could choose whether or not to study for. This was my life. And the life of my innocent sister. The one with the earmuffs. I couldn't assume that Corelli would know everything, either. That was clear. He might, but then again he might not, or he might forget or he might get interested in some hot dogs, or a game of Parcheesi.

It's on your shoulders, I told myself. Like it or not, you're alone on this one. You're not a child anymore.

I felt like one, though.

On Monday I had my first session with Mr. Dunfee's Divorce Group. Mr. Ryder, my guidance counselor (blue eyes, tan skin, short gray hair, wears college sweaters, doesn't like to admit that people get problems), called me down to his office and told me that instead of my chosen special for this semester, The

Writings of James Thurber, I had been switched, un-
beknownst to me, to Dunfee's Divorce Group. My mom
had recommended it. She must have told the school
about the Whole Divorce Thing. It was like her. She's
so aware of child development IN GENERAL. I'm sure
she told Mr. Ryder to be on the lookout for any disrup-
tions in my study habits. If she could go that far, why
couldn't she go the extra step of admitting that an ir-
revocable upset to Jenny's and my lives would be the
by-product of her own unresolved stress and the stress
of my father? Denver must be cold in December.

For whatever reason, Q mod on Monday I found
myself in Mr. Dunfee's room with a bunch of crazy
kids (me included). There's no age separation in the
sessions. Kids from all four classes are there. There
were about twenty kids on that first day. Maybe half
of them I knew. Haverman was there and Marion and
Amy and C.J., and this junior named Vivian who's
in my art class. There was also a tiny girl with a spinal
problem of some kind who's a freshman. I'm in chorus with her. Because of her smallness she looks about
ten. She's smart, though, and nice and plays the flute
beautifully. She also has a beautiful voice. I didn't
know her parents were divorced. I was sorry to learn
that. It seemed to me that her spinal problem was
enough of a thing to deal with without a divorce, too.
I guess it wasn't. Life is hard to understand sometimes. I really and honestly believe there's a pattern
to it, but sometimes it's hard to see. Like this man I
heard about once, who was struck by lightning seven
times and lived and then shot himself. There was
something he was to have learned, but I don't think
he learned it.

I hadn't been in Mr. Dunfee's room for about a
year, since I was a freshman. He was my guidance

counselor at that time. I remember I liked him, but I found him naive, unabashedly poetic, like a Hall-mark card. He's definitely a borderline nerd, overly helpful, with suspicious-looking hair. I think it's a piece.

The room was large, with travel posters on the walls, some nice windows, two tables, some chairs, and no desks. I found that refreshing. The buzzer rang. I sat down next to Haverman, who was sitting on the floor. "Coconuts are mammals," he said.

"I don't think so."

"No. They are. Listen. They're furry and they give milk."

"Hello, students," said Mr. Dunfee. His toupee was poor, his belt was too tight, his pants surprisingly high at the waist.

"Hello, Mr. Dunfee," said the kids. They were sit-ting on the tables, or on the floor, like me and Hav-erman. This was around the time when it was cool to leave your workboots unlaced. There was this whole row of legs dangling off one of the tables, not one pair of boots tied.

Mr. Dunfee was plowing ahead with his opening remarks. "Some of you are new today and some of you have been here for a while."

"That's right, Mr. Dunfee." A group of kids spoke in unison, like a Greek chorus.

"Some old, some new."

"He doesn't have all his dogs barking," whispered Haverman.

"But old and new together make a group," contin-ued Mr. Dunfee. "I think you'll find that just by sharing some of your thoughts here, a lot can get accom-plished. I think we tend to think sometimes when we get in shaky situations . . ."

"You're a shaky situation," muttered Haverman.

"We think we're alone. We're not alone. None of us. I think we learn that here. We're all in the same big boat. A little leaky maybe, in need of some paint, but we've each got an oar. And we're gonna row."

"Not me," said Haverman. "I've got blisters."

Amy started things off with a question. She was sitting next to Marion, on the table by the window. Amy had on her Calvin Klein jeans and Marion wore pink sweatpants. (Success at the Denim Mine?)

"I have a question," said Amy.

"Yes," said Mr. Dunfee.

"How do you introduce your mother's boyfriend if you're, like, out or something, and you meet someone you know? Like, what do you say?"

Haverman had the answer. "You say, 'Hi there. Nice weather we're having. I'd like you to meet this jerk who's screwing my mother.' "

General laughter and giggling.

Mr. Dunfee cleared his throat. He didn't care for Haverman's answer, but he tried not to show it. He folded his arms and looked down at his shoes. Then he took a few steps toward the windows. "I'm sure many of us have had the wish to respond in just that way, or perhaps in some way similar." He turned, looked up at the ceiling, then retraced his steps away from the windows. "Can anyone think of another response? Perhaps something a bit more constructive?"

"Just say, 'This is Jim,' or Jack, or whatever the hell his name is," said Marion. She swung her pink legs forward and back from off the side of the table. "You don't owe any explanations."

"True," said Mr. Dunfee. He was thoughtful.

"Let your mom describe her own sex life," said C.J. He was twisting a large rubber band in trellislike formations between his fingers.

"Yes, well," said Mr. Dunfee. He seemed uncomfortable.

"I had a really bad time last night." The voice came out of nowhere, forceful and immediate. It was Vivian. I knew she was upset, involved in her own thoughts, her own world, unaware of our common boat, unaware of her oar, unaware even of the need to row. She was feeling only pain. I understood that. I knew it well. She was sitting just behind me. I turned around to see her there, her arms around her knees. She was wearing blue jeans and a jean jacket and small earrings, silver, I think. There were these deep circles under her eyes and her eyes were teary, like any minute all these tears would spill out. I turned back and stared at this poster of Venice. It had a large, curved bridge.

"Would you like to talk about it?" said Mr. Dunfee. He seemed happy to be changing the subject.

"It was bad," said Vivian.

I could almost feel her intensity through my back. It was strange to hear somebody being honest at school. Normally, you never hear that. I stared at the bridge and listened.

"I want to die," she said. I knew she meant it. There was this pause and then she went on. "Well. I was hanging around and stuff, watching TV and it got late, like eight, and I started to worry 'cause my mother wasn't there and she never stays out without telling me. My dad's not home anymore, so I was alone and I was getting really creeped out. Anyway, I go upstairs to get something, my hairbrush, I think, and

I hear this crying. I look in my mom's room and she's lying on the bed with just a slip on, and it's cold and she's lying there and she's crying. I got so scared."

Vivian was crying herself now as she told all this. It made me think about finding Mom asleep in her suit and thinking she was dead. Vivian kept talking. She kept crying, too. It made me want to cry.

"She didn't stop and she wouldn't talk to me, or anything," said Vivian. "I said, 'What's wrong, Mom?' But she wouldn't answer me, so I just left. I was crying, and I didn't know what to do. Oh, God. She didn't even come down for supper. I'm very upset about this. I just . . . I don't know. Now I'm supposed to take care of my mother and I can't even take care of myself."

That did it. It wasn't sympathy for Vivian. Well, it was that, but mostly she had hit too close to home. I was crying, and I'll tell you, if there is one place in this entire universe I do not want to cry, it's in school right there in front of Marion's pink legs and all the unlaced workboots and Amy's Calvins and Mr. Dunfee's toupee and C.J.'s rubber band extravaganza and Haverman's coconut updates and the fluorescent lights and the linoleum and that poor, sweet girl with the injured spine.

CHAPTER
24

Dad called from Denver. He said he wouldn't be back for another week because he had to go to Salt Lake City. It interested me that he said "back." Normally, he would have said "home." "I won't be home for another week." Not it was "back." I guess that was because, in his mind, he was never coming home. Once more Jenny refused to speak to him, or even take off her earmuffs to find out who was on the phone. She knew, of course.

When I was talking to Dad he said an amazing thing. He said, "Don't worry. I'll definitely be back for Christmas." Christmas! I had forgotten completely about it. It was coming in less than two weeks. The inescapable fact had totally escaped me. Christmas had always been a major event in our family. Stocking presents would take half the day to open, and then would come the BIG presents, the turkey, the pie with ice cream, cranberry sauce, cider, eggnog, an enormous tree, decorations, lights, candles, singing, the works. Dad would always play his guitar. He didn't play anymore, normally, but on Christmas he would play. The four of us would huddle together and sing Christmas songs on Christmas Eve with just the lights on from the tree, all the other lights out. We'd sing together until after midnight. Mom has a beautiful voice. Jenny always liked the singing. She especially liked staying up so late. She couldn't have slept anyway. She had to stay awake all night to listen for the reindeer on the roof. She always heard them, too. One year we made a stained-glass window, all of us on the living-room floor—surrounded by scissors, tape, glue, construction board, and all the colors of see-through gel paper—designing, cutting, pasting, laughing, all the while listening to Handel on the stereo, or the *Nutcracker Suite*. Mom's Christmas bell looked like a potato, but Jenny cut out a flying dove that was virtually perfect. We put it in the center. Christmas! How could I forget? The best time a family could have. But now there was no family. What would Christmas be like this year? I couldn't bear to think. "I'll be back for Christmas." What difference did it make? "Back" was not important. Salt Lake City, or the Mt. Kisco Holiday Inn. Who could care?

After I hung up from Dad I went out and sat in the garage. I had intended to take a walk, but it was too cold once I got out there, and I didn't want to be in the house, so I chose the garage. I sat on the wooden garbage-bin ledge and stared at the dirt on the floor, the random flowerpots, the lawn mower, the cardboard boxes, the stacks of newspapers, the rakes, the shovels, the tires, and all the various discarded junk. It was all pretty depressing, the stuff that needed attention, the mess that needed to be cleaned. I should have done it. Normally, Dad and I would have worked on it together, but this year we were both too busy. The worst thing was my old bicycle. I spotted it over in the corner behind some other junk. It was so small, a red two-wheeler, rusty, unwanted by anyone. I had hardly used it. What was its purpose? Why don't we use what we have? I thought of my family.

I gave Corelli a few more days. Mom had gone to a PTA meeting at school, her first visible trip out of the house in days. Jenny was watching TV, still wearing her earmuffs. I sat at my desk by my fish, picked up the phone, and dialed.

I hope he's there, I thought.

I was doing this thing I often like to do, where I hang my hand over the top of my fish tank and let the fish nibble on my finger.

"Did you come up with anything?" I asked Corelli when I got him on the phone.

"Nothing definite."

"What about grounds?"

"What about 'em?"

"What do you think they should be?"

"A lotta possibilities."

"Like what?"

"Emotional deprivation, child abuse, mental suffering, malpractice."

"Which would be best?"

"I don't know yet. We can't rush into this. You know what I'm saying?" Corelli coughed. It went on for some time. It sounded like he was choking to death almost. Then he stopped.

"Are you all right?" I asked.

"Yeah." He sounded unconcerned.

Roscoe, my biggest and most brazen fish, swung by and nipped my finger in transit. I love that feeling. I glanced down at my law notebook, which was open in front of me. "I was wondering."

"Yeah?"

"What about the best interests angle?"

"What about it?"

"I was reading about how custody decisions have to be made in the best interests of the child."

"Right."

"I was wondering if that would help us. Like, the best interests for Jenny would be for both my parents to have custody in the same house. That would be in her best interests."

"No good."

"Why not?"

"The shared custody is all right, but not in the same house. They couldn't force that under best interests. It gets obscure. You know what I'm saying?"

"No."

"What if there's fights? It would be argued that that would not be in her best interests."

"The fights wouldn't last."

"Hard to prove."

"It's true!"

"Doesn't matter."

"What's true doesn't matter?"

"Not in the law."

"I don't believe that."

"Suit yourself."

I pulled my hand out of my fish tank and dried it on my jeans. Then I searched through my notes. I knew there was another point. I just couldn't remember.

"Don't worry," said Corelli. "I'm workin' on it. I promise."

I spotted the other point. "There's something else," I said.

"What's that?"

"Interested and affected parties."

"Yeah?"

"I read that children are supposed to be treated as interested and affected parties whose welfare should be the prime concern of the court."

"That's true, but the court's determination is not gonna be yours. In my opinion, that is. You're asking me."

"Who else am I going to ask?"

"Ask whoever you want. There's other factors."

"Like what?"

"The rights of your parents."

"To mess up Jenny's life?"

"That's not the way they see it."

"That's the way it is!"

"Take it easy, kid. We're gonna get something. I'm telling you. We got one chance, and it's gotta be right."

Roscoe was staring at me, his nose pressed up against the side of the tank, treading water with his tail. He wanted something. I think it was my finger.

"Keep reading," said Corelli. "There's something in that interested and affected party angle. I'm not sure what. It's not head-on. It's related. Somehow. I don't know. I gotta think."

"Okay."

"I'll talk to you in a few days."

"Right."

"Listen. Chris?"

"Yes?"

"If you start getting crazy come over for a game of Vectrex. We'll listen to Beethoven. It clears the head."

CHAPTER
25

I used to have this recurring dream. I had it mostly when I was sick, like with a fever, but I had it other times, too. I'm on this sheer rock face, taller than the Empire State Building, in my pajamas, holding on to this long rope that's attached on top. I have a paper cup and a tiny, toy-sized pick. It's my job to chip away at the rock, or granite, until it's gone. The dream always gave me the screaming creeps. I would wake up with the feeling that I was shrinking, totally disoriented and creeped out by the overwhelming and totally senseless task of moving a mountain with a paper cup and a tiny, toy-sized pick. I bring it up now because that was the way I was feeling during that particular week before Christmas. I remember it distinctly, Christmas decorations in town, lights up on neighbors' trees outside, Christmas carols on the radio, chorus rehearsals, concerts, parties at school—things I normally like, but this year it was different. It was one of the worst times I can remember. A gigantic wave of hopelessness had washed over me. I was like a half-dead person. Nothing mattered. Nothing could be done. A paper cup and a tiny, toy-sized pick. Chip, chip, chip. My will was low. I was listless. Wait for Corelli.

That was the best I could do. But who knew what that would bring? I knew he wanted to help—I no longer doubted that—but could he? I didn't see how. I had read my *Rights of Young People* backwards and forwards. Nothing seemed to apply, or, if it did, for some reason nobody interpreted it that way. I thought of reading other books, law books, research books, but then, somehow, I didn't. What would I find? Would I even understand them? I doubted it.

I began watching TV with Jenny. We didn't speak, just sat, side by side, Jenny with her earmuffs and Funny Bunny Richardson, me with a bag of taco chips and a jar of peanut butter. I also slept a lot and progressed, zombielike, through a sea of homework ("Most sponges live in salt water"). I had forgotten the purpose of life, if, in fact, I had ever known what it was. With Dad away, Mom in the tub or napping, and Jenny not speaking, we had settled into a kind of half-life routine. Somewhere, some inside voice told me I should do something, that there was a sense to life, there was a reason, there were things worth fighting for that a person could win, but it was a small and distant voice. On one level it scared me. Like, I've heard about this dangerous thing that happens to people in the snow sometimes. If they're out too long and it's freezing, they can get tired and so cold that they just want to lie down and rest. It feels like the sensible thing to do. They just lie down for a little rest and they never get up. Sometimes you need a rest but, at a time like that, it's the worst thing you can do. I thought about that and worried if it applied to me, but basically I just felt hopeless. How could I make a difference? My parents had their own lives to live. Who was I to say what they should do? Why would they listen? Chip, chip, chip.

To make matters worse, Corelli was going to Vermont. He called to let me know, and to give me his phone number up there. He and Carol would be leaving the day before Christmas and spending the week. He assured me that he would be working on things from there, but the thought of his being away added to my general sense of despair.

In some ways life went on as usual. It was, of course, the week of the Christmas dance. Zeus was due in from Detroit and Marion was all excited. She accosted me at the bus stop one morning with this entire outrageous scheme. I should take Amy to the dance and we should all go together in this limousine her father was renting for the night with champagne and a TV set and a chandelier. It was outrageous for many reasons. First of all, Amy and I, although good friends, had not been going out together, she being involved with a six-foot-two-inch junior football player, who would have killed me. It was also outrageous because it was virtually the last thing I would have chosen in my condition. Well, nearly. The thought of loud rock music, crowds of hysterical people, and oddly placed, unnecessary chandeliers was too much to bear. I mainly wanted a good night's sleep.

"I can't," I said. I was kicking at clumps of ice, or caked snow, trying to keep the circulation moving in my toes.

The bus stop in December is worse than the bus stop in November. Eskimo territory. Marion didn't seem to mind. Her thin jean jacket was totally unbuttoned, her running shoes buried deep in snow. "Why not?" she said.

"I have a lot on my mind."

"So what?"

"So I don't want to."

"You'll love it."

"No, I won't." I spotted Ronald way up at the top of the hill, a tiny, distant figure, moving toward the bus stop.

I hope he makes it, I thought.

He often doesn't.

I looked for Haverman, but he was nowhere to be seen. He hadn't been in school for a couple of days. I'd heard nothing from him. I had the feeling that something was wrong. Normally, I would have called him, but in my condition I hadn't been thinking about other people.

"Trust me on this," said Marion.

"I'm not up to going. What can I say?"

"Please?"

"No."

"Come on."

"I wouldn't be very good company."

"Sure you would."

"No, he wouldn't," said Amy. She wore gloves and held her gloved hands up over her ears. She could have used Jenny's earmuffs.

"See?" I said. "She understands."

"She's kidding," said Marion.

"No, I'm not," said Amy.

"She's not. She doesn't want to go. I don't want to go. End of subject."

"Tim's in Florida," said Marion.

"So what?"

"So Amy doesn't have anybody to go with."

"I don't want to go, anyway," said Amy.

"Zeus wants to meet you," said Marion.

"He'll have to wait."

"He's coming tomorrow."

"Great. Did that guy regain the use of his fingers?"

"Not yet."

"Time will tell."

"He told me he's with the Mafia."

"Who's with the Mafia?" said Amy. "The one without the fingers?"

"Zeus," said Marion. "But I don't believe him." She turned to me. "Do you?"

"How would I know?"

"But, like, what do you think?"

"I don't know. For God's sake."

"Mr. Personality," said Amy.

"How would I conceivably know whether Zeus Pitkin is a member of the Mafia?"

"You don't have to be rude."

"I'm not rude. I just don't have the vaguest idea. Nor do I care, to be perfectly honest."

"I still think you two should come to the dance."

That afternoon, when I went into the kitchen to make my after-school snack, Jenny was sitting under the kitchen table with a paper bag over her head. I understood the impulse. I ignored her for the moment and moved to the fridge. I opened it and stared blankly inside, looking for something to strike my interest. I took a couple of chocolate grahams, then shut the fridge and moved to the cabinet. Why is it I never get tired of tuna fish? I could eat it every day and usually do. I took a can out of the cupboard, then reached for the can opener.

"It's not fair," said this voice from underneath the paper bag.

"What's not fair?"

"I can't hear you."

Here we go again, I thought. She must have the earmuffs on underneath the bag.

I opened the tuna.

"She's a big stupid," said the paper bag.

"Who is?"

"I can't hear you."

"If you want to have a conversation, take off the earmuffs."

"I can't hear you."

I dumped the tuna into a small metal mixing bowl, not unlike Bozo's, only smaller. I mixed in some mayonnaise, then got out the rye bread.

"What?" said Jenny from underneath the bag.

"I didn't say anything."

You could tell she wanted to talk, but couldn't get herself to admit she could hear. There was a long pause while I made myself some chocolate milk. Then this tiny voice came out from inside the paper bag. "I can't be Dancing Rudolph."

She was talking about the Christmas play at school. She was going to play Rudolph, who, I assumed, was going to dance. I had promised to do her make-up.

"Why not?" I asked.

"I can't hear you."

"I'm not talking to you anymore."

"But I have to be! She promised and now she says, 'Noooo. You can't be Dancing Rudolph.' "

I scooped out a glob of tuna and put it on the toast.

"I have to be!"

Just then Mom came in with all this brown fabric and a twisted network of white pipe cleaners. She wore a light blue sweatsuit and her glasses and carried her sewing box. Her hair was all kind of stringy. She looked tired, which was surprising considering her quota of naps, thinner, too. The Whole Divorce Thing was taking its toll. "Have you seen Jenny?" she asked.

"She's under the table." I sat down with my tuna and my chocolate milk.

Mom set her stuff down on the table and bent down to talk to Jenny. "Jenny, sweetheart, we need to measure your costume."

No answer.

"Sweetheart. Take the bag off your head and come out. We have to work on the antlers."

"I can't be Dancing Rudolph."

"Why not?"

"Because."

She answered, I thought. Not much of an answer, but an answer nonetheless.

At that point Mom did a nice thing. She got under the table with Jenny. "Why can't you, sweetheart?" she said.

"Because," said Jenny.

"Because why?"

"Mrs. Young said."

"What did she say?"

" 'Nooooo. You can't be Dancing Rudolph.' "

"Why did she say that?"

No response.

"Take the bag off your head so we can talk."

Jenny reached her hand up very slowly and removed the bag. She was crying and still wore the earmuffs.

"Why don't you take off the earmuffs, too?" said Mom. "We can talk better that way."

Jenny shook her head. "That's the whole and only reason."

"What is?"

"That's why. 'Nooooo. You can't be Dancing Rudolph.' "

"I don't understand."

"That's what she said. 'Nooooo. You can't be Dancing Rudolph. Not unless you take off those ear-muffs!' "

"Wouldn't that look better?"

"No."

"Rudolph doesn't wear earmuffs."

"Sometimes he does."

"I don't think so."

"You don't know."

"How could we attach the antlers?"

"We could only stick them on."

"Did you suggest that to Mrs. Young?"

"Yes."

"And what did she say?"

" 'Nooooo. You can't be Dancing Rudolph.' "

The whole conversation was starting to get to me. It was giving me a kind of creeps. I can't explain it. I tried concentrating on my sandwich, then stared at the residue of Nestlé Quik, floating on top of my chocolate milk. It made me somewhat cross-eyed.

Jenny continued. "She says I won't hear how the dancing steps go and when to jump, but I know everything and I can hear her."

"You can hear through the earmuffs?"

"I can."

"Can you hear other things?" I asked.

"No."

"Want some chocolate milk?"

"Yes."

"You heard me. You hear everything. It's all pretend." I got up to get her the milk.

Mom took off her glasses and rubbed her eyes. I noticed they were still puffy.

I wonder if she cries in the tub, I thought.

The idea served to further depress me.

If she's so unhappy about the divorce, why do it? I thought.

"You've wanted to be Dancing Rudolph for a very long time," Mom continued. "Chris is going to give you a red nose with makeup from his kit, remember?"

"I remember."

"You have to think of Mrs. Young."

"No, I don't."

"She's your teacher and it's hard for her when you don't answer. She doesn't know if you understand."

"I do."

I bent down under the table and handed Jenny her chocolate milk. I figured I'd give it one last try. "You want my advice?" I said.

"Maybe."

"Yes or no."

"Yes."

"Take them off now, and when the play's over, if you miss them, you can put them back on. That's what I would do."

"You wouldn't wear earmuffs in the first place."

She had me there.

CHAPTER
26

Grampa called after supper. Mom was napping so I picked up the phone.

"Are they going through with it?"

"Hi, Grampa."

"It's me."

"I know." I was doing the dishes and had the receiver between my ear and shoulder. It was uncomfortable with my neck twisted to the side that way, but I wanted to get the dishes over with and I needed the use of my hands. "How are you, Grampa?"

"I'm all right. What's happening?"

"Dad moved out."

"Oh, no. What's the matter with him?"

"I don't know, Grampa."

"He hasn't called me. Not a word."

"I'm not surprised."

"When do we go to court?"

"I'll let you know as soon as I find out."

"I'm ready."

"Thanks, Grampa."

"What the hell's happening with Christmas?"

"I don't know. Things are a little disorganized."

"You're telling me. Wait a minute. I have to put on my slippers."

"Grampa?"

He had disappeared. He often did that. He would call up and then leave to do things. I felt bad about not even thinking about him in regards to Christmas. He must have felt so neglected. Before, he would always drive over and spend the day with us, but now, with his eye operation, he would have to be driven.

I wonder if Mom or Dad arranged anything, I thought. Probably not.

Mom appeared, half awake, at the door. "Who's that?" she said.

"It's Grampa. He wants to know about Christmas."

"Oh, God," she said. "I forgot all about him."

"I'm back," said Grampa.

Mom leaned against the side of the door, one hand holding her head. "Tell him I'll call him tomorrow. I don't know what we're doing."

"Could Mom call you tomorrow, Grampa? The plans are a little unformed."

"It's going to be a funny Christmas," said Grampa.

"Funny is not the word for it."

"For what?" said Mom.

"Nothing. Listen, Grampa, we'll call you back, okay?"

"Sure. I've got stocking things."

"Great."

"What else have I got to do? My stereo broke."

"Can you have it fixed?"

"I'm going to do that."

"We'll call you, Grampa."

"I love you, Chris."

"I love you, Grampa."

• • •

Haverman's parents were getting divorced again. Both his father, married to Sherry (the one who cooks cheese), and his mother, married to a lawyer (she only marries lawyers), announced impending divorces in that same week before Christmas. This would make four marriages for each, or seven all together. Haverman's mother was planning to stay in Bedford (same house, new lawyer), but his father was doing a stranger thing. He was marrying an ex-aerobics-dancing teacher who was moving to Venezuela. Haverman went into near collapse when he heard about it, which is why he seemingly disappeared for all those many days. He returned to school on the last day before Christmas vacation. I wondered why he hadn't stayed out that day to aid in his recuperation. He looked awful. I saw him first in homeroom. His face had a slightly green color to it. He looked as if he hadn't slept for at least a week. He also looked like he had acquired some bizarre strain of liver ailment, because of his general skin color and deep, sunken eyes.

Either liver or drugs, I thought. Let it be his liver. A highly curable liver condition, that was my hope.

"What happened?" I asked when I first saw him. He was sitting at the back of the room, slumped over in his chair. "Are you all right?"

"How do I look?"

"You look terrible."

"Work it out from there."

"Are you sick?"

"Shhhhhh," said Dr. Gomez, my Spanish/homeroom teacher. She's quite short, with complicated hair piled up on her head. She always wears these white, ruffly blouses and very high-heeled shoes. She has this air of being very correct all the time, while constantly making mistakes. "Now!" she said. She picked up the attendance sheet, held it high above her nose, then remembered she didn't have her glasses and returned to her desk.

"What's going on?" I whispered to Haverman.

"Life is a joke."

"How do you mean that?"

I never got the answer. Dr. Gomez had located her glasses and began taking attendance with a forcible cheeriness I held decidedly suspect. I think she would really like to have been sipping margaritas in a night-club in Spain, or Mexico, at the very least.

I learned about Haverman's divorce problems at Dunfee's Divorce Session later that day in Q mod. Mr. Dunfee already knew about them. He asked Haverman to come up and take a seat in the front. Then Mr. Dunfee sat down next to Haverman and took hold of both Haverman's hands. This put Haverman off to begin with. Mr. Dunfee looked deep into Haverman's eyes. "Close your eyes," he said.

Haverman closed his eyes. Mr. Dunfee paused for a long, significant moment. At last, he spoke. "How do you feel about both your parents getting divorced for the third time and your father moving to Venezuela?"

"Ah, bad," said Haverman. He was seriously doubting Mr. Dunfee's sanity. You could tell.

"You feel bad," said Mr. Dunfee. He was still holding Haverman's hands.

"Bad," said Haverman.

"Bad," repeated Mr. Dunfee.

"Not good," said Haverman.

"Not good," repeated Mr. Dunfee.

"Can I open my eyes now?" said Haverman.

Mr. Dunfee ignored his request. "It's okay to feel bad."

"Can I open my eyes?"

"When bad things happen we don't feel good."

"I don't. Can I open my eyes?"

Mr. Dunfee dropped Haverman's hands and turned to the rest of us. Haverman opened his eyes.

"We all feel bad at times," said Mr. Dunfee. "I felt bad when I didn't make the Little League."

Not that again, I thought. Mr. Dunfee had told it to me the year before. It was all about when he was eight years old and lived in this small town and how he wanted to be in Little League and his mother had bought him this baseball hat and then he didn't get picked. It was sad in a way. I don't mean to put him down. God bless him. He got me started on my journal, and I thank him for that. It helped me at the time to really look at what was going on. Thank you, Mr. Dunfee.

After a brief cupcake party in art, school was officially over for Christmas vacation. I missed the old excitement. School vacation had always meant more to me than almost anything known to man, or woman. This year I couldn't feel a thing, except maybe the promise of getting more sleep. I was not in good shape.

That afternoon Jenny had her Rudolph Show. It was actually a Christmas show, as I mentioned earlier, but since Jenny was Rudolph, or Dancing Rudolph to be exact, she called it the Rudolph Show. I wondered why she didn't call it the Dancing Rudolph Show, but then she's full of surprises. She had decided to take off the earmuffs. I thought she would. I knew how much she wanted to be Rudolph.

After school I did her makeup. It was simple, just

a light face with reindeer whiskers and a bright-red nose. She looked so cute. She wore her brown, furry reindeer costume that Mom made, with tights, ballet shoes, a fluffy tail, the twisted pipe-cleaner antlers, and her bright-red Rudolph nose.

Dad was there. He had called the night before. Mom must have told him about the performance. He sat in the back. It was so strange, them sitting apart. I went back and sat with him about halfway through the show. I didn't know where I belonged. I didn't feel right with either of them.

One thing interested me. Mom had her hair done. Why did she do that? I thought. Was it purely for Dancing Rudolph? Could it be because she knew, or suspected, that Dad would be there and she wanted to look good? Please, God, let that be the reason.

I wasn't in the mood for a show, but I have to admit it was adorable. Dancing Rudolph was a definite highlight. He danced around this large paper tree with decorations which was surrounded by presents. After circling around the tree several times, he picked up various presents and danced with them. Later, he joined in with Santa and the elves and sang "We Wish You a Merry Christmas.." I was sitting next to Dad at that point, and his eyes started to tear up. After the show, Jenny came running out in her costume. She ran towards him, jumped up into his arms and hugged him for the longest time. Afterward, he gave her a T-shirt that said "I SAW THE GREAT SALT LAKE." She hugged that, too.

CHAPTER
27

Christmas was a disaster. To begin with, we had a blizzard. Dad had planned to go over and get Grampa, but driving that kind of distance was impossible. Grampa would have to spend Christmas alone, with the unopened stocking presents and his broken stereo. It made me want to cry.

The plan was for us to have two Christmases. Mom told us, trying to make it sound like some great and spectacular thing. "You'll have two Christmases this year," she said. We were in the kitchen, finishing up an uninteresting supper built around Weight Watchers frozen chicken breasts. "We'll have a Christmas here, and then Daddy will pick you up and you'll have another Christmas with Daddy."

"One Christmas is enough,"said Jenny. She was shoving her rice around in circles through her low-cal, white-colored gravy.

"This year you're going to have two!"

"That's stupid and wrong," said Jenny.

"You'll have to accept it."

"Bunny won't."

"There's nothing we can do about it, sweetheart. We'll be doing things a little differently."

"Not me."

"We all will."

"Trudy got bad breath," said Jenny. "She stuffed lima beans up her nose and they rotted."

"That's nice," I said.

"It wasn't," said Jenny. "The doctor had to pull them out with a pinching stick."

"Can we talk about this later?" I hadn't finished my chicken.

"He said it wouldn't hurt, but it did. They always do that. They say, 'This won't hurt,' and it does."

"I don't think that's true."

"Trudy said."

"I don't think so."

"They try to pull one over on you."

"Put one."

"What?"

"Put one over. You don't pull one over. You put one over."

"Trudy said."

"I don't care what Trudy said. She's wrong."

"You're wrong."

"Can we not argue?" Mom was getting desperate. I couldn't blame her. I was in a rotten mood, which was not exactly what we needed that night.

After supper I made the mistake of passing through the living room. I say mistake because it caused me to view our pathetic, spindly runt of a Christmas tree. Mom had bought it in haste from the tiny tree man in the empty lot by the side of the Texaco gas station. There were a few lights on it, but that was all. The amount of presents was pitiful. I didn't care about it from that standpoint, because I didn't want anything, except my family, but the sight was so depressing. It was like nobody cared, like everybody was somewhere else. In a sense that was true.

I had bought almost no presents. A Mr. Potato Head for Jenny, a blouse for Mom, a record for Grampa (*Ella Fitzgerald Sings Cole Porter*), and a sweater for Dad. I had gotten them in a big rush on Friday night at the mall. It was awful there, everyone blank-eyed and desperate, attempting to complete their last-minute shopping. I wished I could have skipped the whole thing. Mom made a stocking for Jenny, but that was it. Neither Mom nor I wanted stocking presents. Dad would have to make do with his sweater and a handmade cardboard frog-shaped desk blotter from Jenny.

It pains me to describe Christmas Day. We opened our presents, which took about ten minutes. Then I stayed in my room, just lying on my bed until Dad rang the bell at twelve-thirty.

Why did Dad ring the bell? I thought. Because it's not his house anymore! Not in his mind. He's gone, remember? Nooo! I have to call Corelli! We have to do something!

Dad and Jenny and Bunny and Mr. Potato Head and I all went over to the Holiday Inn in the blizzard to have our second Christmas, while Mom took a bath, or a nap. I'm not sure which.

I hope she doesn't cry, I thought. No turkey, no eggnog, no cranberry sauce, no singing. Her day would be different—WQXR, a bath, and a jelly tumbler full of brandy. Not my idea of Christmas.

Jenny was pretty hyper. Bunny and Mr. Potato Head had this huge fight on Route 117. Mr. Potato Head had to be locked in the glove compartment. He didn't even get to come into the Holiday Inn for

Christmas number two. I envied him. The way I was feeling I would rather have spent Christmas in a nice glove compartment.

When we arrived at the Holiday Inn, I told Dad I had to go to the bathroom. "I can't wait till we get upstairs," I told him. "You and Jenny go ahead."

They got into the elevator and I went to the lounge area to call Corelli. Once more, I used Dad's credit card. I shouldn't have.

"Merry Christmas," said Corelli.

"Merry Christmas," I said. "Listen, Corelli, don't stay the week. Please. Come back. We have to do something!"

"I'm workin' on it."

"We don't have grounds!"

"We will."

"When?"

"We got over two weeks."

"We don't know that. Mom said about a month. That could mean anything."

A woman wearing a lot of perfume and holding a small poodle was waiting to use the phone. I nodded and smiled in a way to suggest that I knew she was there and that she wouldn't have to wait long. It didn't seem to work. She adjusted her poodle and made a type of sighing noise.

"There's nothing on the calendar for the first week of January," said Corelli.

"What calendar?"

"The court calendar. I checked."

"What about the second week?"

"I don't know."

"There better not be."

"Relax now. Don't worry. You listening to Bee-
∗hoven?"

"I always listen to Beethoven."

"Keep it up. I'll see you next week."

I hung up, thereby freeing the phone for the poodle woman. She looked a lot like her dog.

When Dad opened the door to his room I was greeted by the sight of this two-foot-tall pink Christmas tree. It was hideous. No tree at all would have been a gigantic improvement. It was shiny, virtually glowing with this bizarre type of paint. There it was, sitting up on the dresser next to the room service menu and a complimentary shoe cleaning cloth, a depressing still life if there ever was one. It was depressing, too, because I knew Dad had gotten it for us. He had made a kind of effort. I wished he hadn't. Also on the dresser were two presents. Jenny got a Rainy Day Activity Kit with Magic Markers and stickers and coloring books, and that type of thing in it. I got a jacket. It's actually terrific, although I couldn't get excited about it at the time. It's a waterproof, safari-style jacket, which advertises that you can wear it under a waterfall, hardly necessary in Bedford, but kind of neat. If I'm ever under a waterfall, I'll know what to wear. Dad had gotten it in Denver on his trip. Dad liked his sweater, and it fit, so that was good, but there was this incredible strain between us. It was like neither of us could think what to say.

"I love my sweater."

"I love my coat."

"I got it in Denver."

"I know."

"Did I mention that?"

"No."

"How did you know?"

"It says so on the label."

"It does?"

"Right here."

"So it does."

Long pause.

"How's school?"

"We're on vacation."

"Of course. How was it?"

"When?"

"When you were there."

"It was all right."

"That's good."

"How's work?"

"It's all right."

"That's good."

It was downhill from there. Jenny got more and more hyper. She insisted on putting Rainy Day Activity stickers on Bunny's face and vest, and he didn't like that, so she threatened to put him in the glove compartment with Mr. Potato Head. She was being totally unreasonable. Dad and I stared at the snow, put on our new clothes, watched Jenny torment Bunny, then took her down to the restaurant where we had inferior fried chicken. After that we came back to the room and watched TV. It was altogether so bleak, so desolate, us there at the Holiday Inn, watching television and waiting for the night maid to bring in the chocolate mints, Mom at home, crying in the bathtub, Grampa sitting off alone in Connecticut beside his broken stereo. It was not my favorite Christmas.

CHAPTER
28

The rest of vacation was a blur. I spent the time in my room with my fish. I had trouble sleeping at night, so I would sleep late in the morning and wake up with half the day behind me. I remember writing a lot in my journal. We were supposed to write something each day, which I found myself doing. As I did that, I found myself really getting into it. I wrote a lot about what happened when we first learned about the divorce. It was a type of solace, writing all that stuff down. I would lie on my bed, or sit at my desk, writing, glancing now and then at my fish and listening to Beethoven. I listened to all the symphonies that week. Then I moved into the piano concertos. Arthur Rubinstein. Dad had made the tapes for me off a record set we have. We used to listen to the tapes in the car a couple of years ago, when we did things together. The smallest errand was an event. A trip to the Smokehouse in Mt. Kisco for smoked salmon took on the coziest proportions. Beethoven on the Saw Mill and a fistful of pine nuts. I WANT MY DAD!

Dad went away again, in the large, geographical sense. He went to Seattle. Mom pretty much stayed in the tub. Jenny made up with Bunny, and the two of them spent hours in her room with her Rainy Day Activity Kit, making various signs. Most of them said MOM, or DAD. She taped them up all over the house. MOM on the stove, DAD on his dining-room chair, MOM on the tub, DAD on his kitchen chair, MOM on her kitchen chair, DAD on his recliner chair by the TV, MOM on the bathroom door, DAD on the door to the basement (for obscure reasons known only to Jenny), DAD also on the Ovaltine jar. (He loves Ovaltine.) On the door to Mom and Dad's bedroom she put MOM AND DAD. I thought that was telling. On top of the dining-room table she put a sunshine smiling sticker saying NO MORE FITES. It permanently damaged the finish.

Corelli came back toward the end of the week. Thank God. Otherwise I'm not sure I would have made it. He called after New Year's, saying he thought he had something. We arranged to meet that same afternoon. Marion was away so I took Bedford Taxi. I found Corelli inside the garage.

"Corelli?" I said. I wasn't sure it was him because all I could see was the end half of these legs sticking out from under a beige Mercedes.

"He can't hear you." Joey was down at the other end of the garage working on an ancient and decidedly bashed-up green Chevrolet.

"Hi, Joey."

"He can't hear you."

"Is it him?"

"Yeah." Then he shouted. "HEY, ARCHIE, YOU GOT COMPANY!"

"I'm comin' out," I heard from under the Mercedes. The legs started moving out, then the chest, then the head. It was Corelli. "Hey, Chris. I think I've got something."

"So you said."

Corelli began tinkering with something just be-hind the front wheel. I couldn't see what it was.

"Can we talk?"

"Sure." More tinkering.

"Can we talk now?"

"Let's take a walk."

We left the garage, followed by Bozo, and headed for this area by these old deserted train tracks. The blizzard had stopped, but there was still some snow and it was cold. We crossed the street, then started along by the tracks. Bozo was delighted. I don't think he often got a midafternoon walk. He soon was lead-ing the way.

"There's a divorce action pending, right?" said Corelli. He wore his dark green mechanic's suit. There was a large wrench in his left front pocket.

"Right," I said.

"Well, we don't hit it head on."

"We don't?"

"We can't. There's a proceeding, right? Now in this proceeding there's going to be a judgment."

"Right."

"The divorce will be granted, or the divorce will not be granted. You follow me?"

"Yes."

Bozo spotted a squirrel. His ears pulled forward like when he saw the Grape-Nuts. He stopped still. The squirrel must have seen him because he headed full speed ahead up a nearby tree.

Corelli put his hands in his pockets. "Our ques-tion is, how do we get into that proceeding. See, at this point, nobody in there's gotta listen to a damn thing we say."

"They don't?"

"What are they gonna do, listen to any damn fool that walks in off the street? They can't do that. They gotta set a thing."

"A thing?"

"A procedure. And that's what they did. You gotta get accepted into a case as a necessary party."

"You just thought of that?"

"I knew it, but I was thinking of a different tack. Hear me out."

"Go ahead."

"Okay. We gotta get accepted into the case as a necessary party. If we don't do that, the court's not gonna entertain any application in your behalf at all." He sat down on a rock ledge several yards from the tracks, then called to Bozo to let him know we had stopped.

Bozo stopped instantly, then turned to review the situation. I sat down next to Corelli. Bozo ran back and stared at us. We had made a poor choice. He wanted to be on the move.

"Sit down," said Corelli.

Bozo sat. Corelli continued. "Point in our favor. The court must have before it all people necessary for a proper decision to be rendered. Okay. We prove you're necessary and you're in."

"How do we do that?"

"We go to that proceeding."

"You mean the final divorce thing?"

"It's not gonna be final. Not if we get accepted."

"What if we don't?"

Bozo got up and walked off in the direction of a cluster of trees. Corelli didn't notice. "I think we will," he said.

"You think so? What the hell is that? My life is on the line here, Corelli. Don't get vague with me!"

"I think it's gonna work! You want guarantees? You're on the wrong planet."

"If they don't accept us, that's it. There's nothing we can do."

"It's our best shot. I'm telling you. Your interested and affected party angle got me thinking. You ever want to be a lawyer?"

"No."

"Good for you."

Bozo returned, carrying a large rock. He stood in front of us with a look of pride.

"Drop it," said Corelli.

Bozo stared.

"Drop it!"

No response.

"Crazy dog," said Corelli. "He loves rocks. Look at him. He's got flat teeth from carrying rocks. No points on 'em anywhere."

WHAT ABOUT MY LIFE?

"Drop that rock!"

Bozo stared, the rock held firmly in his dog jaws.

"He won't drop it," said Corelli. "He's got it from now till suppertime."

"I don't know, Corelli," I said. "Can't there be a plan whereby we have some kind of alternative? We leave it to the last minute and then try this whole thing, and if it doesn't work we're dead. I don't like it."

"In my opinion it's our best shot. You asked me. That's my opinion."

I was not reassured. "So we go there, we just show up, and then what? What do we say?"

"I gotta work that out."

"When?"

"We got at least a week."

"And then what?"

"If we're lucky? They put the whole thing off, two, maybe three weeks. Then we present our case."

"Which we don't have."

"We will! Procedure, Chris. It's ninety-nine percent of the law. You gotta know it. You gotta follow it. You gotta play the game."

I was shivering. The combination of the cold and my overall nervous state had my teeth virtually chattering.

It's up to you, I thought. It's on your head. One wrong move and your life will be altered for time and eternity. God help me.

Corelli put his arm around my shoulder. "I know it's hard, kid," he said. "You're in a tough spot. I hate to see it."

I was looking at Bozo. He was sitting now, but he still had the rock. It must have been heavy.

"Good dog," said Corelli. He patted Bozo on the head. "Good rock."

"Bozo lay down, loosened his grip on the rock, then held it between his paws. He put his head down on the snow, heaved a sigh, and slept. Corelli patted me on the back. "What can I say? Who the hell knows in life—you know what I'm saying?"

"I do."

"I think it'll work out. I wouldn't say so if I didn't."

"I know."

"So what do you say?"

I couldn't answer. I looked at Bozo with his rock, the tender way he cradled it with his paws, the snow, the old, half-broken tracks, Corelli's worn-out workboots with the broken laces, the large oak tree where the squirrel had made his escape, the clouds forming out in the distance, high above the on ramp to the Taconic Parkway.

"All right."

I heard the words, not realizing, at first, that I was the one speaking.

"Good," said Corelli.

I was filled with panic, a deep-seated terror, a blank zero in the center of nothing. Part of me wanted to take it back, to beg him to reconsider, but I said nothing.

All right? I thought. Am I crazy? Why did I say that? I'm agreeing to a plan that makes no sense— to me, at least. Am I a coward? When the chips are down am I afraid to stick up for what I believe in? Am I confused? Exhausted?

Another thought intruded on these: Inspiration. Could that be what it was? Inspiration? Intuition? A feeling—a hunch? Had my very own Obi-Wan just tapped me on the shoulder? Had Yoda just whispered in my ear? Had I done the very bravest thing? Had I listened?

CHAPTER
29

Throughout the following days I tried desperately to make some sense out of Corelli's plan. It made no sense to me, the plan itself or my agreeing to do it. The uneasiness continued, the fear. Then, on the last night of vacation, I read something that seemed to apply. I was in my room with my fish, listening to Mozart, trying desperately to unwind by sketching from this wildlife animal book. It's a very thorough, scientific book on all types of animal life in Africa. What hit me was what it said about escaping from an angry rhinoceros. The man who wrote the book had been on several expeditions in Africa, so he had pretty much firsthand information. Here's what he said. If you're faced with certain death because of being attacked by a charging, angry rhinoceros, the only way to survive the situation, save shooting the rhino in the head with a BIG gun, is to remain still until the last minute. You stay right where you are and wait until the rhino comes within five or six feet of you, then you jump out of the way very fast. The rhino literally cannot see you, because his head is down in position, ready to impale you with his horn. Before that, he can see you. He can change his direction, veer toward you wherever you go, but at five or six feet it's too late. His head is down, his direction locked in. Jump out of the way and you're safe. The trick is to have the guts to stand there until the last minute. It seemed to me, on that dreary night, as I sat alone in my room with my fish and my Mozart and my enormous fear and dread and self-doubt and depression, that maybe that's what Corelli's plan was like. Like the rhinoceros was the impending divorce and the courageous and only thing to do was to hold our ground, do nothing until the last minute when we could have the most certain effect. We weren't ignoring the danger. We had a plan. At the present moment stillness was a part of it. It sounds silly now, farfetched and irrelevant, but I remember that after reading about the charging rhinoceros I had my first night's sleep in weeks.

School started the next morning. When I went downstairs to make a protein drink, Jenny was sitting at the kitchen table. She had her nightgown on, and was eating vanilla wafers out of her Roadrunner lunch box. The box was open in front of her, filled with nothing but vanilla wafers. Bunny was in her lap.

"You're up early," I said.

"So it seems." She stuffed two wafers into her mouth, one after the other. There hardly seemed to be room.

I started mixing my drink.

"I'm not going to school," she said.

"Why not?"

"It hurts my eyes."

"Why's that?"

"No reason."

"Okay." I was in no mood to argue.

She began taking the wafers out of her lunch box and stacking them in neat piles on the table. "I think of Daddy at school and it's bad," she said. "I get sad and I have to cry, but I don't want to so I squeeze inside my eyes, and no tears come but it's only hurting."

"I know what you mean."

"You have that, too?"

"In a way. I have headaches." I had finished making my drink and was drinking it down. It tasted good. There was a raw egg in it, but you couldn't tell. "Try not to worry," I said. "I'm working on it."

"Trudy has a new cat."

"That's nice."

"You bet." She dumped the remaining wafers from her lunch box, destroying the neatly stacked piles. "She's so cute. I only want to squeeze her. She has pussy-willow toes."

At school things were back in full swing. Mr. Pucci informed me that I had to put up my art show, which would entail matting over thirty pictures in three days; Haverman informed me that I had to do all the makeup for *The Fantasticks*; Mr. Story informed me that I had to help collect empty soda cans for the Empty Soda Can Refund Drive; Mr. Marrone informed me that I had two tests to make up in social studies; and Marion informed me that I had missed the greatest experience of my lifetime by not going to the Christmas dance. She accosted me in the Library in L mod. "It was the absolute greatest," she whispered with feverish intensity. "We went to Friendly's and the Midnight Diner, and then we hung out in the lobby of the Holiday Inn."

I wondered if she had seen my dad.

"It was fantastic. Zeus wanted to go to Rye Play-land, but they close it for the winter."

"Why should that stop him?"

"There's a fence."

"Too bad."

"You should have come. I was so tired I threw up."

"Maybe next year."

Three days after that simple conversation I had the greatest shock of my life. I was in the bathroom in just my pajama bottoms, throwing cold water on my face, as I do every morning to wake myself up. When I turned off the water I heard my mother on the phone.

"Well, call him," she was saying. "What do you mean who? Beanie, or whatever the hell his name is. Your lawyer. Call him and find out."

Find out what? I thought.

"Because I couldn't reach you," she continued. "I'm calling you now, aren't I? What do you care? You don't have to be there anyway."

Be where?

"They moved it up. What can I tell you?"

A chill ran through my body.

Oh, God.

"So it's today. What difference does it make?"

Oh, God.

I stood transfixed and shivering, cold water dripping from my face and hands, too stunned to reach for a towel.

Oh, God.

"You might thank me for trying to reach you at all. I didn't know you cared."

I reached for a towel.

"Call me tonight."

I dried my face and hands and ran from the bathroom into Mom and Dad's room. Mom was standing by the phone. She had just hung up.

"What's going on?" I said.

"What?" She was in a daze.

"What's going on?"

"Where's your shirt?"

"Who was that?"

"Dad."

"What happened?"

"It's today."

"The divorce?"

She didn't answer. She looked completely lost. She was wearing her long, white, ruffly robe with the tiny flowers on it.

"I thought it was next week."

"They moved it up. They said they might do that."

"And you just found out?"

"They told me a few days ago."

"Why didn't you tell me?"

"I'm sorry. It's at twelve o'clock. I need you to watch Jenny this afternoon. I don't know how late I'll be."

Oh, God.

I was flooded with panic and desperation. Things were crashing down on me from every side. I had to think, but my mind went into this kind of locked place, like it jammed. All I could feel was my heart pounding. It felt like it was pounding everywhere in my body, not just in my chest, but in my hands and my arms and legs and stomach and head, like my whole body was one gigantic heart, pounding and beating in terror.

We're not ready. We're not ready. Oh, God, we're not ready.

"Can you take care of Jenny?"

"I can't! No!"

"I'll call Evelyn." Mom was in a world of her own, unaware of my desperation. "Maybe she can play with Trudy."

"Right." I ran from the room, not knowing where to go. I was thinking of Mom, standing by the phone, so lonesome in her robe.

She doesn't want the divorce, I thought.

In that instant I knew.

I threw on my clothes and left the house. I had grabbed my jean jacket, which was a mistake. It was twenty-nine degrees out.

Don't go to school, I thought as I ran down Elm Ledge. Get to Corelli!

I ran practically the entire way to Bedford Taxi. Fred, the head taxi man, was inside the tiny one-room taxi office, huddled over his coffee and his radio microphone.

"I need a cab!" I said. I was so out of breath, I could hardly get the words out.

"Where to?" said Fred. He wore a muffler. It was what I always saw him wear in the winter, the same sweater and the same muffler. He never seemed warm enough.

"Millwood," I said.

"Jack'll take ya."

When I got to Corelli's I paid Jack and literally leaped out of the car. Nobody was outside, so I ran into the garage. I came in so fast that I scared Bozo, who didn't recognize me momentarily and started to bark.

"Quiet!" said Corelli. He was working on a car in the back, drinking coffee while he worked.

Joey was dozing in the office.

"It's today!" I said, out of breath and desperate.

"What?"

"Today! Twelve o'clock!"

"Oh, Jesus!"

"Oh, God, what are we going to do?"

Corelli was stunned. He stopped all movement, stood absolutely still, then his mind started going a mile a minute. "You gotta get your Grampa!"

"Grampa! I forgot all about him!"

"You gotta get him!"

"He's in Connecticut!"

"Get someone to drive you."

"What about you?"

"I gotta go over my notes." He swallowed the remains of his coffee, threw the Styrofoam cup toward a trash bin, missed the bin, ignored that, and started taking off his mechanic's suit. He had his jeans and sweatshirt on underneath. I thought of him in court, dressed like that, jeans and sweatshirt. He looked like a sculptor, or a dishwasher, or a guy that loaded crates at a dock. "Get your Grampa!" he said.

I spotted Joey, dozing in the office. "Can Joey drive me?"

"He's gotta stay here. I can't leave the place alone. HEY, JOEY!"

Joey shifted position, then opened his eyes.

"Get up! I gotta go!"

Bozo ran toward us, tail wagging, ready.

"You stay here!"

Bozo dropped his head. His tail stopped wagging.

"Who's gonna drive me?" I said.

"Don't you know anybody sixteen?"

"Marion!"

"Marion, fine. Get Marion!" Corelli started out, calling back over his shoulder. "Meet me at the court-house!"

"Where's that?"

"White Plains." He had almost reached the door. "Call information! Get the address! Front steps, a quarter to twelve!"

I felt like I was in quicksand—my life, my future, dissolving, sucking me in by the feet.

"Have we got grounds?"

"Kind of." He was gone.

Kind of? God help me.

The rhinoceros had caught *us* with our heads down, unable to see. He was already upon us. Too late to get out of the way.

Bozo stared at me from over by a stack of old tires, awaiting an explanation. I couldn't help him.

CHAPTER
30

Speeding east along Route 84, past Danbury, Marion narrowly missed hitting two orange, barrel-like construction-marker tubs.

"The primary thing is to get there," I said.

"I know," she said, but she didn't slow down.

Needless to recount, Marion had been delirious over the idea of driving me to Connecticut. When I called her from Corelli's I didn't give her the details. I just told her that I had to get to Connecticut, fast, that it was an emergency, that I'd tell her what it was about later, and would she cut school and drive me. What would she say? You know Marion. Miss Dramatic Intrigue of Westchester County.

"That is totally awesome," she said, navigating the double rows of orange tubs and inverted funnel-shaped markers.

I had just told her the complete and gruesome story. "Slow down, will you?" The speedometer read seventy. "Too fast! There's tubs!"

She pulled back to sixty-five. "I can't believe you are actually doing this. Like, it's totally blowing my mind."

"I haven't done anything yet."

"What do you mean? You got a lawyer. You planned this whole big thing. It is so excellent!"

"It may be disaster. We're not prepared."

"Oh, God!"

"What is it?"

"I have to sneeze!"

"So what?"

"You close your eyes when you sneeze."

"For a split second."

"That's all it takes. We'll hit something."

"No, we won't."

"We will!"

"We won't. Slow down and sneeze."

"I heard if you open your eyes when you sneeze they explode out of your head."

"Just sneeze, okay? I've got the wheel."

She sneezed and we proceeded east to Southbury.

As we turned into Heritage Village, I realized I hadn't told Grampa we were coming.

I should have warned him, I thought, but then where would he be? Walking Peterson? (That's his dog.) He's either walking Peterson, or he's at the grocery store, or he's inside. He can't drive. He can't be far.

We turned left into the row of condominiums on the hill opposite the gray wood board shopping plaza and the Timbers Restaurant. I remembered we ate there just when Grampa moved in. They had a gigantic buffet with a five-foot-tall swan in the middle, carved out of ice. We had a good time, but we never went back.

I rang the bell. Grampa opened the door. He wore his bathrobe over slacks and a pajama top. Peggy Lee was singing on the radio. The reception was poor.

"Chris!" said Grampa. He gave me a big hug. He was so happy to see me. It made me sad. I knew how much he missed me when I wasn't there.

"Hi, Grampa," I said.

"Peterson, down!" Grampa grabbed Peterson's collar. He was whining and generally leaping all over me and Marion. He's a small, wiry, little dog that Grampa found several years ago at a railroad station. Grampa says he's some rare and unfamiliar breed of dog found only in Africa, but I think he's a mutt. He's a sweet dog but he hardly ever quiets down. It's like he thinks any minute he's going to be dropped back at the tracks. Only when he and Grampa are alone and quiet, if Grampa is sitting or resting, then Peterson will lie down and sleep a deep and grateful sleep. Grampa loves him a lot, and I know Peterson loves Grampa. Once Grampa shut Peterson in the bedroom for some reason and Peterson carved great slashes in the bedroom door with his nails, trying to get out.

"Down, Peterson!" said Grampa. He pulled back on Peterson's collar. Peterson still lunged up, his front paws totally off the ground, wheezing and gagging from the pressure of the collar on his neck.

"I don't mind him," said Marion.

"He shouldn't jump on people," said Grampa. "It's not right."

"This is Marion," I said.

"Hello," said Marion.

"Hello, dear," said Grampa. "He'll quiet down in a minute."

"Grampa," I said, "we have to go to court!"

"Now?"

"Right now! They moved the hearing. It's today!"

"Today?"

"At twelve."

"Damn fools! Down, Peterson! There's a good dog." Grampa dressed in a hurry and we left. Peterson accepted that, for some strange reason. He didn't even bark.

"How long does it take to get to White Plains?" I asked as we began heading west on 84.

"You're asking me?" said Grampa.

"Whoever knows."

"I don't know," said Marion.

"I don't either," said Grampa. "I've never been there. Well, that's not quite true. I was there once. Macy's, I think, but I didn't go from here. Where the heck did I go from? I got pillows."

"I think it's about an hour and a half," said Marion, "maybe two."

I looked at my trusty Rolex, a hand-me-down from Dad. Ten-fifteen. An hour and a half was perfect. Two was disaster.

There were numerous traffic snarls on 84 and a major tie-up on our way south. A truck had gone off the road and was lying on its side on the grass in the center of the highway.

Let no one be hurt, I thought. And let this clear, please. Please!

Ambulance sirens, blue flashing police lights, seconds ticking by. I started to sweat. I had never known such tension.

Please, God, let us get there on time, I kept repeating silently, over and over again. It was virtually a prayer.

I didn't dare look at my watch. The last time I looked it said eleven-thirty.

We'll never make it, I thought. How can we? Don't let it end this way, please!

WHITE PLAINS! The sign, the turn-off.

"Where's the courthouse?" asked Marion.

I pulled out the directions I had gotten when I called from Corelli's. "Left," I said. "Right at the first light."

"I never came this way," said Grampa. He seemed to be enjoying the outing despite the desperateness of events. "I think I came from Riverdale."

"Left at the gas station," I instructed. I was shaking, sweating, my head was pounding. I was afraid to look at my watch. We took our left, and, up ahead, several blocks down, was the courthouse.

"Did we make it?" said Marion.

I looked at my watch. It was eleven fifty-six.

"We'll make it," said Marion.

"We're not there yet."

Marion sped through a stop sign, then pulled to a screeching halt in front of the courthouse. Corelli was on the front steps.

"Go!" said Marion. "Run!"

Grampa virtually jumped out of the car. Corelli spotted us from up on the steps. "Where the hell were you?" he shouted.

"Connecticut!" I shouted back. "Remember?"

Corelli turned and ran up the steps. Grampa and I followed. Grampa can run surprisingly fast. Corelli burst through the doors of the courthouse. "This way!" he shouted.

There was a group of people waiting by the elevators. We followed Corelli in the other direction, off to the right and up a flight of stairs. I looked back to see how Grampa was doing. He was puffing for breath, but he looked happy. "I'm coming!" he shouted.

On the second-floor landing Corelli veered off through a door and ran down the corridor. We followed.

What time can it be? I thought. It must be after twelve. Is it over? Does it happen in a minute? I thought of the electric chair.

Along the sides of the corridor a lot of people were sitting on benches. Corelli stopped midway down in front of a large door. "What's happening?" he said. He seemed to be speaking to no one in particular, to the walls, to God.

No one answered. They looked confused, or like they didn't care.

Corelli nodded at the door. "Who's in there?"

And then, just then, and I swear this, the door opened and a man stuck his head out and called, "Stephen Mills!"

My heart beat in my throat.

"Stephen Mills?"

"That's us!" said Corelli.

"Wait a minute. Who . . . ?" said the man, but it was too late. Corelli had already barged past.

CHAPTER
31

The room was smaller than I thought it would be. In the center, behind a table, was the judge. Near him was a stenographer woman and behind her, a sheriff with a noticeable gun. There was a flag to the left of the judge. Facing the judge, up at the front of the room, was another man, tall, thin, in a tan suit. Next to him was my mother. She had on a blue dress. My heart tripped when I saw her.

"Your Honor!" shouted Corelli. He was moving toward the judge, out of breath, running almost. "We want to make a motion to intervene in this case!"

Mom turned around. She was startled. Then she saw me. She looked stunned, instantly disoriented. I wanted to go to her, to hug her, to tell her that I loved her, but of course I didn't. I inched up closer to Corelli. Grampa followed.

"Who is this?" said the judge. He also spoke to no one in particular, to the walls, to the voice of higher reason. He had a beard and looked as if he hadn't gotten enough sleep.

"I don't know, Your Honor," said the man who had opened the door.

Corelli moved forward. I noticed he had changed

his clothes. He looked halfway decent, nothing fancy, but acceptable. He wore a nubby knit tie, but it wasn't quite straight. He looked in my direction, motioning me forward. Grampa moved up with me. Mom just stared.

"This is my client, Christopher Mills," said Corelli, "son of this lady here." He turned to me. "Is this your mother?"

"Yes."

"Right." He turned back to the judge. "And this is the boy's grandfather, Mr. Macintyre Mills."

"How do," said Grampa. He nodded agreeably at the judge. Then he nodded at Mom. She stared in disbelief.

The judge seemed irritated. Our interruption was decidedly not part of his afternoon plan. (Delay in a scheduled game of golf?) Mom kept staring at me. Corelli cleared his throat. "On behalf of my client I would like to make a motion to intervene."

The judge appeared to ignore him. He turned to Mom. "Is this your son?" he asked her.

"Yes," she said. She was definitely in shock.

What is she thinking? I wondered. Does she hate me?

"What's your name?" The judge was speaking to me.

"Christopher Mills," I answered. My voice cracked. I was basically panicked.

The judge turned to Corelli. "What legal basis do you have for intervening in this case?"

Corelli thrust his hands deep into his pockets, the way I do when I'm nervous. "Necessary party, Your Honor," he said. He moved forward. I could see him shifting into a higher gear. "Being that the court must have before it all people necessary for a proper adjudication to be rendered, and being that my client has pertinent and necessary information to be included in said adjudication, we respectfully request the court's permission to present our argument."

I could tell he was nervous, but his thinking was incredibly sharp. He was on top of every thought, in the very center of reason, unwavering, and real. I felt a whole new respect for him.

The judge was not convinced. He stared with a kind of stony expression at Corelli. "In what way is your client necessary?" he asked.

Oh no! I thought. Did we cover that? Does he know? Is this the part we didn't get to figure out? Please, God, let him have an answer.

Corelli took his hands out of his pockets. "My client is an integral part of this family unit," he said, "and would thereby seriously be prejudiced by any adjudication in this proceeding. He is also in possession of information crucial to the outcome of this case. We seek to enumerate said information, Your Honor, by gaining the court's permission to present our argument."

The thin man in the tan suit didn't like that. The veins in his neck started to puff out. "I respectfully submit!" he said. He was going to say more, but Corelli didn't let him.

"I'm not finished," he shouted.

"Gentlemen!" said the judge.

"Your Honor!" said the man in the tan suit.

He must be my mother's lawyer, I thought. No wonder he doesn't like Corelli.

"Gentlemen," repeated the judge. He took a drink of water from the glass on his desk. He seemed confused, but he was trying not to show it. "This procedure is highly unusual."

"Listen, Your Honor," said Corelli, "I respectfully submit that final judgment on the pertinence of my client's testimony can only be made subsequent to its presentation."

I loved his wording. It was really impressive.

"CPLR, Section 1012(a)(2)," he continued, "which deals with intervention as of right, clearly requires that intervention be permitted when a person will be bound by a judgment, and his interest would not otherwise be protected. My client, Christopher Mills, will be bound by any judgment rendered by this court that effects a change in his parents' marital status, and, with all due respect to my colleagues involved in this case, they are bound by the terms in their retainers to represent the interests of the parents, not the children. Any decision made here will so affect the life of my client and his sister that my client must be included." Corelli moved up closer to the judge, his tone more personal. "What are we talking about? One week, two? A short delay in the dissolution of this marriage. The parties have been married for over fifteen years. Surely they can wait another two weeks in consideration of their children's welfare. I understand that this is highly irregular. In fairness to all parties, we would request that a stay of two weeks be granted so that all parties can prepare argument on this matter." He stopped, staring intently at the judge.

No one said a word. My mother's lawyer stared at his shoes. The judge cleared his throat. He looked at his papers, although he didn't appear to be reading. Grampa smiled and nodded to himself. He liked what Corelli had said. So did I. I had no idea Corelli would come off like that. Popcorn, bare feet, dogs with rocks, a mistrust of the law, a love of Grape-Nuts, and out of all of this comes a brilliant mind, a command of things legal, and a gigantic heart. I felt this great love for him as I watched him stare down the judge. His look was so fiery, so relentless, so demanding. Then I looked at Mom. She was crying. I felt this pang of guilt.

"Is it your desire to intervene in this case?" The words seemed to be coming from the end of a tunnel, unimportant, distant. And then again. "Is it your desire to intervene in this case?" It was the judge. He was talking to me.

"Ah, yes, sir." That didn't sound right. "Your Honor."

"Do you honestly believe you have information that must be presented to the court before a proper decision can be made in this matter?"

"I do."

The judge took a deep breath, then let it out slowly. My heart was pounding in my ears. Mom was still crying, searching in her purse.

She needs a Kleenex, I thought.

The judge began to speak. "There may be some novel legal issues here," he said. "I'm not going to preclude a motion being made to intervene on whatever grounds you want to make it on."

What does that mean? I thought.

"I may deny that motion," he continued, "but I will not deny permission to present it."

Corelli jammed his fist into his hand. The judge turned to Mom. She had found the Kleenex. "Mrs. Mills, the court must dispose of this issue before a divorce can be granted."

Mom blew her nose. The judge turned to Corelli. "You have two weeks to prepare your argument and submit your application to the court."

Two weeks! The words went directly into my chest. It was like a fire, or a sudden dip on a roller coaster.

Two weeks! Two weeks! We did it!

Corelli stepped forward. "Your Honor, may an order issue, appointing the boy's grandfather guardian *ad litem* in this matter?"

"So ordered," said the judge. "See the clerk and a time will be set for oral argument on this motion. Case adjourned."

"Now you're talking!" said Grampa.

I love that guy.

CHAPTER
32

Out in the hall I had my first chance to talk to Mom. She and her lawyer had left the hearing room first. Me and Corelli and Grampa followed. I hugged Corelli, hugged Grampa, then moved toward Mom. Her lawyer had led her over to a bench where they were sitting together. He was apparently filling her in on all sorts of strategic details, while she didn't appear to care. That's the way I interpreted it, anyway. She had stopped crying, but was still blowing her nose.

"I'm sorry, Mom," I said.

She reached up and hugged me.

Thank God, I thought.

Her lawyer gave me this incredibly mean and irritated stare, but I ignored him and just hugged Mom, she sitting, me standing.

"I'm sorry," I repeated.

"Why didn't you tell me?" she asked.

"I did."

"No, you didn't."

Did I not tell her? I couldn't remember.

"I told Dad. He didn't believe me."

"You didn't tell me."

"I'm sorry. I had to do something. It's wrong, Mom. This whole thing is wrong."

"It's really none of your business," said her tan, thin lawyer.

"I disagree," I said. I thought of saying more, but I decided against it. I just held on to Mom.

When we left the courthouse Marion was waiting on the front steps. "How'd it go?" she shouted when she saw us come out. She raced up the stairs to meet us, two steps at a time.

"Good," I said.

"Great! Want to go back to Connecticut?"

I'd forgotten about Grampa. In my mind I was going home with Mom, to talk with her. I needed to explain. Grampa was holding Mom's arm, her lawyer on the other side. I looked for Corelli and found him at the bottom of the steps. He was waiting there alone. I think he was uncomfortable with Mom.

"Let's go, Grampa," I said. "We'll take you home."

"Right-o," said Grampa. "Want to stop for a sand-wich?"

"Okay."

We got Grampa home in record time, sandwich and all, returning him to a grateful Peterson.

"I'll keep you posted, Grampa," I said when we parted at the door.

"Want some ice cream?"

"No thanks, Grampa."

"It's chocolate."

"I want to get back to Mom."

"Right-o," said Grampa. I could tell he was dis-appointed.

The understatement of this or any year would be to say that Dad was not pleased. I sensed trouble when

Marion dropped me off. His BMW was parked in the driveway.

When I got inside he and Mom were in the living room. Mom was sitting in the desk chair in her gray sweatpants and sweatshirt, and Dad was kind of pacing. He had a suit on and a tie that was loose at his neck and a trench coat. He must have just come from work.

"Hello," I said.

"How dare you?"

I moved into the living room. My feet felt heavy, like cement. There is nothing in the world I hate as much as Dad's being angry, only the thought of losing him. I guess it's the same thing.

"I'm sorry, Dad," I said.

"Don't tell me you're sorry. Tell me what the hell was going through your mind."

"I want us to be together."

"That's not possible."

"I don't believe that."

"Well, I'm sorry, but it's true. And I'll tell you something else. What goes on between your mother and me is our business. Not yours, or anybody else's."

I couldn't take it. I was so tired. I felt so misunderstood.

NOBODY UNDERSTANDS!

I started yelling. My face was burning, my insides tearing, my life was a joke. Nothing mattered. I stood there and shouted, right in his face. "I DID IT BE-CAUSE I LOVE YOU! I LOVE THIS FAMILY! I WANT IT TO WORK!"

"Come on, Chris," he said. "I know you're upset, but for God's sake, you had no right to interfere. If you have something to say, then say it, but don't go sneaking behind our backs with lawyers!"

"I told you!"

"When?"

"That first night when you were leaving. You said, 'Where are you going?' and I told you. I said, 'I'm going to see my lawyer.' "

"I don't remember that."

"Well, I did. You didn't believe me!"

"Now it's my fault!"

"Stephen, please!" said Mom. She hates it when Dad yells at me.

Dad turned to Mom. "Well, what do you think? You like what he did? You like this? More scenes, more fights, more tears? Is that your idea of a good time?"

"DON'T FIGHT ANYMORE!" I yelled. "I CAN'T STAND IT!"

"Calm down," said Dad. "Think about it. If you hadn't gotten into this thing we wouldn't be fighting now, would we? It would have been settled. We could have gone on from here."

I looked Dad square in the eye. "Where to?" I said.

"Don't be smart."

"I'm trying to save my family!"

"We've tried that."

"You have not! You haven't put any time into making this family work. You, or Mom. Not lately."

"Now, wait a minute!"

"You haven't! Jenny doesn't even know what a family is! I know. We had that. We had it and now it's gone! Nobody cares!"

"That's not true," said Mom. She was still in the desk chair, sitting in a twisted way. She looked uncomfortable.

"It is! Everybody's going their own way! Like your tennis and your haircuts and your whales! Reading to other people's kids at the library! What about reading to Jenny? She needs you! Not things! She doesn't want things! She wants you!"

"It's been a difficult time."

"First take care of us! Then worry about the world! You're never here, you or Dad! How can we have a family?"

"Now, wait a minute," said Dad.

Was he taking her side, or defending himself? A little of both?

"I'm here," said Mom.

"You're in the tub! Or taking a nap! That's not here! You're not available! I mean, you made the antlers, but that was it! It's not enough!"

Mom was crying now. She spoke deliberately. She was upset, but there was a strength underneath. She meant what she said. "I have always wanted to be a good mother. I have always wanted that. And I have always wanted to be a good wife. I do other things because I need to. I've seen the loneliness of women who don't develop their talents. Their children grow up and leave them, their husbands have their work, and what do they have? They become embittered, and I have always believed it to be their own damn fault."

"I don't mean don't do anything! Of course do something! Do different things, whatever, but don't get so tangled up. You get all caught up and you forget about us!"

"I never forget about you."

"Well, it seems that way. It's the same with Dad. The family should come first!"

Mom was staring hard, her eyes wide, filled with tears. I was upsetting her. I hated to do that, but I couldn't stop. "There's your whales and your summer kids and your articles and your hair and your school stuff and your tennis and your jogging and where do we come in?"

"Your mother is a damn good mother," said Dad. It was the first nice thing I'd heard him say about her in months.

"When she's here!" I said.

"I think you've said enough," said Dad.

"And where are you? You're so busy making money, you don't have time for anything else!"

"That's not true!"

"And don't say you did it for me!"

"You don't know my motives!"

"Then tell me!"

"I did do it for you! I did it for you and your mother and for Jenny! And I plan to continue, whether you like it or not!"

"I DON'T NEED THINGS!" I was crying harder now. I felt this deep frustration at not getting through. "If you did it for me, then why didn't you ask if I wanted it? Why didn't you say, 'Hey, Chris, do you want all this stuff, or would you just like an old sweatshirt and a dog and a father who has time to be human?' YOU USED TO BE MY FRIEND!"

"That's enough now, Chris!"

"WHAT ARE YOU DOING WITH YOUR LIVES? RUNNING AROUND IN YOUR JOGGING SUITS, KEEPING FIT? FIT FOR WHAT? FIT TO WATCH OUR FAMILY SELF-DESTRUCT? THE WORLD IS FALLING APART! WORLD WAR THREE IS ALMOST HERE AND YOU FEEL A SLIGHT EMPTINESS! IT'S TOO LATE! THERE'S NO TIME!"

"I want a bush baby." Jenny was standing at the foot of the stairs, her clothes on backwards, holding Bunny.

"We're talking to Chris now," said Mom. "We'll discuss that later."

"They come from Africa."

"Don't interrupt."

Jenny sat down on the bottom stair.

"I want to say something," said Dad. He took off his trench coat and put it over the back of his leather chair. "I want you to listen to me, Chris. I want you to hear me and I want you to remember. You understand?"

"Yes."

"It makes no difference whether you believe it, the truth remains the same. The work I've done, the long hours, the trips away from home, I did it for you. I have always wanted to provide for my family. I always have and I always will. Not even a divorce can change that."

He was telling the truth. I knew it. And I also knew he would never understand what I meant.

"I'm sorry, Dad," I said. "I know you want to take care of us. It's just we're not together. Nobody's happy. We used to be happy. I want it to be like that. I want it to be like Monhegan."

"How did we pay for that?"

"I know. But what about now?"

Dad heaved a big sigh. Then he looked down at his shoes, just like my mother's lawyer.

What happened? I thought. We're leaving our lives' decisions to a court, to a stranger, to some judge who doesn't care, or know us, or get enough sleep even.

I looked at Dad. He was still staring at his shoes. Mom was still twisted up in the desk chair. She had stopped crying, but she still looked really upset. I felt this love for them. It swept through me, unexpected and deep.

They mean so well, I thought. What happened? Maybe they just don't love each other. There's nothing I can do. I said too much and even that was meaningless. Who's to know what's true?

It was the blackest moment of my life. I felt shame and fear and hopelessness. I felt lonely and stupid. I felt about two years old. And then, miracle of miracles, the most wonderful thing happened. It was like the sunrise after the darkest night. Dad hugged me. It was like melting, dissolving in a cloud. He felt so big, so thick, so substantial. It seemed like he was ten times bigger than me, like some big, protecting giant. I remembered back to when I was little and he used to sometimes wash my hands for me, to get tough dirt off, or paint, or stains from berries. I remembered how big his hands seemed then, how tiny mine felt inside his, how protected.

"I love you, Dad," I said. I held on to him and cried.

"I love you, Chris. I'm sorry I got so angry."

"I want a bush baby."

I heard the words, but I didn't look up. My face was buried in Dad's stomach.

CHAPTER
33

At four-thirty that same afternoon I went up on the roof to clean the drains. Dad had suggested it. After our whole scene was over and he was ready to leave, he mentioned that I had been neglecting the drains, or rain gutters, which, of course, was true. In a way I was pleased when he brought up my negligence. He didn't say it in a mean way, just as a fact. He said he was aware of what we'd all been going through, but the drains still had to be cleaned and it was my job, which it was. Is. What pleased me most about Dad's mentioning it was that he was showing an interest in the house. He had been totally ignoring the house and everything to do with it. It seemed like he was thinking, I don't live here anymore, so let them do what they want. His noticing the clogged drains was a positive step, as far as I could determine, even if it did mean climbing up there and poking around. It turned out to be just what I needed, a chance to do some physical work, to breathe some nice air, to let my mind go, to deal with a small, specific thing, some matted leaves. I could handle that. I began to relax. As I worked, I thought about the day, about the talk with my folks, about how much I loved them. I was just finishing up the last drain when I spotted Jenny down below, circling around and around the big oak tree. She had put her earmuffs on and was carrying Bunny. Her clothes were still on backwards.

I have to talk to her, I thought. Tell her about today, reassure her if I can. The earmuffs are not a good sign.

I finished the drain, took a firm grip on my drain cleaning pole (I made it by sawing off the bristly or sweeping part of an ancient broom), climbed down off the roof, and approached the tree. Jenny looked at me, but she didn't stop, or say anything. She just kept circling. I shut off my Walkman. I always listen to music when cleaning the drains, usually *Alexander Nevsky* or the sound track from *Close Encounters of the Third Kind*. Although different, they're equally good for roof work. I stopped by the tree. "How's it going?" I asked.

She ignored me, making another circle around the tree.

"Want some ice cream?"

She looked at me, but kept moving. "I can't hear you," she said.

"Want some ice cream?" I shouted.

She stopped and gave me a long stare. "You came from the roof."

"I was cleaning the drains."

"You're a roof man."

"In a way."

"You came from the roof."

"Not originally. You want some ice cream?"

"Okay."

"I'll take you to Lickety Split."

We started walking. "Why'd you put on the earmuffs?" I asked.

"I can't hear you."

I stopped walking. So did she.

"Look, Jenny, I can't stand the whole earmuff thing. If you want some ice cream then take off the earmuffs."

She stood totally still except for twisting Bunny's left ear. "Bunny wants ice cream."

"Then you'd better take off the earmuffs."

With her free hand she pulled off the earmuffs and handed them to me. "Here," she said.

We started walking.

"Bunny almost died."

"What happened?"

"He didn't want to be living anymore because everything is so crazy, so he shut himself in the clothes drawer with a pillow on his head."

"Is he all right?"

"He's living, as you can see."

"I see."

"He wants to run away."

"Where to?"

"He's not telling."

"I went to court today."

"Did you walk there?"

"No. I stopped the divorce for two weeks. Me and the lawyer have to plan things out, but there's a chance we can stop it forever."

"Parents shouldn't get divorced until the children are dead."

We reached the end of Elm Ledge and turned left. A squirrel ran in front of us. A woman came out of a nearby house carrying a large folding chair and a banana. (Plans for a picnic?) I looked at Jenny. "Don't worry, okay?"

"I want a bush baby." She was doing it again.

Whenever things got really tough around that time she'd tune out, change the subject. I had no doubt that she wanted a bush baby, but the timing was odd.

"How come?" I asked.

"Because."

"They're from Africa, aren't they?"

"Oh, yes. They go on their feet."

"They go on their feet?"

"Yup. They're completely cute and furry like a cat would be, or a monkey, or both of those, and they have the biggest eyes. They can leap so far you would not believe it."

"Really."

"And they make the loudest noise in the world. I'm telling you because we heard it in this movie at school, like EEEEEHHHHH!" She shrieked, making this incredibly loud, bush-baby sound. "Like EEEEEHHHHH! Everybody leaves them alone 'cause they don't want to hear that sound, EEEEEEHHHHH! They stay out in the very deep of night, and they have big and enormous ears, and they go on their feet."

"What do you mean by that?"

"They make peepee on their feet."

"I didn't know that."

"You do now."

"I guess I do."

"And do you know why?"

"No."

"Can you even imagine? In your big and gigantic roof man's brain, can you even think of it?"

"I can't, no."

"It's because they only want gripping power. They make peepee on their feet, and then they have these feet that are so sticky they never fall."

"I see."

"It's a good way."

"I wouldn't try it."

"I won't," she said, but I could sense her disappointment.

When we got back home Grampa called. He was excited about our successful morning in court and wanted to know how Mom and Dad were taking it.

"Not too well," I told him.

"If things get too rough you can come and stay with me for a while."

"Thanks, Grampa."

"I mean it."

"I know you do."

"What happens next?"

"We have to work on the case."

"What do I do?"

"Sit tight."

"I could die sitting tight," he said. "It's not healthy."

"It won't be for long," I reassured him. "We need you in court in two weeks."

"Thank God," he said. "A fellow likes to be needed."

"You're not a fellow," I told him. "You're my grampa and I'll always need you."

"Let me know if you want to come to Connecticut."

"I will."

"It's pretty in the snow."

Just before dinner Mom asked me if I would consider dropping the whole thing. I couldn't believe she would ask me that. Didn't she know how serious I was, how hard I'd worked, how much it meant to me?

My own mother doesn't know who I am, I thought. The single most important thing in my entire life and she wonders if I wouldn't just consider dropping it.

"No," I answered. I was pulling clean silverware out of the dishwasher. She was washing lettuce.

"Your father's going to try and stop you."

"He can't."

"He's talking to his lawyer."

"So am I."

After dinner I went up to my room to call Corelli. I fed my fish, then sat at my desk to dial.

"You were great," I told him when I got him on the phone.

He was oddly distant. "We'll see," he said.

"What do you mean we'll see? You were fantastic."

"I didn't do anything."

"We're in the case!"

"Right." He sounded depressed.

"What's the matter?"

"Now we gotta work."

"We've been working!"

"That was nothing."

Roscoe was attacking one of the smaller fish. I tapped on the glass to distract him. "What's our next step?"

"We gotta have a meeting."

"When?"

"Tomorrow."

"Tomorrow night?"

"Yeah."

"Regular time?"

"Right."

"Okay. And thanks, Corelli."

"Thank me later."

CHAPTER
34

At the next Dunfee Divorce Group session things became complex. It started with Mr. Dunfee reciting the Alcoholics Anonymous Prayer. "God grant me the serenity to accept the things I cannot change, the courage to change the things I can, and the wisdom to know the difference," quoted Mr. Dunfee. His pants seemed tighter than usual. His belt was on a looser notch. Holiday eating had taken its toll. "Food for thought," he added. He meant the prayer. Then, for some strange and undesignated reason, he called my name. "Chris."

"Yes?"

"What's your reaction to that little poem?"

"My reaction?"

"Does it bring up any feelings?"

"Kind of," I said.

"What feelings does it bring up?"

"I think the wisdom part is the hardest."

"Can you tell us more about that?"

"Well, I think the serenity is good when you have to not do something and the courage is good when you have to do something, but knowing which is which is the hardest."

Mr. Dunfee moved to the window and peered out

for reasons unclear. "That's an interesting point," he said. "Does anyone agree with Chris?"

There was what you might call a general agreement. A lot of kids said things like "sure" and "definitely" and "oh, yeah." Then Marion spilled the beans. She was sitting up on a table next to Amy in her sweat pants and a new pair of purple Adidas. "Chris, you gotta tell," she said.

Amy swung her legs back and forth from over the side of the table. "Really," she said. Marion had no doubt filled her in on the details.

Mr. Dunfee was still over at the window, still looking out at something, although nothing appeared to be there. When he heard Marion's comment he turned to me. "Something you'd like to share, Chris?" he asked.

"Not really." I had decided to keep quiet for the time being. I didn't especially feel like answering a lot of questions and hearing a lot of people's reactions to my own personal business.

"Oh, come on," said Marion. "You gotta tell."

"Really," said Amy.

"There's nothing to tell."

"Oh, sure," said Marion. "He just sued his parents. It happens every day."

"Really," said Amy.

Mr. Dunfee moved away from the window. "Well," he said. He was looking right at me. "Any truth to the comments?"

I didn't want to get into it, but lying appealed to me less. I don't like to lie in the first place, and in the second place, since Marion had actually been at the courthouse, she would know I was lying and it would get incredibly complex.

"What say you?" said Mr. Dunfee.

"I didn't sue them yet."

"You're gonna," said Marion.

"I'm in the process."

Mr. Dunfee stuffed his index fingers into his belt. He was trying to look casual, but it wasn't working. He was desperate to know the details. "That's an interesting approach," he said. "Care to share your experience?"

"Not really."

Mr. Dunfee removed his fingers from his belt. Then he looked at the floor. "All right," he said. "That's fine."

You could tell it wasn't. He would have killed to know the details. Well, not killed entirely, but he would have gone pretty far. I don't think his life is all that interesting to him.

"I took him to court," said Marion. "First we had to pick up his grandfather in Connecticut because he's the guardian. Chris has a lawyer and they went into the hearing and they stopped it for two weeks, and now they have to work out how to sue them. Tell them, Chris."

"You just did."

Mr. Dunfee put his fingers back in his belt. "That's an interesting approach," he said.

How many times is he going to say that? I thought. The famous Dunfee Broken Record Torture.

"How do you do that?" It was Vivian, the girl who lost her hairbrush and found her mother crying in her slip. She wore the same jean jacket and silver earrings, although the circles under her eyes were slightly less pronounced.

"You talking to me?" I asked.

"Yes."

"I got a lawyer."

"Where'd you get the money?" said C.J. His right cheek was all swollen out from an unsuccessful attempt at hiding seventeen sticks of gum between his inner cheek and rear molars.

"I got him cheap," I said.

"How much?"

"A dollar."

"Good price."

"He's crazy," said Haverman.

"He got me in the case!"

"Alert the media."

"That's not a bad idea," said Marion. "People should know."

"That's an interesting thought," said Mr. Dunfee. His hair was looking different for some reason. I couldn't place it.

Is it on at a different angle? I thought. Farther forward?

He fingered the stack of ditto sheets on his desk, then turned to the group. "Any reactions?"

"I think it's great," said Marion.

"You said that," said Haverman.

"What's eating you?" said Marion.

I wondered, too. Haverman was always there with the bright remark, but there was a different tone in his voice. He was definitely in a bad mood. (The return of The Old Fish People?)

I'll have to talk to him after class, I thought. I hadn't seen him for days.

"Anyone else?" asked Mr. Dunfee. "Vivian? How does it strike you?"

"I don't know," she said. "Brutal."

"In what way?"

"In a brutal way."

"I see. Had the thought occurred to you?"

"To sue my parents?"

"Yes."

"No."

"It didn't occur to you."

"No."

"You just accepted it."

"I wanted to kill myself."

"You wanted to kill yourself," said Mr. Dunfee, "but you didn't."

"There's the proof," said Haverman. He pointed over at Vivian.

C.J. snapped his gum.

"What was that?" said Mr. Dunfee.

"Mice," said C.J. He had hastily divided his gum into segments, storing one segment on each side of his mouth. Now both his cheeks were puffed out. He looked like a winter squirrel.

Mr. Dunfee turned suspiciously. "What?" he said.

"Mice," said C.J.

"Mice?"

"In the walls."

"What?"

"Mice. In the walls. They get into the wiring."

"It didn't sound like mice."

"It never does," said Haverman.

"It sounded like explosives," said Mr. Dunfee.

"Mice," said Haverman.

"Does someone have caps in here, or a cap pistol?" No answer.

"I would not like to hear that again."

"Who would?" said Haverman.

"Mice," said C.J. "I'm telling you."

"That was mice?"

"Cheese traps," said Haverman. "It gets them every time."

CHAPTER 35

"We'll continue," said Mr. Dunfee. He was still fingering his ditto sheets. The room was quiet. "Amy. How does it strike you?"

"What?"

"The approach Chris is taking. How do you feel about it?"

"I think it's great."

"Is it something you ever considered?"

"Not seriously."

"Did you ever think of it in, shall we say, perhaps, a wild and wishing type of way, in retaliation, in anger?"

"I don't think so. See, like I'm not putting Chris down 'cause I think it's great what he's doing, and, like, it's right for him, but for me it was different. Like, I got really mad when it happened, like when I first heard about it, and, like, I wanted to run away, or kill myself, or do something, you know, like, to make them stay together. I thought my life was over. But then they got divorced and it was really like the beginning. There were no fights and my mother would smile sometimes and we started playing cards and going shopping and going to the movies and now when I see my dad it's like better with him, too. Like,

I'm not saying for Chris, but for me it would have been a mistake to sue them. It would have been fighting a change that was good, out of fear, because I didn't know what it would be like. In the end it was going to be better for everybody, but I didn't know that. You know what I mean?"

"I think I do, yes," said Mr. Dunfee. "Fear of the unknown. 'There is nothing to fear but fear itself.' Who said that?"

"You did," said Haverman.

"I mean prior. Who am I quoting?"

Somebody answered that question, but I wasn't listening. I knew it was Roosevelt (the one who said it, not the one who answered), but more importantly I was upset by Amy's comments.

Did I make a mistake? I thought. Am I fighting a change that would really be good?

"Further thoughts?" said Mr. Dunfee. He turned to Haverman. "Any feelings?"

"Pick a category."

"With respect to Chris's action. Are you having any feelings?"

"I'd like to jump out a window."

"Would you care to elaborate?"

"Well, yeah. I mean there's a hell of a lot of us going through this divorce thing, over twelve million at the present moment in the greater US of A. Where does that leave us, the poor stupid ones who didn't do anything about it? If it's so easy, why didn't we all sue our parents and live happily ever after?"

Just then I noticed that the sweet girl with the injured spine had her hand raised. She was crying.

"Yes, Mollie," said Mr. Dunfee.

She spoke quietly through her tears. "My parents got divorced two months ago," she said. "I wanted them to stay together. I really thought they should, but I didn't say anything. I feel now . . . I feel that . . . I like Chris, but I'm feeling now that I hope he loses."

"You hope he loses."

"I do. In a way . . . because . . . because if he wins, then I have to always feel . . . always wonder if I could have done something, too. I would never know if I had been brave enough, or if I had enough courage like he did, if I could have stopped them. I'm worried about that right now. I feel so bad. I like Chris, but now I want him to lose. That wouldn't help me."

"No."

"And it would hurt him. But I can't help it."

"It's all right. It's the way you feel."

"Could he win?"

"We never know in life." It was definitely Hallmark time. "Life hands us what it wills, and picks the times it wills it."

"Can I quote you on that?" said Haverman.

Dunfee ignored him. "Somewhere we find the strength."

She knows that, I thought. Watch her smile, hear her laugh, listen to her play the flute, then think about her twisted spine. She knows about life and what it hands you sometimes and how to manage. I couldn't bear the thought of having upset her. "Can I say something?" I asked.

"Of course," said Mr. Hallmark.

"I think everything is different. You can't judge one situation by something else. See, I think a lot of times people have to get divorced. Either they made a mistake in the first place, or one is really mean to the other, or they don't love each other, or there can be a lot of reasons. I think you always want them to stay together,

or mostly, I would think—and if you feel that way I
think you have to tell yourself the truth. I think inside
you know. Kids know their parents pretty well, better
than parents know their kids a lot of the time. You
have to be honest. You have to ask yourself, 'Do they
belong together? Did they ever get along? Do they now?
Can they again? Did we ever have a family? Can we
get it back?' Questions like that. I think you have to
ask yourself and answer straight. Should I let go of it
and let it be, or should I fight for something they're
going to find out later and wish somebody'd told them?
See, that's the way I feel. In my case that's the way I'm
feeling and I have to go by that. I'm not a hundred
percent sure, but it doesn't feel like I'm just desperate.
I am desperate, but I'm also thinking of them. If it
wasn't that, then I think I should keep quiet and live
through it and find out that it was really the beginning,
like Amy said. I know that happens a lot of times. I
don't know. A lot of times there's nothing we can do
and there shouldn't be, but I think you can tell if you
ask yourself straight. You know what I mean?"

Mollie had stopped crying. She was looking right
into my eyes. Girls don't usually do that. I returned
her stare, deep and steady. It was like we were the
only ones in the room. "Do you think your parents
belong together?" I asked her.

For a long time she didn't answer. She just stared
straight into my eyes. Then she spoke. "No," she said.
She sounded sad, but relieved, too, deep down where
it mattered. She continued to look straight into my
eyes. "It wasn't the way I wanted it to be, but that
was in my mind. It was my idea. It wasn't connected
with what they could do."

"Is it better now?"

"It's quiet," she said. Then she smiled.

CHAPTER
36

I didn't get a chance to talk to Haverman until just before art. I was in the large room at the end of the hall, right in front of the art room, desperately trying to mat my pictures. I had gotten an extension from Mr. Pucci that amounted to three extra days, but I was still drastically behind. I was on the third mat (twenty-seven to go), pressing down with full strength on my X-acto knife, when Haverman popped out of the photo lab. He's a good photographer, although he mostly shoots old shoes and parts of things that you don't know what they are. I spotted him heading off toward the cafeteria.

"I have to talk to you," I said.

He stopped and looked at me but he didn't say anything.

"Are you okay?" I asked.

"Time will tell."

I set down my X-acto knife and my ruler and sat back down on the floor. "I'm sorry about your parents," I said.

"Me, too."

"Do you hate me?"

"Why would I hate you?"

"I don't know."

"I'm just in a generally foul and inconsolable mood."

"I can tell."

"I'll live. A questionable benefit."

"I wish I could do something."

"What could you do?"

"Nothing."

"That's my point." He moved closer to where I was working and looked down at the picture I was attempting to mat. It was a pencil drawing of part of the windshield of Dad's BMW. It was rather like one of Haverman's photographs, come to think of it.

"Nice," he said.

"Thanks."

"What's that?" He had moved his attention to an abstract done by the girl I was doing the art show with. For reasons I cannot imagine, she had tried to copy Andy Warhol's work. It was basically a large pink tomato, well done, but strange. That was my view, anyway, but then, hating Andy Warhol's work to begin with, I may not have been the best and most impartial judge. I saw a picture of him once, in some totally useless magazine. He had all this bushy white hair sticking out, and was wearing an immense muffler over a tuxedo. He looked like his own art project.

"A pink tomato?" said Haverman.

"It's not mine."

"Glad to hear it." He took a cinnamon donut out of his zip-up sweatshirt pocket and began to eat. "The show's Friday, in case you forgot."

"What show?"

"You forgot."

"What show?"

"*The Fantasticks*. Makeup? Chris's job? Ring a bell?"

"Oh, right."

"You forgot."

"I have a lot on my mind." I picked up my next drawing, a pen and ink of a garlic press, simple, but decently rendered. I couldn't figure out how to mat it.

"You'd better be there," said Haverman. He finished the donut, then reached into his pocket and took out an apple.

"I'll be there."

"You've got a lot on your mind."

"I'll be there!"

"Swear to God and all the moving creatures?"

"If I'm alive, I'll be there."

"What if you die?"

"You'll have to do your own makeup."

Haverman bit into the apple, taking nearly half of it in one bite. "I got a new stereo," he announced through the juicy apple section.

"A consolation prize?"

"It would appear. Excellent speakers."

I moved back up onto my aching knees, picked up my knife and my ruler, and resumed my work. Twenty-seven mats to go. I had to keep moving.

"I perceive an upward trend," continued Haverman.

"In what respect?"

"Number one was a watch, number two was a tape deck, number three is a stereo."

"Maybe next time you'll get a car."

"I'm counting on it."

I was excited about my meeting with Corelli. I had a totally new perspective of him since the hearing. I was impressed and I was grateful. I wanted to bring him a present, but there wasn't time. With the mats and homework and dinner I was rushing like crazy as it was. I found a bar of chocolate by the phone in the kitchen and I took that. Mom and Jenny were over at the Beckners' so I didn't have a chance to ask Mom about it. I remember hoping that she had gotten it for me and not for her own bedtime snack. She sometimes eats chocolate at night, particularly when she's depressed. I realize now as I'm writing this that I never did ask her about that. Sorry, Mom.

When I got to Corelli's, courtesy once more of Bedford Taxi, I heard Beethoven coming from the apartment upstairs.

Fourth Piano Concerto, I thought as I got out of the cab.

I climbed the long, creaky, and unstable flight of stairs and knocked on the door. No barking.

Where's Bozo? I thought.

Corelli opened the door. He was wearing jeans and an undershirt. "Hi," he said. "I gotta get my shirt." Then he left the room. I didn't have time to say hello.

Bozo nuzzled my hand. He knew about the chocolate.

"Why didn't you bark?" I said.

I guess he knew me.

The card table was still set up in the corner near the kitchen. It was covered with law books, many opened, others stacked in piles. There were notes, too, lots of pens, pads, pencils, and odd scraps of paper.

He's working, I thought. That's a good sign.

Corelli came back into the room wearing an unbuttoned and slightly wrinkled shirt. He was buttoning up the buttons. "You want something?" he asked.

"Like what?"

"I don't know. Ice cream? Something like that?"

"Okay."

"After we work."

How unlike him, I thought. Normally, it's popcorn and Vectrex, Grape-Nuts and recorders, anything but getting down to it.

"I brought you this," I said, holding out the chocolate. Bozo followed it with his nose.

"How come?" said Corelli.

"It's a present. I wanted to get you something more substantial, but I didn't have time."

"Chocolate's good. Ooh! Semi-sweet. Thank you." He took the candy and began to unwrap it. Bozo stared with pleading eyes. "NOT FOR YOU," said Corelli. "How come you got me a present?"

"I'm grateful for what you're doing."

"What am I doing?" He took a bite, then offered me some.

"Thanks," I said.

"You bought it."

Bozo was drooling heavily on the rug.

"GET AWAY! GET OUT OF HERE!"

Bozo shrank into himself and went under the card table to lie down.

"You were great at the hearing," I said.

Corelli took another large bite of chocolate and looked down at his shirt. "Crap," he said. Then he went into the kitchen.

"What's the matter?"

"Damn thing's wrinkled."

"Your shirt?"

No answer.

I followed him into the kitchen. "You're so good," I said. "You have to practice."

"Why?" He was at the sink, splashing water on his shirt front.

"You can help a lot of people."

"I can fix cars."

"Do that, too."

He turned off the water, then patted his shirt front.

"What are you doing?"

"Dries straight." He moved past me and left the kitchen. I followed. We sat down at the card table, disturbing Bozo, who was still underneath, trying to become invisible. He seemed embarrassed about the chocolate.

"Okay," said Corelli. He glanced at his notes, then at me. "Sit down."

I sat.

"We're gonna do something now," he said.

"What's that?"

"Just answer my questions."

"All right."

"Don't get upset."

"Why would I get upset?"

"You tell me."

I didn't understand him, but that was often the case. Corelli returned to his notes, then looked up rather suddenly at nothing in particular, his eyes focusing inward. "Listen to that," he said. "Listen to what he does there." He meant Beethoven. "He just changes keys. For no reason. He does what he wants."

"Yeah."

"Doesn't care what anybody thinks."

"He didn't."

"What?"

"He's dead."

"Oh, right."

CHAPTER
37

Any other time I would have loved to discuss Beethoven. I had no one to talk music with anymore, not since my father had pretty much stopped talking to me. I missed our music talks so much. Dad and I have the same tastes. Beethoven, Corelli, Mozart, Stravinsky, and Spyro Gyra. I can't talk music at school. They'd put me away for insane opinions. Here was a fellow Beethoven lover, but I had other things on my mind. "Do we have grounds?" I asked.

"You couldn't rush him either," said Corelli. "He didn't give a damn."

"Who didn't?"

"Beethoven. You know how long it took him to write the Ninth?"

"Six years."

"Right! You know stuff."

"So do you."

"I know nothing." He turned the pages of his legal pad, reviewing his notes.

Bozo shifted position under the table and made a kind of low-pitched, moaning, wheeze-type sound. He was feeling sorry for himself, or so it seemed. Corelli put down his pad. Then he stared at me hard. He looked deeply and intensely into my eyes, the way Mollie had done earlier, only sharper. Then he spoke. "Why are you against your parents' divorce?"

Why is he asking me that? I thought. He knows.

"Answer the question."

"I told you."

He kept staring at me, like he didn't know me almost. "Answer the question," he repeated.

I felt confused. My mind was blank. Bozo put his head on my foot. Corelli kept staring. "Answer the question."

"You know why."

"Tell me."

"I told you."

"Tell me again."

"It's a mistake."

"Who says?"

"I say."

"Who are you?"

"I'm their son."

"That gives you the right to pass judgment?"

"I think so."

"Why?"

"I don't know."

"You don't know."

"No."

"And yet you proceed to pass judgment."

"I don't know if I'm passing judgment, I'm just right!"

"How do you know that?"

"I just know!"

"*How* do you know?"

"I just do! I'm right!"

"They say you're wrong."

"They're wrong!"

"How do you know?"

My heart was racing, my palms had started to sweat. Bozo got out from under the table and moved across the room. He couldn't stand the tension. Neither could I. Corelli's eyes pierced through me, relentless, demanding. "Answer the question."

"What question?"

"How do you know your parents are wrong?"

"I just do!"

"That's not good enough!"

I lost it. I broke down, tears and shouting, the whole thing. It was a total embarrassment. "What the hell are you doing?" I shouted.

"Wait a minute now," said Corelli. "I told you not to get upset."

"What are you doing?"

Corelli got up and put his arm around my shoulder. "I didn't mean to scare you," he said. "These are the things they're gonna hit us with in court. We gotta be ready."

I couldn't stop crying. He had brought out all my fears. Bozo got up and rested his head on my knees.

"Stop crying now," said Corelli.

"I'm trying," I said. "I'm sorry."

"Don't apologize."

"Are they going to question me?"

"They might."

"I hope not."

"Who cares?" Corelli still had his arm around my shoulder. It was comforting. My crying began to subside. "Ever hear of the devil's advocate?" he asked.

"I think so." I had, but I couldn't remember what it meant. I mainly wanted a Kleenex.

"Well, I'm playin' it." Corelli sat down next to me. I rubbed my draining nose with the back of my hand.

"See, you gotta articulate. I know you're speaking the truth, but they don't know that. We gotta take the truth and poke all the damn holes in it we can think of. We gotta beat them at their own game. I'll get you a napkin." He went into the kitchen and came back with a paper towel. "All we got," he said.

"That's okay." I blew my nose.

Bozo still had his chin on my knees. His eyes were so deep and brown and understanding. Dogs have so much devotion. People should be more like that. I patted Bozo on top of his head, on the bony part between his ears.

I wish I had a dog, I thought. Then I thought of Jenny and her allergies, and then just of Jenny and how I had started this whole anti-divorce thing in her behalf. The whole thing felt like a lie.

I didn't do it for her, I thought. I did it for me.

I felt this wave of embarrassment and then this peculiar desire to share it with Corelli. I still don't know why. Maybe because he was the only one I had, or so it seemed at the moment. He was checking his shirt.

"Is it dry?" I asked.

"Not yet."

"I feel so bad."

"Don't."

"I keep saying I'm doing this for Jenny and it's not true."

"Doesn't matter."

"I feel like a baby. I'm fifteen years old and I've got this deep voice and sometimes I just want my mom and dad. I want them to *be* there, you know? It seems so childish."

"Who knows."

I gave another blow on the paper towel. Corelli patted his shirt front. "Damn thing's still wrinkled."

"You could iron it."

"I hate to iron."

The door opened and Carol came in. She had on a blue peacoat and jeans and carried a bunch of flowers. Bozo went over to greet her. "Hello," she said. "How's it going?"

"I scared him," said Corelli. He was still checking his shirt.

"How'd you do that?" Carol moved over to Corelli and gave him a hug.

He patted her on the arm. "I'm mean."

Carol unbuttoned her coat, then sat down with us at the card table. She still had the flowers. "I'm rooting for you, Chris," she said. "I was thinking of calling the paper, the *Patent Trader*, or the *Reporter Dispatch*. Would that be all right?"

"Sure."

"People should know what you're doing."

"We didn't do anything yet," said Corelli. He was pulling on his shirt, presumably to aid in the de-wrinkling process.

"He shouldn't quit the law," I said. "He's too good."

"He doesn't like it."

"Why not?"

"Ask him."

I turned to Corelli. He was looking up again, eyes inward like before, wrapped up in the music. "Listen to what he does there!" he said. "God, he's great! You wanna know ultimate truth? Listen to Beethoven."

When I got home Jenny was asleep and so was Mom. I went into the kitchen to have my nighttime snack and there on the kitchen table was an envelope.

CHRIS it said on the front, so I figured it was for me. I poured myself some milk, took a handful of chocolate grahams from the fridge, and sat down to read. I hadn't seen the envelope at suppertime. It wasn't Mom's handwriting and it certainly wasn't Jenny's, so I figured it must have been delivered while I was at Corelli's. I later learned that this was true. Inside the envelope was a note. It was on this nice notepaper with a drawing of a bird just about to land on a branch. This is what it said:

Do not believe it because I have said it.
Do not believe it because you have read it,
do not believe it because some sage has been
inspired or thought he was inspired, but
believe it when you know it in your heart.
                                        (Buddha)
            Thank you.
            Mollie

CHAPTER
38

The Fantasticks was a huge success. Backstage was chaos beyond belief, but somehow the actual performance looked as if reasonable people who knew what they were doing had actually rehearsed. So I was told at any rate. I was backstage the whole time, doing makeup, helping people change their costumes, and locating desperately needed and chronically elusive props. Haverman was the hit of the show. His "Rape" number brought the house down, as they say. Not one of his various parents was there. I felt bad for him in that respect. I wondered why they didn't show. His father was presumably in Venezuela with the ex-aerobics-dance teacher, but what about his original mother, or lawyer number three, or Sherry of the sweating cheese? Somebody should have been there. I boil it down to selfishness, but that's only my opinion.

On Saturday morning Helen, our cleaning lady, woke me up by calling at eight o'clock and asking to be picked up at the station. I reminded her that I was too young to drive and then went in to wake up Mom. I tried to go back to sleep after that, but it was useless. I had to mat my pictures, I had to clean my fish tank,

I had to write in my journal, and I had to call Corelli. We had ten days left. We had to have our grounds!

"Did you ever know about cranberry juice?" Jenny stood by my bed in her yellow pajamas with the feet, holding Bunny and drinking a large glass of cranberry juice.

"What about it?" I turned my head slightly on my pillow, still keeping the covers up under my chin.

"It's very bitter."

"I know."

"It makes your mouth all squeezed up and pointy."

"I know. It gets you in the lemon glands."

"What's those?"

"Nothing."

"But what?"

"I made them up."

"Why?"

"No reason."

"You want some?"

"What?"

"Cranberry juice."

"No."

"You could have mine."

"I don't want it."

"You want breakfast?" (A sign that she was hungry.)

"I'll be down in a minute."

"You will not."

"I will."

"Not you." She took a big swallow of cranberry juice. Most of it went down the front of her pajamas. "You're a lying thing."

"I'll be down in a minute."

"You always say that, but that's never what it is 'cause you say you'll be down in a minute and it's no minute. It's maybe only five, or ten, or fifty hundred hours."

"I'll be down in a minute."

Jenny brought about five or six stuffed animals to breakfast. She put them on the kitchen table, circling the food. Bunny was on her lap.

"Why'd you bring all your animals down?" I asked, serving up the eggs.

"I didn't."

"Looks that way to me."

"Better get your eyes checked."

"Why'd you bring so many?"

"They may be dying."

"How come?"

"They're very sad."

"Why?"

"They won't say."

"They're not going to die just because they're sad."

"They might," said Jenny. "I feel it with my bones."

"In your bones. You don't feel something with your bones. You feel it in your bones."

"It's all bones," said Jenny. She offered Bunny some orange juice. He didn't seem to want it.

"Are they upset about the divorce?"

No answer.

I figured they were. "I'm still working on it," I said. I took a long sip of coffee. I don't drink coffee often, but sometimes I feel the need. "I've been talking to the lawyer and telling him the reasons why Mom and Dad should stay together. He has to figure everything out and write it down. He's doing that now."

"How do you know?"

"That's his job."

"Maybe he's brushing his teeth."

She had me there.

"Right. Well, yes. I don't know what he's doing this minute, but during these next ten days he's doing it."

Mom arrived with Helen. They were conversing in the entrance hall. "You'll be sure to do the baseboards and vacuum in the corners."

"I always do."

Sounds of Mom going back upstairs, Helen banging around in the utility closet, singing "You Only Live Twice."

Jenny offered Bunny some toast. I finished my Popeye egg, while attempting to explain things further to Jenny. "The lawyer writes down all the reasons and makes them legal and the judge reads them and decides."

"Why should he decide?"

"That's the way they do it."

"What if he's stupid?"

"Judges usually aren't."

"What if he is?"

"We're out of luck. But don't worry. Whatever happens, we'll be okay."

"Bunny won't."

"Sure he will."

"He has a plan."

"What's that?"

"Only something."

The phone rang. It was Grampa. "Ready to come to Connecticut?" he asked.

"I'll let you know," I said. "Mom's been pretty quiet and I haven't seen Dad."

"We could watch some tapes on the VCR. You could bring it along."

"I'd like that, Grampa. When this is all over we'll do that."

"No reason to wait."

"I have school. And I have to work with Corelli."

"Right-o. Don't let your father push you around."

"I won't."

"Stick up for your rights. And Jenny's, too."

"I'm doing the best I know how."

"You're doing great," said Grampa. "Don't let me fool you."

After breakfast I cleaned my fish tank. Then I tried to get Corelli on the phone, but I couldn't reach him. I figured I'd work on my mats. I had seventeen to go, but I definitely needed some grapefruit juice. I left my room and headed down the stairs to the kitchen. As I neared the bottom of the stairs I heard Mom and Dad in the den. Dad must have arrived while I was involved with fish maintenance. I had been listening to Steely Dan on my tape deck, and with that and the door closed, I was in another world. I didn't even know Dad was there. I had heard from Mom that he might want to take me and Jenny to the movies, but that was tentative.

"I don't like it," my dad was saying.

"One paper."

"Today the *Patent Trader*, tomorrow *The New York Times*."

I sat down on the stairs. I guess you could call it eavesdropping, but I couldn't help it.

"Who do you suppose his lawyer is?" asked Dad.

"I don't know."

"My mechanic."

"What mechanic?"

"My mechanic!"

"Your car man?"

"That's right."

"His lawyer is your car man?"

"How could he do that?"

"You mean Chris?"

"I mean Corelli."

"Life is full of surprises."

Jenny came out of her room. She still had her pajamas on and was carrying Bunny. She also wore her earmuffs. She crawled up into my lap and sat there, legs dangling down. I put my arms around her tiny waist.

"I talked to Davis this morning," said Dad.

"Who's that?"

"Beanie Davis? My lawyer?"

"Oh, right."

"He wants to talk to Chris."

"What for?"

"Talk him out of this thing."

"Oh."

"The bottom line is we have to be civilized."

"It's a little late for that."

"What do you mean?"

"Nothing."

"What was Pillman's reaction?"

"Who?"

"Isn't that his name?"

"Whose name?"

"Your lawyer."

"Pilsner."

"Whatever. What was his reaction?"

"Mild shock."

"I thought of grounding him."

"You thought of grounding who?"

"Chris. Our son?"

"Oh."

"I talked to Beanie about it."

"You're on a first-name basis?"

"I can do it, of course, but it's pointless. I can't deny him right to counsel."

"Does he wear a beanie?"

"Who?"

"Beanie Davis."

"Not that I know of."

"I wonder where he got the name."

"I wondered that, too. Maybe from college."

"Maybe."

"I never saw him wear a hat of any kind."

"To each his own."

"Right." My father laughed.

My father laughed! It was the first time I'd heard that in months. Then Mom laughed! They were laughing together! I hadn't heard them laugh together in years, not that I could remember. They always had the same sense of humor. I remembered how often in years past they would laugh together at things that no one else would think was funny.

It's still there, I thought, that same sense of humor, that tiny sense of the ironic. They never lost it. It's just been buried under a lot of junk.

Helen moved through the downstairs hallway, dragging the vacuum cleaner. She wore tight blue jeans, a wig, a straw hat, and a T-shirt that said "Anything Goes" in large red letters across the front.

"Beanie suggests we talk to Corelli," said Dad.

"Your car man."

"Right. I thought we'd have him over for brunch."

"Over where?"

"Over here."

"You don't live here anymore."

"Do you want to solve this thing, or do you want to let it drag on for another six months?"

"Who does the shopping?"

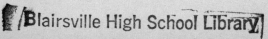

"What shopping?"

"Who buys the food? Who sets the table? Who does the dishes?"

"It's my idea. I'll take care of it. What should I get?"

"You take care of it."

"God, this is complicated."

"Like life. You want some coffee?"

"Ah, yeah. Thanks. Where are the kids?"

"Upstairs."

"I thought I'd take them to a movie."

"Fine."

"The more time away from the Holiday Inn the better."

"How is the old Holiday Inn?"

"Great."

"Can you open a window?"

"No. The air's dry as hell."

"Why don't you get a vaporizer?"

"That's not a bad idea. My sinuses are killing me."

"I hate that."

"Me, too. I'll get a vaporizer."

"I would."

"I will. Thanks. How's tomorrow?"

"In what respect?"

"For Corelli."

"Your car man."

"Right."

"Fine."

"God, he's a great mechanic. I'd hate to lose him."

"Is that your main concern in all of this, losing your car man?"

"Of course not. What a mess. It's so damned complicated. Maybe we should forget the whole thing."

"What whole thing?"

"The divorce. It's more trouble than it's worth."

"Are you serious?"

"No."

CHAPTER 39

Corelli accepted Dad's offer to come to brunch. "Why the hell not?" he said when I asked him about it on the phone.

"It's going to be incredibly weird."

"You gonna have bagels?"

"I guess."

"Smoked salmon?"

"Probably."

"I'm comin'."

Dad and Jenny and I picked up the groceries on the way home from the movies. I can't remember what we saw. That's how bad it was. I do remember stopping at the Smokehouse, however, and getting smoked salmon and also a whitefish. Corelli would be pleased. Apparently Dad had asked him if he wanted to bring someone and he had said sure, so I expected Carol. The next morning at eleven-thirty they arrived. Mom was still upstairs and Dad was in the kitchen, so I got the door.

"Come in," I said.

"How's it goin'?"

I took their coats and hung them up in the hall closet. Corelli was pretty dressed up, for him, anyway. He had on a pair of tan cords, a long-sleeved cotton shirt (ironed), and a gray sweater vest. Carol looked really nice in this blouse and skirt. She carried a coffee cake in a metal baking pan.

"She made it," said Corelli, nodding in the general direction of the cake.

"Great," I said. "Thank you."

"My pleasure," said Carol. "Can I take it to the kitchen?"

"This way." I led Carol to the kitchen. Corelli followed, but then got caught up in the den where Jenny was watching cartoons. She had her earmuffs on and her kitty slippers. Her hands were handcuffed to each other with these toy metal handcuffs from her Sheriff Mike's Big Work Kit. The kit also included a badge, but she wasn't wearing it. She sat on the floor, watching *Bugs Bunny*, holding a shoe box on her lap. Bunny was inside, or so she had told me earlier.

"That's my sister, Jenny," I said as we headed through the den.

"Hello, Jenny," said Carol.

"She won't answer. She pretends not to hear anybody when she's wearing her earmuffs."

"I understand," said Carol. "Earmuffs cover your ears. It makes it hard to hear."

"That's right," said Jenny.

We moved into the kitchen, leaving Corelli with Jenny and Bugs. Corelli's eyes were glued to the TV set as Bugs headed, blindfolded, for the side of a cliff.

Dad was at the sink, in his jogging suit, measuring cups of water into the electric coffee maker. True to his word, he was doing everything himself, or with my help, to be exact. He has trouble getting everything ready at once, even coffee and cream. I introduced him to Carol. Then Carol and I put the cake on the table.

It was one of your stranger meals. It had this unreal quality, like a disjointed dream. I couldn't believe
it was happening, not really. Mom was in a quiet
mood. She said practically not one word. Dad was
nervous, having to synchronize all the serving and
the readiness of food, plus dealing with the basic
problem of convincing Corelli to drop the Whole Divorce Thing without running the risk of losing his
mechanic. It was a lot. Jenny had livened things up
by handcuffing herself to our large rocking chair.
Bunny, it seems, had done something or other with
the key and was now in deep winter hibernation in
the shoe box, so he could tell us nothing. I brought
Jenny and the shoe box and the chair to the table
just to keep things moving.

"So tell me," said Dad. He was serving Corelli a
large helping of scrambled eggs. "What's the word on
these so-called brushless car washes?"

"They're a lot of crap."

"Really?"

"They got all kinds of abrasive grit and junk in
there."

"I was afraid of that. Enough eggs?"

"I'll have a little more."

"What about rustproofing?"

"What about it?"

"Is it a good idea?"

"I don't like it."

"Why not?"

"They do more damage making holes to apply the
rustproofing than the natural process of rust itself.
Weakens the frame."

"You don't say?"

Is Dad going to mention The Subject at all, I

thought, or it is going to be two hours of car maintenance?

The phone rang. "I'll get it," I said.

It was Beanie Davis. I disliked him immediately. He has this very insisting and gravelly voice. "Chris Mills," he said.

"This is Chris."

"Beanie Davis, your father's attorney."

"Oh, yes. Hello."

"What's all the silliness?"

"What silliness?"

"The intercession. You know what I'm talking about."

"I don't think it's silly."

"You can't win. You know that, don't you?"

I felt suddenly tired. I sat down on the high stool we have by the kitchen counter near the phone. He spoke so fast, I could barely understand him. "No judge will force two people to care about each other. That's psychological, not legal. See what I'm saying?"

I could hear sounds from the dining room. The brunch was still underway. "Don't they rustproof at the factory?"

"Some do."

I turned off the electric coffee maker. A brown crust was starting to form on the inside of the glass pitcher.

Beanie was not letting up. "They're not compatible," he continued. "Their incompatibility vitiates your efforts. See what I'm saying?"

"No."

"You're a smart kid." He didn't sound like he meant that. "Why do you want to make trouble?"

"I don't."

"That's what you're doing. Legal fees alone will be an unnecessary hardship."

"Don't charge them."

"What?" He was horrified to the depths of his being."

"If you don't think it's fair, don't charge them. Unless you need the money."

"That's not the point."

"What is the point?"

"I'm trying to tell you, if you'd listen a minute. You're wasting everybody's time here."

"I don't mean to offend you, Mr. Davis," I said, "but I don't think that's true. I've thought about this very carefully and I sincerely believe I'm doing the most important thing I could possibly be doing with my time. I'm trying to save my family. If I'm wasting your time I'm sorry about that, but I really don't think there's anything I can do about that now."

He hung up.

"Mr. Davis?"

He was gone. I was rid of him. For a week, at least. I returned to the table. Dad was just getting into The Subject. "You really take this law business seriously?"

"Pretty much." Corelli helped himself to a piece of Carol's coffee cake.

"Well," said Dad. "You learn something every day."

"If you're lucky."

"Right. If you're lucky. Well." Dad was clearly nervous. "How's business?"

"Which one?"

"The law business," said Dad. "I know about the garage. You're the best. I mean, who the hell can fix cars these days? And they charge an arm and a leg."

"It stinks."

"Right. How's the law business?"

"Okay."

"Do you have many clients?"

"About one."

"One. Well, I guess we know who that is."

"I guess so."

There was an awkward pause. Dad pushed his scrambled eggs around on his plate. He looked at Corelli. "Let me put my cards on the table."

Corelli stared at Dad, but he didn't say anything.

"You don't mind?" said Dad.

"I don't mind."

Mom spoke for the first time. She was staring at Jenny's untouched food. "Eat something, Jenny," she said.

"I can't hear you," said Jenny. She was still handcuffed to the rocker. With her free hand she opened the shoe box on her lap, peering in to check on Bunny.

"Someone in there?" asked Carol.

Jenny stared at her.

"It's hard to hear when you're wearing earmuffs."

"Very hard," said Jenny. She shut the shoe box.

"You're handcuffed to a very big chair."

Jenny stared at Carol, then she nodded.

"Did you put the handcuffs on yourself?"

Another long stare. Jenny shook her head.

"Who did it?"

"Bunny did it."

"Does Bunny have the key?"

"Not anymore."

"Where did Bunny put it?"

"Somewhere deep."

"Where was that?"

"In the toilet."

"Can he get it out?"

Jenny shook her head.

"Why not?"

"It's flushed."

"I'm going to be blunt," said Dad.

"Who's stopping you?" Corelli took an additional bagel.

"You haven't got a chance in hell."

"We'll see."

"Why don't we just admit the thing's not feasible and stop right here?"

"You want me to drop the case?"

"In essence, yes."

"In essence?"

"I do, yes."

"It's up to my client."

"With all due respect, he's in no position to judge the consequences here."

"Why not?" I said.

Dad ignored me. "Chris is emotionally involved. He can't be objective."

Corelli stared at Dad. He was about to say something. It was important, I could tell. He paused, deep in thought. Then he spoke. "Can I have some more of that fish?"

CHAPTER
40

The art show went rather well. Miraculously, I managed to get my stuff acceptably matted and hung by three o'clock on Monday when there was this sort of opening. My partner, the Andy Warhol Girl of the Pink Tomato, sent out invitations to all the teachers and to her family and friends, so quite a lot of people came. She also got some sodas and I brought cookies (Pepperidge Farm Milanos, if I remember correctly). It was rather festive. Both Mom and Dad came, which pleased me a lot. I had expected Mom because she said she'd be there and she tends to keep her word, except in marriage commitments. Also, she had been cutting down a lot on her mad dashing around, so I figured she would have the time. Dad's being there really surprised me. He hadn't said a word about coming. It was right in the middle of his workday, so I had counted him out. When I saw him I was stunned.

Two days later I had my next meeting with Corelli. He asked me to come to the garage after school so we could go over stuff while he was working. Things were piling up for him at work and we were down to the wire. In a matter of days we would be presenting our case and WE DIDN'T HAVE ONE! We were both getting desperate.

Marion drove me over. She had broken up with Zeus on the weekend so I had the benefit of a total recap of the situation. "It's over," she said. We were pulling out of the senior parking lot.

"What happened?"

"I got bored with the whole thing."

"Bored with the Mafia?"

"Who knows if he's in the Mafia."

"My point exactly."

"What do you mean?"

"He may be in the Mafia. I don't find that boring."

"Well, you know."

I didn't, but I wasn't going to mention it. Breaking up with Zeus struck me as the sanest move she'd made in months. Who cared if her reason was senseless.

When Marion dropped me off I didn't see Corelli. I did see Carol over by the Coke machine. She was sitting on a large can, or tub of some kind, drinking a Coke. Bozo was at her feet. "Hi," she called out as I got out of the car. "Did you find the key to the handcuffs?"

"We got them off with my Dremel," I said. I moved over to where she was sitting.

"Kids," she said. "You gotta love them."

Bozo got up and nuzzled my hand. I had saved him a Milano from the art show, which, needless to say, he was aware of. He snapped at it like it was his last morsel of food in this present existence.

"Corelli's in the office," said Carol. She had on jeans and workboots and a large red-and-black lumber jacket. "He's settling a bill or something. You want a Coke?"

"Sure." I reached into my jeans pocket for change, but she was already up at the Coke machine.

"My treat," she said.

"Thanks."

"My assistant teacher was out sick today. I need a vacation."

"So do I," I said. "And we just had one."

"Life gets to a person."

"You're telling me."

She handed me the Coke and sat down. I sat next to her on this wooden crate. Bozo was giving me the third degree, demanding additional Milanos.

"How's it going?" asked Carol.

"We don't have much time."

"He'll make it. He always does."

"Why doesn't he practice? Does he talk to you about it?"

"He says it's gaps." She turned up the collar of her lumber jacket and raised the zipper.

"What kind of gaps?"

"Gaps in what should be and what is." She took a long swallow of Coke. "Too much idealism can discourage a person."

"I know the feeling."

"Six years ago he lost a case. He knew the guy was right. He cared about it a lot, but he lost. He nearly had a nervous breakdown. But don't worry. He's the best. He's just an egomaniac with a big heart "

"I know. I love the guy."

"Me, too." She took another sip of Coke. "So. He'd rather fix cars."

"I can understand that."

"He says with cars everything is simple. You find out what's broken and you fix it. With law it's not so simple."

"I'm finding that out."

When I finished my Coke I went into the office. Bozo followed. (The Great Milano Lure.) Corelli was by the cash register in the midst of a conversation with a trendy-looking man in pressed blue jeans and a leather jacket. "You don't use lacquer?" the man was saying.

"Not unless you're crazy."

"Why not?"

"It stinks." The man thought about that for a moment, thanked Corelli, and left.

Corelli reached into the cooler. "Want some ice cream?"

"No thanks." I mainly wanted to get to work.

Corelli pulled out a chocolate pop. He let the cooler lid bang shut, then tore at the Popsicle wrapper with his teeth, the way he had the first time I saw him. "Grab those," he said, pointing to a stack of books near the register.

I picked up the books, then followed him out behind the garage where he crawled in underneath a dusty, rose-colored turbo SAAB. I sat down on the ground by the car. Thank God the sunlight was bright out there, or we would have frozen. As it was, it was kind of nice. Bozo settled down between us. He had two reasons, the Milanos and the ice cream.

"You gotta read to me," said Corelli. He began pounding on something underneath the SAAB. "Start with the blue book."

I couldn't see the blue book at first. I saw brown, tan, gray, and black, but nothing in blue. "It's not here."

"Look under the dog."

I reached in under Bozo and there it was.

"The place is marked," said Corelli. More pounding.

"Can you hear me under there?"

"Yeah."

I started to read. " 'A child may sue and recover damages for a violent beating, willfully exceeding reasonable punishment.' "

"Go on."

" 'It has also been proved that a child can sue his parents for negligence resulting in his injury.' "

"That's the area," said Corelli. He slid out from underneath the car. "The brown book over there."

There was a brown book on the top of the stack by my right knee, but the title was odd. "*Know Your Exhaust System*?" I asked.

"The other one." Corelli was rummaging through a bunch of tools on the ground. I found the other brown book at the bottom of the stack. It had a more promising title. *Symptoms of Emotional Damage or Injury as Recognized in the State of New York.*

"They got emotional starvation?" asked Corelli.

I looked in the table of contents, found "Emotional Starvation," and turned to the appropriate page. Bozo made a long-suffering, wheezelike sound, then began vigorously chewing on a tiny patch of fur right where his left leg joins the rest of his body. I would have said he had fleas, but it was too cold for that. I began to read. " 'Emotional starvation, like emotional abuse, is the most difficult type of abuse to detect and is perhaps the most tragic.' "

"They got symptoms?" Corelli was now working with a wrench, still under the car, but further front.

"Symptoms" was the next paragraph. I kept reading.

" 'Symptoms. Child refuses to eat, or eats little and is very frail.' That's Jenny!"

"She's not frail."

"She doesn't eat."

"She's in good health. It won't hold up."

" 'Child is unable to perform normal functions for a given age, such as walking, talking.' She can, she just won't."

"It's not the same thing."

I continued reading. I felt we were close. " 'Child displays antisocial behavior. May be abnormally unresponsive, sad, or withdrawn.' "

That's it!

"That's it," I said. "That's it! She cries a lot, and what about the earmuffs?"

"Kids cry. They do weird things."

"No, Corelli! This is it! I know it!"

"No good. It's got holes."

"What holes?"

"I'm telling you."

I felt a wave of panic.

He doesn't want to find anything, I thought. He's afraid to settle on anything for fear it won't work.

Bozo was making clicking noises with his flat front teeth. He was now working on the identical patch of fur on the other leg. I returned my attention to the brown book, scanning its pages for additional thoughts. "What about malpractice?" I asked.

"They're decent parents."

"They can be, but they haven't been lately."

"Hard to prove."

"WE NEED GROUNDS!" I shouted.

Corelli had stopped working. He sat, motionless, leaning back against the car in his green mechanic's overall suit, surrounded by his tools and rags, his dog and his law books, he looked beaten. "You tell me," he said.

"You're the lawyer!"

"The law's got holes."

"Now, wait a minute, Corelli. I tell you the truth about something and you tell me there's not one legal ground to base it on? I don't believe that!"

"Sue me."

"The law's for justice! It has to back me up!"

"Not necessarily." He sounded listless.

"Don't you care?"

"I'm not interested in the law," he said. "I'm interested in what's right, and the two don't have a hell of a lot to do with each other."

"I don't believe that! There must be a way! You just can't find it!"

"Get yourself another lawyer."

"I want you!"

"She ready?" Jerry Ritzer, the law student I met that first day I met Corelli, appeared suddenly from around the side of the garage. He wore an open trench coat with the same three-piece suit he had worn that first day, or so it seemed. "Seven months to the bar exam," he said.

"Right," said Corelli.

"You know Fordham's got the highest number of passes on the first try?"

"Great," said Corelli. He was clearly disinterested.

"I'm gettin' nervous." Ritzer lit a cigarette.

I breathed in, trying to get a good, deep breath, trying to calm myself.

"That's some case you're working on," said Ritzer. "I read about it in the paper."

"Right."

"How's it goin'?"

"Great," said Corelli. He got up, brushing the dirt from his overall suit. "I'll get your car."

Ritzer shook his head. "Somethin', boy. A case of first impression."

Corelli was checking his pockets. A missing bill, a wrench, a Kleenex?

"When did Mueller reaffirm the lemon test?" Ritzer was staring intensely at Corelli who was still checking his pockets.

"What?" said Corelli.

"When did Mueller reaffirm the lemon test? Was it eighty-four?"

"Eighty-three."

"Damn. Got that wrong on the midterms."

"Doesn't matter," said Corelli.

"I like to be right."

Corelli stopped searching in his pockets. He looked up at Ritzer, stared for a moment, then spoke. "What would you go for?" he asked.

"Where?"

"In my thing."

"Your thing?"

"You read about it. What would you go for?"

Why is he asking him? I thought. He's not even a lawyer yet. Next thing he'll be asking the Coke machine serviceman.

Ritzer furrowed his brow. He took a deep drag on his Marlboro. Then he put his hand on his hip and stared thoughtfully into the middle distance. "That's a tough one."

"Off the top of your head."

"I'll think about it."

Corelli turned and started off toward the garage. "I'll get your car."

Ritzer followed Corelli, leaving me alone on the

freezing ground by the turbo SAAB, surrounded by law books, wrenches, pliers, various other car maintenance tools, and a sad dog with flat teeth. No case, no lawyer, no hope. I felt like a huge, ungainly jelly boy, a useless blob, a beached oyster without its shell.

I should get up, I thought. I should do something. I should go somewhere. But where?

It didn't seem to matter, or, if it did, I couldn't think of why. Bozo looked up at me, not raising his head, just moving his large, sad eyes. I could see the white part underneath. My nose started to itch.

Don't cry. Don't cry. Don't cry.

"WE GOT IT!" Corelli literally came running around the side of the garage, shouting at the top of his lungs. "WE GOT IT! WE GOT IT! WE GOT IT!"

Bozo jumped up. Such excitement could only mean food. A lamb chop, a beef bone, a piece of chicken?

"Got what?" I said. I straightened out my left leg. It was totally asleep.

"Why didn't I think of that?" said Corelli.

"Of what?"

"God bless Ritzer!"

"What?"

"Third party beneficiary of a contract!" Corelli reached out to shake my hand.

"Our grounds?" I asked.

"Damn right!"

We shook hands. That's when I started to cry.

CHAPTER
41

Corelli had an errand to do in Bedford so he dropped me in town. He apologized for not taking me all the way home, but he was late in getting to some supply place or other before it closed. He had an enormous amount of work to do in just a few short days, formulating everything, writing his argument, and putting his blue back together. It had to be perfect. Nervous and excited, we said good night.

It became increasingly clear, as I trudged up Elm Ledge in the semi-darkness, that I needed a peanut-butter-and-jelly sandwich. I hadn't eaten since breakfast, except for the Milanos, and I was starving. I badly wanted that sandwich. I remember it was this burning thing. It verged on the passionate, but there were two problems. One was that it was nearly dinnertime, which seemed to indicate that I should forgo the sandwich in favor of dinner. The other problem was that I had had the same passionate longing for a peanut-butter-and-jelly sandwich the day before and had found, to my dismay, that there was no peanut butter in the house. Worse than that, I had forgotten to put it on the list, or ask Mom to get some, so the terrible chances were there would be no peanut butter in the house when I got home. To make matters worse, my stomach was feeling a little funny from all the excitement and nervousness of the EVENTS. Peanut butter was the only thing I could think of that had this certain, specific, soothing effect. I remember thinking about all this as I approached the house. I was maybe about two houses away from ours when I thought of the jar of peanuts. Then I thought about the hammer. I quickened my steps. Thoughts of smashing dozens of tiny peanuts, mashing them into a crumbling tempting delight, filled my overtaxed brain. Then I saw Dad's car. For some reason that scared me. I can't tell you why. Something was wrong. I sensed it. I kept moving toward the house, all thoughts of peanuts driven from my mind.

When I opened the door I saw Mom in the living room, talking on the desk phone. Dad was standing next to her. They both had jogging suits on. Dad was also wearing a muffler and a jacket. They both looked pale.

"About four o'clock," Mom was saying into the phone. "The maid saw her."

Jenny, I thought.

I closed the door, then moved into the living room.

"I wasn't here," Mom continued. "I got back at five-fifteen. Or about five-fifteen. Maybe five-thirty. Five-fifteen or five-thirty."

I looked at Dad. He paid no attention to me. He was staring at Mom, listening to every word she said into the phone.

"Completely sure," said Mom. "She's not here. All right." She hung up the phone, then turned to Dad. "He said we should stay in the house."

"That's crazy."

"That's what he said."

"What happened?" I asked.

Mom looked at me. It was a blank look, like she didn't see me, or was looking through me, or something. "Have you seen Jenny?" she asked.

"No," I said. "What happened?"

"She's, ah . . . not here." She sounded so vague. I suspect she was in a form of shock.

Dad kept staring at her. "Did she say anything? Did she leave any hints about where she might be?"

Mom shook her head.

"What about Trudy? Did you call Evelyn?"

"I called everybody."

Bunny's plan, I thought.

"Do you know anything, Chris?" said Dad. "Did she say anything to you?"

"Bunny had a plan."

"Did she say what Bunny's plan was?" Dad was so intense. It struck me funny in a way, his intensity over the plans of a stuffed rabbit.

"He was going to run away."

Dad turned to Mom. "What about Trudy? Did you call Evelyn?"

"I called everybody."

"We'll look for her."

"The police are calling back."

"The hell with that," said Dad. He zipped his jacket. "We can't wait around here forever."

"We'll miss their call."

"We'll call them. We'll look for her and we'll keep checking back."

I began to have a series of dark and sinister thoughts about what could be happening to Jenny. I wondered if Mom was doing the same thing with her head. I knew we shouldn't be doing that. It would immobilize us, for one thing. We had to move. Fast.

"Let's go," I said. "We'll find her."

Mom didn't respond. She just looked from one to the other of us like she didn't know what to say.

"Come on," said Dad. "Unless you want to split up, two of us go, one stay here."

"No," said Mom. "Let's stay together."

MY FEELINGS EXACTLY.

Mom got her Eddie Bauer jacket from the hall closet, Dad collected two flashlights, and we hurried out. It was odd. I felt scared about Jenny, and at the same time there was this wonderful aspect to the three of us working on something together. There we were, one unit, one thought in mind, one idea, one dream. It hadn't been like that for years.

There was some moonlight, but not a lot, because it was partially overcast. I remember my feet were freezing. Normally I don't have that problem, not to that extent, anyway. It must have been my fear. We checked the bushes, the trees, the garage, everywhere. Mom kept calling to Jenny.

"I don't think she's here, Mom," I said.

The three of us got into the car and drove off. Mom and I shone the flashlights out the windows while Dad drove. He drove slowly. Mom kept calling to Jenny.

She may never answer, I thought. Life can be like that. Everything seems so solid, so sure, but it can change overnight, in an instant.

In that moment everything seemed so precious to me, my life, my mother, my father, my sister, my fish. There, in the dark, driving through the night, against the recommendations of the Bedford police, staring into the vastness for a tiny figure who could be anywhere, my feet numb with cold, something exceedingly basic was clear.

Everything is a gift, I thought. You don't own it.

And if you don't take care of it, you lose it. Life is like that. Everything. It's a gift. A gift from God?

Mom began to cry. "Oh, God," she said.

It startled me to hear the word. My inner thoughts and hers, one thing.

"We'll find her," said Dad. He was gripping the steering wheel with both hands, which was unusual for him.

We drove around for about an hour before we stopped to call the police. They hadn't heard anything. Mom wasn't crying anymore, but she seemed in shock. She didn't answer right away when you talked to her.

"We'll keep looking," said Dad. "All right with you?"

Mom didn't answer. I pulled forward on the seat and held my flashlight out the window. "Let's try the station," I said.

I remembered standing with Jenny on the platform, holding her tiny hand, waiting for the "big and gigantic train," as she termed it, to rush past us with its "terrible wwwhhhsssh." I always had to tell her not to stand too close.

We didn't find her at the station. After that we went over to the Beckners' to see if she had shown up there. She hadn't. We checked the schoolyard, Gristedes' parking lot, Leonard Park, the firehouse, Lickety Split, virtually everywhere we could think of. There was no sign of her. Dad lit up a cigarette. "We'll drive through town again," he said. "Maybe we missed her."

We headed back into town. This time we checked all the parking lots and the areas in back of all the stores, not just the storefronts and the street. My feet were colder than ever. I stamped them up and down on the floor of the car in a futile attempt to restore normal feeling. Mom got out a Kleenex. She blew her nose. DAD PUT HIS HAND ON HER SHOULDER. "We'll find her, Connie," he said. "Don't worry."

The sight of Dad's hand on Mom's shoulder was unbelievable.

He cares about her, I thought, when the chips are down. Why only when the chips are down? If he cares when the chips are down, why can't he care when the chips are up?

Mom turned to him and nearly smiled. It was pretty feeble, and not any kind of big or happy smile, but she smiled. I returned my attention to the blackened night, directing my flashlight into the doorways of the different stores as we passed. Jack's Cleaners, Nora's Flowers, Bixler Real Estate. There was a dog asleep in the entrance way to Country Woman Clothes, but there were no other signs of life. I adjusted my position. My back was killing me. I had been holding it in a straight and stiff position and at a certain angle for over an hour in order to properly direct the flashlight.

What's that? I thought.

Up ahead, near Anywhere, Anyday Travel, a strange form was moving along the sidewalk. The shape was unfamiliar.

"We'll try the house again," said Dad. "Maybe she went home."

Mom didn't say anything.

What is that?

As we approached the moving form it remained unclear.

"What's that?"

My heart started racing a moment before I knew. "JENNY!" we all shouted together.

Dad stepped on the gas, then pulled to a screeching halt at the curb. Jenny stopped walking. She stood still, staring at the car. It was the saddest and most pathetic and sweetest and funniest sight I'd ever seen. There, standing all alone in the dark, in front of Sarah Edwards' Fine Baked Goods and Catering, was my tiny and beloved sister. She wore her earmuffs and her duffle coat with her yellow foot pajamas coming out the bottom. Over her foot pajamas she wore her kitty slippers, and as if all that wasn't enough, she had done a remarkable thing. She had tied all of her thirty-six stuffed animals to herself with belts and string and bits of old fabric. She carried Bunny.

Dad jumped out of the car. "Jenny!" he shouted. He ran over and squatted down by her side. "Sweetheart. Are you all right?"

Jenny nodded.

"What did you do?"

Jenny didn't answer. Mom and I got out of the car. Mom ran to Jenny, knelt down on the sidewalk, and hugged her, her arms reaching around all the animals. "Sweetheart, baby," she said. "What did you do?"

Jenny didn't answer. Mom was crying. She just stayed there, holding on to Jenny and all the animals.

"We were very worried," said Dad. "You must never do that again."

Jenny didn't look at him. "It was Bunny's idea," she said.

"Well, it wasn't a very good one."

Jenny started to cry.

"What's wrong?" said Dad.

"I'm hungry."

"Well, let's get you some food, sweetheart," said Mom. "Let's go home."

"I was only walking," said Jenny.

Mom stood up. She took Jenny's hand. "Why didn't you come home?" she asked.

Jenny didn't answer.

When we got back to the house, Dad made hot chocolate. Mom went upstairs to get some Anacin, and I helped Jenny untie the animals. "You scared us," I said. I was trying to untie a large knot in an old piece of rag that was tied around the neck of a one-eyed panda. "Why did you run away?"

"It was Bunny's idea."

"What was in Bunny's mind?"

"A new life."

"He doesn't like the life he has?"

"No."

"Why not?"

"No family is no family."

I had freed the panda and now needed to cut a knotted piece of twine. I went over to the marble table in the hall and took my Eddie Bauer survival knife out of the drawer. "Bunny has a family," I said.

"You wouldn't notice."

"He has you and he has all these brothers and sisters."

"They're stuffed."

"So is he. And he has a mother and a father and a pretty decent brother, if I may be so bold." I cut the twine. Rusticales, the tiny gray donkey, fell to the floor.

"Bunny doesn't think so."

"He doesn't think I'm decent?"

"No family is no family."

"But he has a family."

Jenny shook her head. At that moment she seemed

somehow so old, so wise, like she'd lived for maybe a thousand years. "It doesn't work out," she said. "It's not in anybody's mind."

CHAPTER
42

It's funny. When a thing finally happens that you've been waiting for forever, it comes as a shock. That's the way it was with the trial, or hearing, or whatever you literally call it. When the morning came, I couldn't believe it. It seemed to have come about all of a sudden, the months of terror and fear and planning dissolved in a wash. A swish-pan of a movie camera and there I was, standing on the cold floor of my bedroom in my bare feet, staring at my fish. Corelli's concerti grossi played loudly on my tape radio, a wake-up selection in honor of you know who. My fish suspected nothing. They stared out from their silent, briny fish world, eyes wide, mouths agape, asking for food.

"Big day," I told them. They didn't understand.

Mom was in a funny mood at breakfast. She burned the toast, undercooked the eggs, and dropped the cereal.

"You okay, Mom?" I asked. I was heading over to the closet to get the dustpan and broom.

"In my way," she said.

"What way is that?"

"It's not important."

"You don't really want the divorce, do you?"

She didn't answer. I began sweeping up the cereal.

"I want it," she said. Then she burned herself on the coffee maker.

"Hold it under cold water."

She moved to the sink.

"You don't seem like you do."

"Do what?"

"Want the divorce."

"I want it because your father wants it."

"What if he didn't?"

"Well, he does, so there's no point in discussing it."

Jenny came in, asking for olives.

"You can't have olives for breakfast," said Mom. She was holding her hand under the cold running water.

"Why not?"

"They're not a breakfast food."

"They are to me."

"You can't have olives now."

"Only why?"

"Because you can't." Mom was not thinking clearly. She looked like she was about to cry. "They're not the kind of thing . . . you . . . have . . . in . . . the morning."

"I do."

"Have some cereal."

"It's spilled."

"Just the Raisin Bran."

"I hate Raisin Bran."

"Then there's no problem. Have the corn flakes."

The hearing was set for eleven. I didn't go to school. Mom and I would drive over to the courthouse together, the plaintiff driving the defendant intervener.

Odd, but cozy. When it comes right down to it, I love my mom more than I can clearly describe.

Grampa was being driven down by some acquaintance of his up at Heritage Village. Not a close friend, he doesn't seem to have any, but someone he talks to sometimes up there. I think he works in the gift shop. He sells books and trinkets, as Grampa put it, something like that, and he likes to travel. That's about all I know about him. Anyway, he had offered to drive Grampa down. Jenny would go to school as usual. Since I didn't go to school that morning, I walked her down to the bus stop. We were both pretty quiet. About halfway down Elm Ledge I had an idea. "I'll tell you what," I said.

"What?" She was clutching her Roadrunner lunch box and a canvas tote bag that said "Jennifer" across the front.

"After school today I'll meet you at the bus stop and we'll go for ice cream."

She didn't look at me.

"And whatever happens at the court, it's not going to change that. One way or the other we'll be going for ice cream. How's that?"

"All right."

"What flavor are you going to get?"

"I don't know."

"I'll be getting chocolate."

I expected her to say something like "News flash," or "What else is new?" but she didn't.

We reached the bus stop a few minutes early. I waited with her as the other kids began to arrive and stayed until the bus came. She didn't speak to me again, and she didn't speak to anyone else, either. I watched her get on the bus. She sat down by a window. I waved to her as the bus pulled off. She didn't wave back.

By five minutes after eleven we were gathered in the courtroom. I sat at a long table between Grampa and Corelli. We were facing the judge. At the other long table, facing the judge also, on the other side of the room, sat Mom (her burned hand was bandaged), Dad, Dad's lawyer, Beanie Davis, the man I'd grown to dislike during our brief telephone conversation, and Mom's lawyer, Mr. Pilsner, the tall, thin one from the first hearing who kept staring at his shoes. It was the same judge. He had the same beard and the same tired expression. I stared at him, directing all my hopes and dreams in a laserlike thought beam, directly into his brain.

Wake up! Be alert! Be fair!

He took a large handkerchief from out of his pocket and blew his nose.

Don't let him have a cold, I thought. No allergies, no sinus irritations, no respiratory annoyances. We need his full attention!

In front of the judge sat an exceedingly small woman with beady eyes. She was the stenographer, ready, I presumed, to write down whatever was said. I also noticed a sheriff, a court clerk, I think he was, and another woman, who I took to be an assistant, or secretary, to the judge.

I adjusted my tie, which had partly come out from inside my blue blazer. Corelli cleared his throat. He seemed more nervous than I was, if such a thing could be possible. He looked like he might not have slept since I'd last seen him two days before. He had on a beautiful gray suit, though. He looked really respectable. Grampa patted me on the shoulder. It was reassuring. It seemed to say he was proud of me right then, at that moment, no matter what happened.

After a few preliminaries, the judge asked Corelli to present his motion to intervene. Corelli stood up. He cleared his throat. "Your Honor," he said, "as my motion papers clearly indicate, my client, Christopher Mills, is necessary to this proceeding. He must be heard. Permit me to explain. Seventeen years ago my client's parents, Stephen and Constance Mills, seated there,"—he pointed over to Mom and Dad—"entered into holy matrimony. They made certain vows. They entered into a marriage contract." He stressed those last two words. "I think we're all pretty familiar with what that entails." He looked directly at Mom and Dad. "The marriage contract basically states that you take each other as husband and wife, that you both agree to live together, in sickness and health, for richer, for poorer, forsaking all others, for as long as you both shall live."

Pilsner didn't like that. "Really, Your Honor," he said.

Corelli pulled a paper from his folder. "Mr. and Mrs. Mills were married at an Episcopal service," he continued. "I have here a copy of the Episcopal vows. Will the court take judicial notice?"

"Certainly," said the judge.

Dad shifted in his chair. Mom stared at her bandaged hand. Pilsner stood up. "Your Honor, this is a hearing strictly on the issue of this boy's right to intervene in this matter. My client's rights to dissolution of the marriage are herewith not an issue."

"Will you let me finish?" Corelli was getting intense. "I seek to point out here that this man and this woman were lawfully joined together. I thought it might be fitting to refresh our minds as to the conditions of their contract, conditions that these two people accepted of their own free will."

"I object, Your Honor." It was Beanie. He didn't stand up. He just sort of grumbled from where he sat, hunched, at the table.

"On what grounds?" said the judge.

"Irrelevancy."

"Overruled," said the judge. He gestured to Corelli. "Go ahead."

Corelli stared at Mom and Dad. "Mr. and Mrs. Mills. At your wedding ceremony, to the best of your recollection, were the vows, in fact, stated as I have outlined for the court?"

Mom and Dad just sat there.

"Answer the question, please," said the judge.

"Ah, yes," said Dad.

Corelli looked at Mom. "Mrs. Mills? Did I have the gist of it?"

"Yes."

"Did you answer freely?"

"Yes."

"How about you, Mr. Mills? Did you answer freely?"

"Oh, come on," said Beanie. He was clearly disgusted, outraged at this waste of his precious time.

"Did you answer freely?" repeated Corelli.

"Yes," said Dad.

"Good," said Corelli. "And what did you say? Did you agree to all that?"

"Object to form," said Pilsner.

"Rephrase your question," said the judge.

"Did you, Mr. Mills, and you, Mrs. Mills, accept the conditions of the marriage contract as I have just outlined them at this hearing?"

"We did, yes," said Dad.

"Mrs. Mills? Did you accept the outlined conditions?"

"Yes."

"Of course you did. And how do we know that? Because I have here the certificate of marriage." At that point he whipped a piece of paper from his folder of papers on the table. He held it in the air. "Here it is. The marriage contract." He turned to the judge. "Your Honor, my client, Christopher Mills, is necessary to this proceeding by reason of the fact that he, along with his six-year-old sister, Jennifer, is a third party beneficiary of this contract!"

"That's ridiculous," said Beanie.

"I'm not finished!" shouted Corelli.

"Gentlemen," said the judge.

"Excuse me, Your Honor," said Corelli. "May I continue?"

"Proceed."

"The mother and father of my client entered into a contract seventeen years ago. It was willingly entered into by both parties. Nobody forced them. Now, I submit that this contract was specifically made with my client in mind. He is a beneficiary of this marriage contract because it is inherent in the traditional marriage contract that both parties contemplate having children."

At this point Corelli quoted a lot of statutes and cases. He talked about the State Domestic Relations Law, giving the rights of people in regards to divorce, quoted something called Black Letter Law, and generally covered a lot of material too technical for me to follow. After that, he described a case in something called the Appellate Division where there was a ground for divorce under the law of fraud. He set down his papers and stared at the judge. "Your Honor, if I say

I want to have children, I want to have a normal family relationship, then I get married and I say I never wanted children, that's a fraud, because when I entered into a contract it was inherent in that contract that I contemplated having children, contemplated the formation of a normal family. Children and marriage are inexorably linked. They have been since the dawn of civilization. So it is with Stephen and Constance Mills. When these two entered into marriage they contemplated having a child. And here he is. Surely, he is no less a beneficiary now than when he was merely contemplated!"

Beanie was getting edgy. He was making involuntary clicking noises with his tongue and teeth. "This is totally irrelevant," he mumbled.

Corelli turned on him. "I'M NOT FINISHED! Your Honor, breach of contract will cause irreparable damage to my client and to his sister. The fact is all too clear. We've seen the torment, the tears, the anxieties created by being shunted back and forth. Schools all over the country are filled with—"

Beanie interrupted. "Could we limit the discussion to the case at hand? The nation's ills are hardly within our jurisdiction."

"Oh, yeah?" said Corelli. He had started to sweat. Perspiration was pouring down the sides of his face. "Well, whose jurisdiction are they?"

"Mr. Davis has a point here," Pilsner suggested.

"NO HE DOESN'T!" shouted Corelli.

"Mr. Corelli, please," said the judge.

Corelli was unstoppable. "The nation's ills are everybody's business! Where do you think the nation's ills come from? The American Mind? The Democratic Process? That's not the thing. They come from people! From all of us! NOBODY TAKES ANY RE-

SPONSIBILITY! This gets me back to what I'm talking about here. These people wanted a family. Nobody forced them. They made a decision. Together! And, under LAW, they accepted the responsibility for that decision. It was a wonderful decision! Is it just that now they turn and willfully, on some flimsy idea of self-satisfaction, disregard these responsibilities and cause irreparable damage to these children? Mr. and Mrs. Mills, I ask you. Do you think that's fair?"

CHAPTER
43

It was Beanie's turn to address the court. He stood over at his table, like a great rock, or boulder, immovable and dense, clicking his teeth, or his bridgework, between sentences. "Your Honor," he began, "my client and the client of Mr. Pilsner here are seeking dissolution of their marriage. They are no longer compatible. We see it all the time. Not compatible. They would know. This youngster wouldn't. His intentions might be good, but he wouldn't know what his parents are feeling. Not really. Now, the question is raised as to my client's responsibility to his children. I submit that far from ignoring this consideration, it has been of prime concern to my client and, I daresay, to Mr. Pilsner's client as well."

Pilsner nodded his agreement. Beanie continued. "It has, in fact, been of such concern that it has been a determining factor in their seeking a divorce."

Another nod from Pilsner. Beanie made a particularly loud clicking noise, as if removing spinach from his rear molars, then continued. "It is my client's conviction that his responsibility to his children will best be carried out by seeking this divorce. What child can successfully be raised in an atmosphere of dissension? No. In the best interests of the children you separate the parents. I question the right of this young man to intervene here at all, but once he does, if he does, he must be shown that his parents do, in fact, have his best interests at heart, as they have those of his little sister. Lastly, I would say that for the court to rule that two individuals remain together in an atmosphere of incompatibility is unthinkable. To rule that they remain together in an atmosphere of compatibility is impossible."

Corelli slouched deeper in his chair. Beanie sat down. Pilsner got up. "Your Honor."

"Mr. Pilsner."

"My client concurs with everything stated here by Mr. Davis. It is her firm belief that it is in the best interests of these children that the marriage be terminated. I think, also, that were we to take this intervention seriously, it would be shocking and inappropriate to entertain the idea of the court making personal and psychological evaluations in the case of sane and rational individuals, forcing them to respond to each other in loving ways. The implications are ludicrous science-fiction scenarios, that I, for one, find no place for in our legal thinking." He was fingering his automatic pencil. "It is clearly not the boy's right, nor the right of this court, to force these two people to live together in harmony. That must be left to a higher power. The court cannot force individuals to do something positive. It can merely attempt to prevent something negative."

Corelli looked up. "That's no longer true, Mr. Pilsner. In exceptional cases—"

"The court can't require specific performance here!"

"This case is exceptional!" Corelli got up. "If I may, Your Honor."

"You may proceed." The judge blew his nose.

"What does my opponent here mean, the court cannot force an order that a marriage shall continue? That's a secondary factor. My client is asking that the court prevent irreparable damage to his sister and himself by not granting this divorce. That's all. Stop something that's gonna cause harm, prevent something negative, as Mr. Pilsner so expertly expressed it. This family hangs in the balance. My client is asking the court to prevent its destruction, prevent irreparable damage to these children. Refrain from granting this divorce and, in so doing, encourage these decent, intelligent, well-meaning, and capable citizens to fulfill the responsibilities that they so willingly undertook to their children, to each other, and to themselves."

"Young man."

A chill ran through my body.

"Christopher." It was the judge. "Would you tell us, please, do you feel you're necessary to this proceeding?"

I looked at the judge. "Should I stand up?" I asked. I felt stupid.

"You may stand."

I looked at Corelli. He gave me a kind of almost smile and a partial nod that said, "Your turn. Stand up and tell them."

I stood up.

Mom and Dad were looking at me. They were proud, I could tell. It was kind of strange in a way, them sitting there, looking at me like I was on my first pony ride or something. There I was, challenging their very life choices, and they were proud.

I looked back at the judge. My mind had blanked

out. For a minute I couldn't remember the question. "Am I necessary?"

"That's right. Assuming that I grant your motion to intervene, do you consider yourself to be in possession of information that would affect the outcome of this proceeding?"

"I do. Yes."

"And why is that?"

"I know something."

Corelli cleared his throat. He was nervous for me.

"What do you know?" asked the judge.

"They're making a mistake."

"How do you know that?"

Panic. Fear.

This is my last chance, I thought. The time is now. It will never come again. I have the floor. I have the court. I have Jenny's life in my hands.

"How do you know your parents are making a mistake?" The judge repeated the question. I must have been standing there in a form of semi-shock. I don't know for how long. "Tell us about it, Christopher. In your own words."

I had no idea what I would say. It was like diving off the high dive, headfirst, for the first time.

Don't be afraid, I told myself. You know this. It's in the center of your heart. Tell them. Be brave.

"You asked me how I know my parents are making a mistake," I said. "I think there's a lot of ways." I took a deep breath, and then, the plunge. "I think sometimes people should get divorced. There can be reasons. But sometimes it's a mistake. I think getting along with another person is a really tough thing, and I think sometimes when people want to get divorced they're fighting hard stuff in themselves and they don't want to deal with that so they say it's too hard, or it's not working, and they back out and maybe start all over again with somebody else. You see it all the time. Some kids in my school, their parents have been divorced two or three times. It gets too much. I think in cases like that, a lot of times, they keep hitting into hard places in themselves, and instead of working that stuff out they just say forget it and leave. Well, in a way it's their lives, but they leave a trail of hurt and it's not right. My parents are about to do that, and they don't need to. They don't even want to. They're going to find that out, but if they go through with this divorce it's going to be too late. That's why the court should stop them. The court shouldn't let people go around hurting other people for no good reason."

"How do you feel the court should deal with this issue?" asked the judge.

"You mean my parents' divorce?"

"Any divorce. How could the court determine with any certainty if the parties involved were, in fact, making a mistake?"

"I don't know. Maybe before people get a divorce you should ask them if they did everything they could to make the marriage work. If they say yes, then fine, I mean, they would know, but if they haven't, then the court should make them honor the law they signed up for when they got married."

"I'm afraid that would be difficult to enforce," said the judge. "People might think they were being honest when, in fact, they were not."

"It's worth a try."

"Threshold inquiry," said Corelli.

"Oh, come on," said Beanie. His disdain was unparalleled in human experience.

"Threshold inquiry!" repeated Corelli. "Your Honor, my client is merely suggesting that in matters of this kind, the threshold inquiry of the court be whether the parents have done everything to make the marriage work. A reasonable proposition, if you ask me."

"This is totally irrelevant," said Pilsner.

The judge kept looking at me. "Do I gather from your statements, Christopher, that you feel your parents have not tried to make their marriage work?"

"Not lately."

"How do you know that?"

"They're my parents!"

I looked over at Beanie. His eyes were wide open, but he appeared to be dozing.

"Mr. Davis over there said I don't know what my parents really feel. Well, I don't think that's true. They want this marriage to work. They've said that to me, both of them. This brings me to something I was thinking about on the way over here. Dad told me something."

Dad looked at me. I began speaking right to him. "Dad, one day when we were sitting out in the car, you told me you were having a lot of problems. You said the only way for things to work out between you and Mom was if you both worked really hard on it. Remember?"

Dad looked uncomfortable. He kind of nodded and mumbled something that was hard to hear.

"You did, Dad."

"Yes."

"Yes. And then you said that Mom wasn't interested, that she was involved in other things. Remember that?"

"I do," said Dad.

I looked over at Mom. She was crying. I don't mean teary-eyed, or anything. I mean crying. Hard.

"Mom."

"Yes." She looked right at me, tears pouring down, straight and clear.

She wants the truth, I thought. What I just said about Dad cut through something. Had he never told her?

"Mom. This morning I asked you if you wanted the divorce. We were in the kitchen. It was after you dropped the cereal, just before you burned your hand. I asked you if you wanted the divorce and you said you wanted it because Dad wanted it. Is that right?"

"Yes."

"Don't you talk to each other? You want the divorce because you think Dad wants it, and Dad wants it because he thinks you want it, but neither of you wants it to begin with!"

Mom was crying harder now. Dad looked at her.

They're hearing this for the first time, I thought. Neither of them told the other one about any of this. Why not? What do people do to each other?

CHAPTER
44

"Is there anything else you have to say, Christopher?" asked the judge. "Hold nothing back."

I looked at Mom and Dad. Mom stared at the table. Dad was kind of staring inside himself. They looked like kids almost.

"I think they're scared," I said. "I can understand that, but it's not a good enough reason to hurt a little kid. Everybody's hurting everybody else in the world and that's why everything's in such a mess."

Beanie took exception. "Your Honor," he said, "the state of the world can hardly be the business of this court, particularly of a fifteen-year-old boy."

That made me mad. "I think it's everybody's business," I said.

Grampa nodded his approval. Pilsner adjusted his cuffs.

"The main thing I have to say is I love my mom and dad very much. I know they love me and Jenny, but stuff just got too much for them, or so they thought. I think if they could just realize that they do love each other and they do know how to be good parents, and that they have responsibilities, and that they can live up to them and be happy doing it, then everything's going to be okay. They're about to hurt a little kid very much, and they don't need to. They can stop themselves, so I think they should. That's my feeling."

I've said enough, I thought, but something drove me on.

"See, I think the world's in really bad shape."

Beanie stood up. "Your Honor, that's irrelevant!"

"Will you sit down until he's finished?" said the judge. He turned to me. "Go on."

I hadn't meant to say all this. I had no choice. "I don't know how much longer we have. I think the world might be over soon, but I think we have to start with making peace in our families. I think if we don't have that, see, if we don't work for that, then nothing else matters. If we do have that, then everything else will come. So I think if my parents, or anybody, can make that real, they have to do that. I mean there's a lot of crazy people in the world, or sick, or just not up to anything, and what are they supposed to do? They do the best they can, but then so should my parents. The ones who can live up to their word should do it. If they don't, who will? My mom and dad could be the best parents in the world, if the court would make it so they had to live up to what they said. I don't know if any of this is legal, but I know it's the truth."

"Thank you, Christopher," said the judge. "Are there any further comments?"

"I got a comment." It was Corelli. He stood up next to me. "I think my client here just made more sense than all the rest of us put together."

Grampa reached over and held my hand. His eyes were tearing up.

Corelli continued. "It's interesting, wouldn't you

say, that although in divorce matters the court must consider what's in the best interests of the children, the children are rarely, if ever, heard from. The last thing I'm gonna say is this. Mr. Pilsner there accused my client of taking a shocking position in this matter. Then Mr. Davis pointed out, not once, but twice, that he is of the opinion that the state of the world is not the business of this court. Well, I find Mr. Davis's position shocking. The state of the world must be the business of this court and of every one of us on this planet. I find a bad thing going on. I'm seeing a breakdown in ethics in western civilization, you'll forgive the broadness of my point here, Mr. Davis, and what I'm also seeing, all too often, in the law is a tendency to accommodate itself to that very breakdown. I think that's dangerous. We got laws oozing around, shifting before our eyes, molding themselves to accommodate the very worst that men and women have to offer. But I'll tell you something else. I feel good today. I feel good because I'm thinking maybe there's some more around like him." He looked at me. "Maybe they can fix things for the rest of us. I hope I'm around to see it happen."

Corelli stared for several moments at the judge, then he sat. Everyone was quiet, even Beanie. I looked over at Mom and Dad. Mom was crying. Dad was looking at her. His eyes were wide and deep. The judge took another drink of water, then he spoke. "Gentlemen. You've raised some important issues here. We're dealing with a case of first impression in this court, perhaps in this nation. In many ways I would like time to consider the points brought up before making an adjudication. However, I know full well, even now, what that decision must be."

My heart was pounding, my breathing shallow. I

wanted to run, out of the courtroom, out of White Plains, out of my life, to drop the whole thing, forget I'd ever started it to begin with. I don't know why. Fear, I guess. Fear of hearing the unhearable.

The judge continued. "The fact that this marriage does not work is not surprising. We see as many marriages, if not more, that do not work, as those that do. It is not the job of this court to figure out why that may be so, merely to deal with the fact, to make the inevitable as painless as possible. It is inevitable that the breakdown of any marriage will cause some pain to the children involved."

Grampa was squeezing my hand. Corelli was slouched in his chair. The judge looked at me. "Young man, your attempt to save your family is laudable, and although I admire your attorney's rhetoric, I might even say, off the record, that I agree with him, I find no legal recourse . . ."

Oh, God.

". . . by which to grant you the relief sought. Therefore, I must deny . . ."

I went totally numb, no feeling whatsoever. Silence. Space. Emptiness.

"He's right."

I heard the words, but they didn't register. "He's right." Two words, coming from a long distance through a tunnel-like time warp.

"He's right." It was my dad.

"Mr. Mills?" said the judge.

"He's right."

I looked at my dad. He was staring at his hands. He didn't look up. Mom was still crying.

"Your Honor," said my dad. He spoke slowly, with a lot of spaces between the words. It was as if he'd learned them a long time ago and had just gotten the courage to speak them out. "I don't know if my wife agrees with me, and I don't know if we could make it work if she did, but my son is right."

Corelli sat up. Grampa squeezed my hand.

"Mr. Mills," said the judge. "Do I infer from your comments that you wish to terminate divorce proceedings at this time?"

My heart literally stopped. I felt no pulse.

"If my wife is in agreement."

"If your wife is in agreement, you would like to terminate divorce proceedings at this time?"

"Yes, Your Honor."

"Mrs. Mills?"

"Your Honor?"

"Are you in agreement?"

The longest pause. Centuries seemed to pass. I didn't breathe. And then the answer.

"I am."

It was like a kaleidoscope, one of those turning, tubelike things you look into, everything shifting, tumbling, rearranging itself before my eyes. Grampa patting my hand, reaching for his handkerchief, Corelli punching me in the shoulder, us hugging, Mom and Dad holding each other's hands, staring at their hands, at each other, Beanie fussing with his papers, Pilsner standing up, looking lost, the judge saying, "Case dismissed, congratulations," then whispering to his secretary about some other case or a dinner appointment, and me just sitting there and crying like a baby.

After a moment I noticed Dad coming toward me. I reached out my arms to him like when I was the tiniest of boys and he would come to pick me up at nursery school. The whole thing came back. How I hated being left there, how the teacher would take me to the sink to get a drink of water in a paper cup to ease the pain. How I'd drink it down and then go and work with the paints, or maybe the blocks, how I'd get into things to a degree, but always part of me would be waiting for my dad to come back. Soon I'd be ready in my snow boots and my outdoor things, standing there by my cubby in the hallway, and the door would open and it would be my dad.

I reached out my arms and he was there.

That afternoon I waited for Jenny at the bus stop. When the bus came she was the last to get off. I was waiting by the big oak tree. The other kids straggled off with their lunch boxes, their construction-paper projects, their extra sweaters and other school things. Jenny carried nothing. She moved slowly toward me by the tree. She stopped a few yards away. I went to her.

"Is it okay?" she asked.

"It's okay."

"We have Daddy?"

"We have him."

She looked up at me and smiled the biggest smile I've ever seen.

POSTSCRIPT

It's summer now. Six months have passed since that fateful hearing in January, and we're a family. It's been hard at times, but undeniably worth it. There's a real connection between us, and a sense of relief all the way around. Whatever difficulties come up, I sense in Mom and Dad a feeling of being in the right place at the right time.

Corelli and Carol got married. I was the best man. The reception was at the Millwood Firehouse, .catered by The Texas Taco. Bozo was there, and so were Mom and Dad and Jenny and Grampa. I'm deeply thankful to Corelli. I hope he keeps up with the law. I expect he'll mainly fix cars, but I also think he'll keep taking the cases of us poor, unpopular ones without any money. I hope so. I still see him at the garage. Next year, when I get my driver's license, I'll visit him more. And Grampa, too. To be honest, I see the handwriting on the wall. My next job will be getting my dad to move Grampa to an apartment or a little house in Bedford, Katonah, at the very least.

If there's one thing I've learned from all of this, it's that anything is possible. This Saturday Dad's taking me to the Metropolitan Museum. I'm going to copy the Kunji painting. I may make a total fool of myself, but, then again, it might turn out all right. I'll never know until I do it. I'm just going to set up my easel and paint.

About the Author

BARBARA DANA was born in New York City. She is an actress as well as the author and has appeared in several plays and films and on television. She and her family have made record albums of folk songs for children, including songs composed by Ms. Dana herself. She is married to actor/director Alan Arkin. They live in Westchester, New York, and have three sons. Barbara Dana is also the author of *Zucchini*, available from Bantam Skylark Books.